Julian
from one author To
another

A Girl in Time

A Novel

by

DAVINA MERRY

[signature]

Drummond Place Publishers

EDINBURGH

Published by Drummond Place Publishers 2017
Drummond Place Publishers is a subsidiary of Scotland Street Press

2 5 7 3 1 2 9 7 5 3

First published in Scotland in 2017 by
Drummond Place Publishers
7/1 Scotland Street,
Edinburgh, EH3 6PP
scotlandstreetpress@gmail.com

Cover Design by Bookmark Studio
Cover Artwork by Hermione Gibbs
ISBN: 978-1-910895-08-5

Typeset in Scotland by Theodore Shack
Printed and bound in Poland

Prelude

I am standing behind the parapet of the Tower, right at the top of the old house. From here I can see over the land to the hills where shadows race, cast by the scudding white clouds above. Far below me stretch the fine gardens that Greville planted, and between the swaying branches of the trees I catch flashing glimpses of the river. I lean against the wall, the stone is warm today in the sun. I think how the house is like a matrix. So many of us have lived here, left it, and then returned.

There are patches of ochre yellow lichen on the stone walls. They remind me of tiny jewels. I pick at some with my fingernail. I have started to realise what I am going to do. I shall write it all down. The idea suddenly enthrals me. I shall abandon the book I am currently working on and write this other story instead. It is like a spring that is wound tightly inside me. It would be a relief to set it free – the chronicle of the people who have lived here and their interwoven lives.

The rooks rise in a great cloud above me and spill themselves into the sky. It is autumn and the wind blows keenly as the evening comes. I turn and go back into the house. I am smiling to myself. I cannot wait to begin.

CHAPTER I

The child lay in the long grass, watching the world through the glistening stems; the world of a perfect summer afternoon.

The bulk of the old house with its defiant tower, and sweep of gravel that led up to it; the sunken garden and the rose beds were all veiled in mystery by these grasses. Butterflies and beetles sometimes obscured his view; this was a secret place where he lay hidden, not even his eldest sister with her commanding height could guess where he might be.

Urchin, the deerhound, lay stretched out by the front door, his nose between his long, elegant paws, ready to leap up and bound with joy whenever anyone appeared 'as they soon will,' thought the child, 'and I shall continue to listen and watch them, like you watch actors in a play.'

The first to disturb the scene that afternoon was his mother, Violet Tarnoch, who appeared from the west side of the house, carrying a flat basket full of flowers. She wore a wide-brimmed hat from under which her long hair had escaped. The dog jumped up and followed her as, with an undulating movement, she went into the house. The child pressed his stomach against the earth and the grass. A moment later his sisters, Theresa and Claire, ran across his vision. They were excited about something, he could see by the way they laughed together, their summer dresses flying out as they ran; they were pursuing their mother. The child, Simon, felt a shiver of excitement. The day had altered its tempo. Vanessa, his third sister, was the last to arrive on the scene. The eldest, she wore a wide-brimmed hat like her mother's. Her long dark hair fell to her shoulders. She was shading her eyes with her hand. He knew she was looking for him:

'S-i-i-imon!' She called him. He let her call twice and then she became impatient. He stood up and waved to her.

'I'm here' he called back.

'Come at once and tidy yourself up' she ordered, 'Father's coming home and Mother says we must all get ready and wait for him in the library.'

He was tearing towards her now, through the sunken garden, jumping the steps as he raced over the lawn. This was the greatest news in the world.

It seemed so long since they had last seen him, Hamish Tarnoch who had won fame in the Great War, about whom they read in the newspapers. Sometimes there were blurred photographs of him on his horse conferring with foreign generals; they wore strange hats with plumes. This always seemed to Simon unreal, and divorced from the father he knew who went riding with them and told them stories of his own childhood at Merlinstone. This news also meant their mother Violet would come out of her dream world and be her carefree self for a while. When their father was away Simon noticed how his mother withdrew from them, and how sad she had looked when no letters arrived for her and how, when some from their father did arrive she seized them and went into her bedroom to read them alone.

Now, upstairs in her large bedroom where the windows looked to the west, Violet sat at her dressing table and tried to pin up her unruly hair. With a desperate yank she seized hold of it and drove in a number of long hairpins. She studied her face in the mirror with objectivity for she only saw what she was facing in her mind; great happiness that her husband was returning and they would be a normal family again. She smiled at her reflection, not realising how young she still looked, seeing only the pictures of what they would all do; the children playing croquet with their father, Simon going down to the river with his father to watch him fish, riding with him over the fields to the hills; her famous husband able to be an ordinary father again. She lifted her chin proudly and screwed some pearl earrings into her ears. The terrible war was over and Hamish Tarnoch was returning heaped with fame and honour. She felt so proud of him.

A small sound made her look round and she saw Simon standing in the doorway.

'Come here my darling' she said softly. He went to her and leant against her. She smelled delicious.

'Father's coming home, Nessa said,' he whispered.

She looked down at him in the mirror; she so glowing and he so small, leaning against her, gazing at her with his long, dark eyes. She bent to kiss the top of his head.

'Perhaps one day you will be great and famous like your father,' she murmured.

He did not reply. It was impossible for him to imagine that he would ever resemble his father. Gently she pushed him away and stood up and shook out her long, cream-coloured skirt, then taking his hand she said 'Come, we will go downstairs and wait for him.'

Downstairs, in the room they called the library, tea had been laid on a round table in front of the fireplace. A piano stood in the corner of the room, draped with a yellow Spanish shawl, and as well as books lining the walls there were several paintings, including a large portrait of Violet Tarnoch, dressed in her riding habit and black jacket, the darkness of the painting enlivened by the crimson collar of the deerhound that stood beside her, a present from her husband when they married - he a venerable forty years and she just seventeen.

The sisters were all three sitting on the sofa gazing at the tea table with longing. There were oatcakes and drop scones and a whole honeycomb on a green and white plate; a chocolate cake and a jam sponge, and frail and delicious little cucumber sandwiches. It was really almost unbearable. Claire, the youngest of the girls and the most lively, sat between her sisters. She had just watched Ishbel, their cook, put a plate of her favourite biscuits down beside the cakes and it was almost more than she could do not to stretch out and take one. But Vanessa had sharp elbows. Simon went over and sat on the wide window seat from where he was able to see the car when it arrived; Violet stood beside him. The clock ticked its deep-throated, important tick and the house creaked and groaned a little in the summer wind. Distantly a door slammed. No-one spoke. They were all straining their ears for the sound of a car engine coming up the lime avenue. Suddenly there it was – they heard the scrunch of wheels on the gravel and they all rushed into the front hall, Violet first, her eyes shining. And there he was, their father, taking off his coat and smiling, and Violet was in his arms and the children pranced and pushed to be hugged as they yelled

'Daddy, Daddy, you're home!'

General Tarnoch was a man of medium height with a natural dignity. His eyes were long and dark and could be enigmatic as well as penetrating. Today they were simply lit with happiness. Behind his large military moustache he had a mouth of great sweetness. His brow was broad and his dark hair, that was brushed back, was thick and powdered with grey. Now he let them take his arms and lead him into the library to the tea table.

There was a silver kettle with a small spirit flame trembling beneath it and a silver teapot beside it waiting to be filled. Violet attended to it whilst the children sat close to their father, plying him with sandwiches and scones so that they could begin eating themselves. When they had finished at last they all went out into the garden clinging to their father's arms.

'Come and look at our garden,' they cried, dragging him away from Violet so that he would see their handiwork with the dahlias and late flowering plants they had been allowed to grow themselves. Violet came up and claimed her husband's arm.

'We are together now,' she whispered to him, 'I pray you will never have to go through another war.'

'I shall be far too old for that,' he replied, 'and I hope our children will not have to either.'

They stood together for a long time, watching the sun fall behind the distant hills.

Later, Simon was to look back to those late summer days as their last ones of real happiness, before their lives as a family changed forever.

Shortly after his father's return he was sent to his first boarding school. He never told his family how homesick he was. Night after night he dreamt of Merlinstone. It was the river that came to him most often; the river he loved so much and where he went to fish with his father. He could feel it in his dreams, the cold water pressing against his knees, and he saw the brown, rushing, gurgling tide push past him like a rich delicious ale, foaming against the banks and then lying still and resting in deep, dark pools where the fish lay against the stones. Above him the trees moved and sighed and showed flashes of the sky. When he woke it was always very early morning, and he would be staring at the dormitory wall reliving the dream and wishing he could be back at Merlinstone.

It was a cold day in March 1924 when Simon was summoned from the classroom and told to go at once to the headmaster's study. With his heart beating rather fast he knocked on the varnished wood door and was surprised to see, on entering the room, that Mr Lucas was sitting at his desk with his head in his hands. When Simon closed the door he looked up quickly, showing his face was pale and his eyes bright with anxiety. Frail spring sunlight flooded the room; Simon could see daffodils bobbing outside beneath the long window.

Mr Lucas said 'sit down, Simon,' and nodded to a chair. There was a long pause. Mr Lucas cleared his throat.

'I am afraid that you are going to have to be very brave,' he said. 'I have some sad news for you.'

Simon looked back at him.

'Yes sir?'

'It is about your father, he has passed away. It happened suddenly yesterday evening whilst he was in London with your mother. They were preparing to go out to a dinner.'

Mr Lucas paused, for a moment he could not go on. Simon felt dizzy, like the time when he had fallen off his pony and hit his head on the hard ground. He could not think. He put his hands to his forehead. He saw the headmaster half rise from his chair.

'Steady boy', he said. 'I'll get some water.' He got up and went over to a jug that stood on a small table by the fireplace and poured Simon out a glass. Simon took it as though in a dream. After a gulp or two he put it down.

'Thank you sir, I am all right,' he said. Mr Lucas returned to his desk.

'I must go to my mother,' Simon said, 'But why has my father died? What happened to him?'

'It appears that he had a massive heart attack,' Mr Lucas replied. 'It was whilst he was dressing for dinner, your mother was with him. They rushed him to the hospital but it was of no use. Now, Simon, we shall have to make arrangements for you to leave for the north tomorrow. Your mother will be returning there before going south again for the funeral so she will need your company. Will you be all right to travel on your own?'

'I shall be all right,' Simon replied, 'but what do you mean about mother going south for the funeral?'

'Apparently your father is to have a state funeral in London before returning north to be buried at his home.'

'Why not Edinburgh?' Simon cried, alive suddenly and full of pain. Lucas leaned over and put a hand on his arm.

'Your father belonged to the nation, Simon,' he said gently 'that is why. It is probably hard for you to understand this.'

General Tarnoch's funeral took place two weeks later with all the expected panoply. It was a cold, grey March day and in spite of this crowds lined the streets to see the coffin go by on a gun carriage to Westminster Abbey. Escorting this came military hierarchy from Britain and France, members of the Royal family, and Simon himself - a small, lone figure who looked young and frail as he marched behind the coffin of his father. Vanessa had wanted to walk with him.

'After all I am the eldest,' she argued, but Violet replied certainly not and Vanessa was angry and sulked throughout the day.

That evening the coffin was taken to the train for the General's last journey back to his homeland. After the family funeral and the wake the Tarnochs gathered together in the library at Merlinstone. They were tired and dazed by grief.

Violet knew that now her husband had died she would be beset by money problems. Without her husband's pay or the money that had come from his many directorships the family would have a struggle to remain at Merlinstone. Violet was determined to carry on her husband's charitable work. She had the idea of creating a museum and she gathered together his uniforms and decorations along with maps, mementos, letters and photographs all belonging to the recent war. These she displayed in glass cabinets that were placed in the hall; creating a sort of shrine for ex-service pilgrims to visit. The children christened it 'The Museum,' and many came, the small amount they paid was put towards the charities.

Years later when she arrived on her first visit to Merlinstone the young Elizabeth de Saint André would enter the Museum and exclaim '*Mais! C'est comme Les Invalides!*' a laughing remark that was to go down in family history.

After the death of the General life for the Tarnoch family changed; with great sadness they had to dismiss several people who had worked for them for many years. There simply was not enough money to pay them. Their cook Ishbel was left with only one girl to help her in the kitchen, and this girl also had to clean the large house. The garden boy had to go as well as the second groom, and several of the General's horses had to be sold. A strange silence came to the house and there was less laughter. Violet grew ill with grief and strain. Vanessa was the only child old enough to help her with her problems and even she was too young to take on many burdens. The result was she started to act older than her years and, always prone to bossiness, she now became annoyingly authoritative which irritated her sisters and frightened Simon. He knew that she expected him to grow up and be like his father, something he also knew he would never be able to achieve.

In his mother's eyes his father was the greatest hero on Earth. She would lie back in her bed against the many pillows and speak of him for hours. She always ended by saying that she knew that he, Simon, would follow in his father's footsteps. Simon knew that almost certainly she was wrong.

CHAPTER II

1939

The plane trees stood limply to attention in the square, and the sash windows in number nineteen were pushed wide open. Three men stood together by these windows, drinking their strong, bitter after-lunch coffee. They were deep in conversation. On the left stood Robert MacMorrow, a small, spare man with a grey moustache; and to the right there was Lionel Everard, pale-faced, wearing a smart dark blue suit. Lionel worked for the Foreign Office.

Between these two, directly facing the street, stood a tall, broad-chested man with a florid face. His prematurely white hair was carefully cut with military precision. This was Ralph Cunningham, the new 'head man', soon to be the Chief of Secret operations. But today, on this sun-filled afternoon, things were still shaping themselves.

'Right, gentlemen, that was an excellent lunch but now back to business', Ralph said.

He drained his coffee cup and with one last deep inhalation of the warm summer air that held the tang of melting tar, he pulled the long sash window down and turned back into the room.

'Shall we be seated?' he asked.

The other two nodded and followed him deep into the shadows of the room where they sat down in comfortable armchairs. For a moment they regarded each other in silence. Then the smaller man, Robert MacMorrow, leaned forward and said

'I think I have got some of the information you wanted, concerning the de Verdurin girl.'

Lionel Everard raised his eyebrows.

'Nothing has been mentioned to her as yet, I presume.'

'Of course not,' MacMorrow sounded faintly aggrieved. 'We have to know much, much more before we move in any direction.'

'It is not all that too soon,' Ralph Cunningham interposed, 'unfortunately.'

They nodded. MacMorrow pulled some papers out of his briefcase and spread them over the low table, shifting his coffee cup.

'Mind if I take off my jacket?' he asked; the room, even in the shadows, had become very warm. Having done this he pulled at the frayed cuffs of his shirt and put his slender finger tips together.

'The de Verdurins are an old Provençal family,' he continued, 'and very much Anglophiles. Their home is a stronghold in a wild and rocky part of Southern France called the Drôme that leads northwards from Provence. The owner, the Comte de Verdurin, is unlike many other French aristocrats. He lives in his chateau most of the year and does not bother much with Paris but I believe he does own an apartment there. The family is one of the very few to slip through the terror and survive, they are pre-Napoleon gentry. They claim, I believe, some kind of link with our own Royal family. De Verdurin is well into his sixties and too old now to take part in combat. He was married to a Swedish lady many years younger than him and she is no longer alive. They had one daughter called Geneviève who has been studying here at Girton College Cambridge. She spends much of her free time staying in rather grand houses in this country. Her mother was a close friend of the Duchess Glengower.'

'Yes, yes,' Ralph Cunningham interrupted impatiently, 'Gloria Glengower is an old friend of mine.'

MacMorrow looked at him quickly over the top of his rimless glasses and poured himself a glass of water. He took a sip and then continued.

'I think the girl, Geneviève, will return to her father and the chateau if there is War.'

'How are they for money?' Ralph enquired.

'Oh, fairly well off I imagine. The Count spends a great deal on the chateau repairing and maintaining it. He owns a large amount of land, mostly scrub and pretty useless, but there is a shooting interest, partridge and wild boar and that sort of thing.'

There was a short pause and then Lionel Everard asked

'What does the girl Geneviève intend to do with her degree, if she manages to get one?'

'I gather she wishes to stay in England for a while and find some kind of a job. More to exercise her brain, I hardly think she can need the cash,' MacMorrow replied.

Ralph Cunningham lit a cigarette.

'She must be quite courageous,' he observed, 'to strike out like this on her own, in a foreign country.'

MacMorrow smiled wryly. 'She will need her courage,' he remarked, 'if there is to be War.'

'Do you think she shares her father's Anglophile enthusiasms?' Ralph asked.

MacMorrow replied, 'I believe father and daughter are close. This coupled with her wish to work in England would indicate that she undoubtedly does.'

Ralph got up from his chair and went over to the large chest that stood against the wall by the window. Opening it he rummaged for a while and finally brought out a map which he unfolded and spread out on the table.

'Provence,' he murmured, 'the Drôme area, here we are. Now let us see if we can locate the Chateau Verdurin.'

'It is near the town of Mont Rouge,' MacMorrow told him.

They all bent over the map. The thin paper crackled as Ralph traced the contour with his forefinger.

'Hell of a country,' he muttered, 'real Mafia land. Look at those cliffs and gulleys. Here, I've got it – the Chateau Verdurin.' It was written on the map in fine black writing.

'Quite a large area,' Ralph continued, 'family graveyard and this block, probably stables.'

'The nearest town with a rail link is here, this place called Apt. You can see the line marked but it does not continue to Mont Rouge, too small a place to merit one I expect,' MacMarrow observed.

Ralph straightened his back and removed his spectacles. There was a long pause whilst MacMorrow picked up the map and folded it. Outside the sun still shone fiercely, but with a greater depth of gold as the day neared evening. The shadow of the iron railings of number nineteen fell over the hot pavement and through these shadows walked Geneviève de Verdurin, as unaware of the men in the room she passed as they were of her. They never saw the pale girl go by, her hair gathered back and knotted behind her head with a black ribbon, a slight smile of expectation on her face. She was excited by the thought of the evening that lay ahead. It was wonderful to be away from Girton College and to be heading that evening for Carlton House Terrace and Gloria Glengower's summer ball. Now she was bound for Montagu Square where she was to stay with Mary Tarnoch, the aunt of her new friend Theresa.

Inside number nineteen the three men concluded their meeting. MacMorrow put on his jacket and Ralph Cunningham stretched his arms and said

'Well, gentlemen, à bientôt.'

They smiled politely and nodded as they went out into the street and hurried on their separate ways.

In her house, number fourteen Montagu Square, Mary Tarnoch awaited the arrival of Geneviève and Theresa. She was the younger sister of General Tarnoch, and she had never married. Her kind, thin face and immaculate white hair that was drawn back into a bun made her appear older than her years. Since the death of the General, Mary had taken a more prominent role in the lives of the three girls and their brother Simon. Vanessa, now married to a young man called Henry Sinclair, had a house of her own where she lived with her husband and their small son Greville. The other two girls, Theresa and Claire, would stay with her but they also liked to go to their Aunt Mary who made them feel even more at home. Tonight Theresa was heading for her aunt's as Vanessa had gone to Scotland where, along with their mother, they tried to keep their family home going for Simon. Theresa had asked her friend Geneviève to stay for the ball. Secretly, although she would have been ashamed to admit it, she was glad she was to stay with her aunt and not with her sister Vanessa whom she found somewhat overbearing at times and inclined to criticise her appearance. That morning she had gone to the hairdresser and parted with her mass of long dark hair in exchange for a fashionable bob. Fascinated, as well as feeling slightly horrified, she had watched the tresses fall to the floor and with them her schoolgirl youth. Now she was a modern young lady and she smiled at her reflection in the long mirror whilst Mr André danced around her waving a hand mirror to show her the new style from every angle. She felt light-headed and smart.

'Wonderful!' exclaimed Mr André, 'you look beautiful Miss Tarnoch.'

Theresa stood up and did a twirl.

Back at number fourteen with her aunt she went upstairs to her bedroom to admire her new dress once again. Mary had given it to her and had been surprisingly understanding when Theresa had chosen a fuchsia pink dress with a dashingly low neck. It swung now on a hanger in her bedroom almost seeming to dance on its own. She took it down and held it to her in front of the mirror. It went wonderfully well with her new hair style, she thought.

Downstairs Mary heard a taxi stop outside the door which she quickly opened; she watched Geneviève de Verdurin step out of the cab, clasping her suitcase in one hand and a large, shiny box in the other. Mary recognised the name of the exclusive Parisian designer. Geneviève paid the taxi and turned towards the door, she was surprised to see Mary standing there instead of some dark-suited manservant. Mary only kept a staff of two; Mrs Trubshaw her cook and Alice her maid, who was out for the afternoon. She would return that evening to help the girls dress for the ball. Mary smiled and held out her hands.

'You must be Geneviève,' she said. Her voice had the faintest northern intonation. Geneviève smiled shyly.

'Miss Tarnoch, can I call you Aunt Mary? Theresa has so often spoken of you.'

'Of course you can. Now come in and put down that case. Alice will take it upstairs for you when she comes in.'

At that moment Theresa came running down the stairs. She flew across the hall and hugged Geneviève.

'It is so lovely to see you!' she cried. Geneviève stood back to look at her.

'Your hair! It's wonderful,' she said, 'it really suits you, Theresa.'

Laughing, Mary led the girls into the drawing room.

'Now,' she said, 'I'll ring the bell and Mrs Trubshaw will make us some tea, or would you both prefer cool drinks? It is a very warm day.'

They chose tea with lemon and the girls sat down together on the large sofa that was covered in an old silk damask that had faded to a misty grey like most of the other furnishings in the room.

'So you have come down from Cambridge, Geneviève?' Aunt Mary observed, whilst they waited for their tea to be brought upstairs from the kitchen.

'Yes,' Geneviève replied with a sigh. 'I shall really miss it all but it is exciting to be free and going into real life!'

'She has beautiful English,' Mary thought, 'and what a striking looking girl!' Geneviève had a pale, cool beauty which was unusual - her eyes were dark, almost the colour of gunmetal, unexpected and at variance with her Nordic colouring.

'Do you know the rest of the family?' Mary asked her whilst Mrs Trubshaw brought in the tea, breathing rather heavily having negotiated the steep staircase that led up from the basement kitchen. She put down the tray with a little crash on the table in front of them. Geneviève shook her head.

'No, Theresa is the only one I have met so far.'

'Well Vanessa, who is the eldest, is up in Scotland but I expect you will meet her husband Henry, he will be there tonight. Simon is in Munich studying Art and German and Claire is still at school. But I expect Theresa has told you all about them.'

'I would love to meet them all,' Geneviève replied politely.

'We'll get Nessa to give a dinner party,' said Theresa, 'and then you shall.'

Later, the girls changed for the ball, helped by Alice who had returned from her afternoon out and had unpacked Geneviève's case and the shiny cardboard box. Her dress was hanging on the back of her bedroom door and Theresa stood and admired it in wonder.

'Oh Geneviève I am so jealous! You can tell at once that it comes from Paris.'

She touched it gently with the tip of her finger. The dress was a simple sheath of pale green satin. Its beauty lay in the cut and the quality of the material. Theresa knew that it would put all the other dresses in the shade.

'Where are we dining tonight?' Geneviève asked whilst they struggled into their clothes.

'With the Netherfields, you'll love them. They are kind of distant relations. Laura and her brothers Mark and Tom are my closest friends.'

Clad now in their dresses the girls left the mirror and went to the window to look out for a moment over the square. It was going to be a beautiful night for the ball. Geneviève took Theresa's hand.

'I am nervous,' she said, 'I may not know anyone there.'

Theresa laughed, 'they will only have to take one look at you, my friend, and they will all be queuing up to dance with you, I shouldn't worry about that. Anyway Henry will be there, my brother-in-law. I am sure that he will introduce you to lots of people. He is my top pin-up man at the moment because he is the only person who takes my future career seriously.'

'Which one is that?' Geneviève asked her.

'Millinery of course, it has never altered. I want to design and make hats.'

'I do take that seriously,' Geneviève assured her.

'Well no-one else does. Even Aunt Mary looked slightly doubtful when I told her; and as for Vanessa, I don't care what she thinks, I am going to train somewhere, somehow. After all, look at Coco Chanel! She managed to do what she wanted. And what about you, Geneviève?' The girl hesitated.

'Well,' she replied, 'I would like to work for an interesting publisher; or maybe, failing that, an author. Do research for them and things like that. I hope that I may stay in England for a while.' Theresa picked up her wrap.

'We had better go and find Aunt Mary.'

On their way down the stairs Geneviève asked her

'Do you believe these rumours about war?' They stopped for a moment on the little half landing.

'I don't know,' Theresa replied, 'sometimes I forget about it and then someone says something and it all comes back, that feeling of uncertainty.'

As they went on down the stairs Geneviève asked Theresa,

'Why does your Aunt Mary live here all alone in this tall house? I would have thought she might have preferred Scotland.'

'Oh,' Theresa replied, 'I expect in bygone days she might have done, but she has lived in this house for years. Originally she looked after my bachelor Uncle Graham. He was my father's brother and he worked in the city and never married. The family regarded him as a bit of a black sheep because he found his career in London and not in Edinburgh. Anyway he died a long time ago – Tarnoch men tend not to live into old age, and Aunt Mary just kind of stayed on.'

In the hall Geneviève stopped once more to examine a painting that hung on the wall beside the drawing room door.

'Where is this?' she asked, 'it looks an interesting house.'

'It is,' Theresa replied, 'it's my old home called Merlinstone. It belongs to Simon now. When he is older he means to live there.'

Geneviève examined the painting a moment longer.

'It is romantic,' she said, 'with that tower in the centre and the snow clinging to the roof.'

At that moment Mary called to them and they went into the drawing room.

'Come in and let me see you both. My! You look smart. Turn round so I can really admire your dresses.'

They obeyed and then stood together by the fireplace, afraid to sit down in case they creased their skirts.

'They are both so different,' Mary thought, 'and so lovely tonight and so young! What unusual looks that French girl has, with that pale hair and those very dark eyes.' There was a quality to Geneviève which Mary found hard to put into words. Was it a strength, she wondered, an almost steely strength that hid behind a veneer of shyness?

Her thoughts ceased as Alice came in to tell them the taxi was waiting for them. In a flurry the girls gathered up their coats and ran out into the street.

Mary called out, 'I almost forgot to tell you, Gwynneth Cotterell will see you home tonight.'

Theresa waved in reply and they were driven off into the summer evening. Pale pink blossom blew in the gutter where the taxi had stood, it looked like confetti. With a little sigh Mary turned and went back into the house.

Henry Sinclair fixed his white tie with an impatient jerk, frowning at his reflection in the dressing table mirror. The evening was far too warm for these formal clothes. Tail coat next, he shrugged it on over his broad shoulders. Lastly he slipped on a gold signet ring that Vanessa had given to him when they married. Even this made him feel hot so he removed it. The roses in a glass bowl by the window drooped, he could hear the plop of their petals as they fell onto the polished wood. They came from his parents' home in Somerset. 'Would I were there now,' he thought. 'Walking in the garden that runs down to the hayfields, that wonderful English smell of grass in the air, and a cooler breeze, surely, than there is here.'

Earlier in the month he had tried to excuse himself from attending Duchess Gloria's summer ball, but she had been adamant.

'No Henry, darling,' she had said, 'absolutely no, you must come. It may be the last big party we ever give in London. I have found a lovely dinner party for you with the Fitzburnhams and although I am miserable Vanessa can't come we simply must have you.'

Beneath the sweetness in tone, the Gloria charm held a steely determination.

'Damn, oh damn,' Henry had thought, as he had heard his own voice waver and acquiesce to her demands.

'Oh well,' he replied, 'thank you, Gloria, I'll be there.'

He picked up his wallet and his house keys and decided to walk to the Fitzburnhams as they lived only a few streets away. He opened the heavy front door and went out into the evening. The fragrant flowers in the London gardens were rampant, pushing their way through the prim iron railings and towering above them in places, waving their branches. Great fronds of syringa that smelt of Spain and orange blossom, lilies holding their heads high, and roses glowing deeply red. Henry inhaled the evening air and felt a little appeased. At least Theresa would be there, he thought, and she could always make him laugh.

Ralph Cunningham arrived a little late at Gloria Glengower's ball. He had refused an invitation to dine beforehand with an intellectual family who lived in Hampstead and had arrived on his own without a partner. Now he walked into the large house in Carlton House Terrace with a feeling of both relief and expectancy. The evening had become a little cooler and he was going to enjoy himself. The front hall was filled with chattering guests. Large stone urns filled with white flowers stood at intervals against the walls and he could hear the music coming from the ballroom beyond.

Gloria herself was advancing towards him through the crowd, holding out her heavily jewelled hands. Long, pale kid gloves were pushed back and dangled beneath her wrists.

'Here you are Ralph, you old devil!' she said accusingly.

'Your Grace,' he bowed low in mock servitude over her hand.

'Don't mock me,' she replied, flashing her famously brilliant smile disarmingly at him. 'As always you are alone, now come with me and let me introduce you to someone.'

She really was looking resplendent, he thought, admiring her pearl and diamond tiara that was set low on her forehead. The rest of her was swathed in oyster-coloured satin, large diamonds glittered around her neck and in her ears. She took his arm and whispered into his ear

'The Prince is here already, dancing with you know who, how about we take the floor?'

'Gloria, you know that I never dance.'

'Not even with your hostess, just for once?'

He laughed and shook his head.

'Then I shall never speak to you again.'

'Oh yes you will,' smiled Ralph, 'but instead of dancing we are going to have one of our very interesting and all too rare conversations at one of those small tables that awaits us well to the back of the garden and which I know, Gloria, you have had placed there for that purpose, beside that enormous climbing jasmine.'

'Well,' replied Gloria 'maybe we shall do that later. First I want to introduce you to one of my guests.'

She smiled again and looked up at him, tilting her head. He returned her look with his steady, solemn gaze and, she noted, the smallest wink.

'She is called Geneviève de Verdurin, and no nonsense, you wicked philanderer.'

'Of course not!' he replied, playing her game, and pretending to be horrified. 'When has there ever been that?'

'No, not perhaps with the younger generation,' she conceded, 'but one must remember that in spite of your prematurely white hair your years are not unduly considerable, and one never knows when you may start.'

'Now, Gloria, that really is quite enough,' he told her and taking her arm he allowed her to manoeuvre him through the hall to the ballroom where a group of people stood by the open doors talking and laughing together.

'There is Tom, I think,' murmured the Duchess, 'those Netherfield brothers are so alike, Henry Sinclair and his sister-in-law Theresa and yes, that must be the de Verdurin girl.'

Geneviève stood at the edge of the group, watching them shyly. 'What amazing hair she has,' thought Gloria, 'it is so pale and with that white skin, but my goodness look at those eyes! And a beautiful dress, it must have come straight from Madame Grés in Paris,' as she came up to the group they turned politely towards her.

'I do hope you are all enjoying yourselves,' she said, 'Henry dear, and Theresa,' she kissed them and held out a hand to Tom, then she turned to Geneviève. 'You must be Mademoiselle de Verdurin, I am so glad you could come, my dear. I used to know your mother very well some years ago. I hear you are just down from Cambridge.'

Geneviève murmured 'yes', clutching her champagne glass so tightly in her shyness that she nearly snapped the slender stem.

'I have someone here who would very much like to meet you,' Gloria continued, and Ralph stepped forward and taking Geneviève's hand said

'I am Ralph Cunningham. I think I know some relations of yours, the de Crepys.'

Ralph explained that he never danced, but asked her to talk with him for a few moments. Smiling charmingly at her, he led her away into the candlelit garden.

Gloria smiled to herself as they moved away. He was so smooth and skilful at putting people at ease. Did he really know these de Crepys, she wondered, and what was his true reason for wanting to talk with this girl? She could wager it was not just because of her beauty.

'Damn!' thought Henry Sinclair, as Ralph and Geneviève left the group, 'I wanted to dance with her myself. Perhaps I'll have a chance later.'

Turning to Gloria he asked her to partner him, which she gladly accepted.

'Such a pity Arnold hates parties so much,' she said as Henry swung her expertly round the ballroom to the strains of the enthusiastic band; others dancing beside them left them a little extra space as though they were royalty.

'He'll be in the library all evening,' she continued, 'talking to his political friends and speculating endlessly on the possibility of war. It is such a jittery time in the House at the moment. No-one can make up their minds about anything.'

They swooped past the band, past the long portraits on the walls of Glengower ancestors, and the urns that spilled over with white roses and lilies.

'You are a wonderful dancer,' she said.

'You flatter me, Gloria.'

She laughed. 'Of course I do,' she replied, 'you are worth flattering.'

'Theresa is dancing with Tom Netherfield,' she remarked. 'She is looking so pretty tonight and they seem to be enjoying themselves. I am glad, it is important we all have a good time tonight, it may be our last chance to dance here.'

Henry nodded; he had been thinking the same thing all evening. It was a pity Vanessa was missing it.

It was opportune, as sometimes things can be, that as Gloria and Henry left the ballroom Ralph Cunningham and Geneviève came out of the garden and into the hall. Ralph gave a polite little bow and said

'Well, thank you, I have enjoyed our conversation.'

He then went over to Gloria and taking her arm said

'Come my dear friend, a glass of champagne for you after your dancing.'

'I really ought to go and dig Arnold out of the library,' she replied.

'That can wait until later on,' he told her.

Henry went up to Geneviève.

'Would you like to dance?' he asked her.

She smiled her slow, rather secret smile.

'Thank you, I would love to,' and she looked at him for a moment, her dark eyes somewhat inscrutable. He sensed that behind her shyness there might lie a strength, and for the briefest of moments he felt a shiver of apprehension. It was as though he sensed a threat, and then the next moment this seemed quite ridiculous. How could she make him feel this when she was so young and shy, although he would never have described her as timid?

'So your home is in Provence, that amount I do know,' he said, smiling kindly at her. They were dancing a quickstep and he avoided holding her too close.

'I want to hear all about it - I love that part of your country.'

'You have been to the Drôme?' she sounded surprised, her voice held only a trace of an accent.

'Oh yes, I know your part of France a little. I went travelling when I came down from Oxford and I have been to Mont Rouge les Bains and seen the name of your home, the Chateau Verdurin, on the map.'

More people had arrived on the dance floor and the band was playing something very fast and wild.

'Let's sit out for a moment or two, it's getting noisy, I would love to talk to you about France.'

'What, again?' she replied with surprising mockery, 'Am I going to spend all evening sitting in the garden? I shall soon be quite drunk on champagne.'

'Ah,' he replied, holding her away from him so that he could really see her face, '

'What about some strawberries and cream instead?'

'He is so full of charm,' she thought.

'That does sound refreshing,' she admitted.

They found a table in the garden; a waiter brought them strawberries and cream and ice cold lemonade. Beside them there was a syringa tree, its scent stealing out into the darkness.

'Mock orange, they call it, because it smells of orange blossom,' Henry said, pulling a branch towards him, and Geneviève knew that whenever she caught that wonderful scent in the future she would remember this evening and Henry saying this.

'You went to our chateau?' she asked him.

'Alas no,' he replied, 'although I suppose I could have, I did have an introduction through a friend who knew your family. It was British diffidence I am afraid, I was young and travelling rough and rather shy about looking people up. I shall never forget that country - so wild with those enormous rocks towering like primeval sculpture.'

'What a pity you did not call in,' Geneviève said, 'my father would love to have met you. He is a great Anglophile and I think he would have amused you. He hardly ever goes to Paris, he just stays in his chateau carrying out endless repairs; it is very ancient and always needing restoration, and he rides for miles over our property dressed like a peasant, in an old blue shirt and a wide hat.'

Henry smiled 'go on, I am intrigued, please describe the chateau.'

Geneviève took a sip of lemonade and leaned back in her chair. The lantern hanging in the tree above them cast a flickering light over her face.

'Well,' she continued, 'when you come near to the chateau, (you cannot see it fully from the twisting road beneath) you find a large archway and a wide courtyard and at the far end of this is the house. It rises up rather majestically, the whole building seems to grow out of the rocks. Inside Papa has left everything more or less as it was in the eighteenth century – the same wall, the same furniture, the same cobwebs! But the house itself dates to much further back than that, the tower itself was built in the fourteen hundreds. There is a beautiful part that has a flagstone floor and no walls. You walk out onto a kind of terrace and you can see for miles over lavender fields and stretches of scrub oak to the mountains. We have our own little chapel with painted walls and our own mail box set in the wall that runs up to it.'

As she continued to describe her home her eyes grew dreamy with memory and Henry felt she was far away from him, and then suddenly she returned with a jerk and laughed at him.

'I am sorry; I am going on too much about it.'

'Not at all,' he replied, 'I am fascinated.'

'Once we had our own private little militia,' she told him, 'they had such a colourful uniform. My father wears it sometimes rather as a joke, I think, like fancy dress.'

'Will you go back,' he asked her, 'when war comes?'

She noticed he did not say 'if'.

'Most certainly,' she answered swiftly, 'I shall have to go back to Papa. But I shall miss England; I so wanted to find a job here, perhaps research for an author, or working for a publisher, something like that.'

'Ah,' Henry looked at her thoughtfully. Then he leaned forward and put his hand lightly and briefly on her wrist.

'I think we shall have war you know.' She looked at him and she did not smile.

'This Mr Ralph Cunningham I talked with this evening, I think he would agree.' Then she asked him a surprising question.

'If there is war, what will you do?'

Not even Vanessa, his wife, had asked this yet. Perhaps she had been afraid of his answer. He looked away for a moment over the garden - the pretty lanterns hanging in the trees; the ladies, their jewels sparkling occasionally in the flickering light, and the men, their white shirt fronts gleaming. The long windows of the house were open and distantly he could hear the sound of the band. He sighed before he said

'I want to do something that is dangerous like most things are in war but that is also interesting. I have promised myself that I shall do this and of course I feel guilty about it when I think of my wife Vanessa and our little son Greville.' Geneviève gave a slight shrug.

'Perhaps it will not happen after all,' she said, 'maybe at the last moment things will be different.'

He changed the subject.

'You must come and dine with us and meet Nessa,' he said. 'She will be back soon from Scotland. Now come I shall take you back to the dancing and introduce you to some dashing partner. I have to go home as I leave tomorrow at an early hour.'

She got up with a reluctance that she hid, and Henry guided her over towards a group of young men who were all hoping they might be able to dance with her.

Gloria Glengower touched Ralph's arm.

'They are going in,' she murmured, 'I expect Henry Sinclair will be on his way home. He works hard and seldom stays late at parties.' They were sitting at their secluded table at the end of the garden half hidden by a cascading white jasmine.

'You have very good night vision,' Ralph remarked dryly. Gloria looked at him for a moment.

'You manipulate,' she told him.

He raised an eyebrow – 'only in times of war,' he replied.

'Hmmm.'

She opened her evening bag and took out a small mother of pearl fan.

'You know, Ralph, that I seldom ask you questions, but just for a moment tonight you gave yourself away when you told Geneviève you know those people you called de Crepy. I felt certain that you did not know them at all.'

'Oh,' he replied, 'I don't think that mattered very much. They are a very *bien connue* French family; the de Verdurins were bound to know them. I had to find some excuse to talk to the girl. Now I think it is high time I too headed for home.' He rose and she took his arm and together they went through the garden and back into the house.

By the time Theresa and Geneviève reached Montague Square, escorted by Gwynneth Cotterell, a friend of Mary Tarnoch's who had managed to stay awake with the greatest difficulty in order to do this, dawn was breaking over London and the sparrows were chirping in the gutters. In spite of their longing for sleep the two girls spent a few moments discussing the evening before they fell onto their beds.

'What did you think of the dinner party?' Theresa asked, 'did you dance with anyone worth remembering at the ball?'

Geneviève was sleepily dragging a brush through her hair.

'There were so many new people,' she murmured, 'so many.'

'Did you like Henry?' Theresa asked. 'Don't you think he's handsome? Nessa is lucky to find a husband like him. They have known each other since childhood and she has really never looked at anyone else.'

'He is charming,' Geneviève replied, careful not to meet Theresa's eyes in the mirror,

'I would love to meet the rest of your family.'

'You will. I'll organize it. Claire will be coming to London soon; she leaves her school this year and Simon will be returning from Munich. You'll love him, he is so gentle and shy. He's been studying Art and German. Why do boys have all the fun? There is never enough money to send us girls anywhere interesting! He went to the Olympic Games and he saw Hitler. He was with that English girl, Simon said, you know the big blonde one who admires him so much. They wrote about it in the papers. Simon said she was gazing up at the Fuhrer as though he were God!' Theresa yawned, 'We must get some sleep, we'll be useless tomorrow, or rather today! Goodnight dearest Geneviève, I'm going to drop into my bed.'

Left alone Geneviève drew back the curtains and looked out at the dawn. She knew that she was not going to be able to sleep for a long time. She lay down on her bed, her eyes closed, remembering and reliving every moment she had spent that evening with Henry Sinclair; and the feeling of bitter disappointment when he had said that he must return home so soon.

'And he is married,' she told herself, 'to the strong-minded Vanessa whom I have never met, and there is no hope for me at all.'

Why did this have to happen, she wondered? Why had she never felt a glimmer of love for any of the attractive boys she sometimes met at Cambridge, or anyone she had encountered nearer to home in France? And now, suddenly, she had been tipped over the edge.

'I must see him again,' she thought, 'I can't help him being married; I simply cannot survive without seeing him.'

When at last she did fall asleep she dreamt that she was dancing again and willing him to hold her closer. It was well after midday before she awoke.

CHAPTER III

Henry Sinclair arrived home with a little time left, he hoped, to snatch some sleep before dawn broke. With relief he went upstairs to his bedroom and removed his evening clothes. The house was almost eerily quiet, not even a water pipe gurgled, and as yet no birds had started to sing to greet the day. Carefully he removed the white carnation from his buttonhole and put it with the languishing roses. Pulling the curtains back he pushed the windows wide open. Once in bed, lying on his back with only a sheet to cover him he closed his eyes but he could not sleep. He saw against the darkness the figure of Geneviève standing by the ballroom door, of Geneviève dancing with him, looking up at him with those dark inscrutable eyes, of Geneviève in the garden, the lantern lights flickering over her face, telling him about France.

'Hell, oh Hell,' he thought, 'why did I have to leave that wretched party so early? She will still be dancing with dozens of those young men.'

But he could not have monopolised her – had he stayed any longer he probably could have only claimed one more dance.

When August came Simon Tarnoch returned from Munich, Claire left her boarding school after her final summer term, and Theresa apprenticed herself to Madame Solanges who ran a millinery workshop in the East End, whilst leading her sister Vanessa, her legal guardian, to believe that she was working in a respectable part of the West End. Mary Tarnoch asked Geneviève to stay on with her if she would like to, and make her house her base whilst she looked for a job. She was fond of the girl and quite enjoyed having some company. Geneviève eventually found what she was looking for, a position as a research assistant to the author Oscar Cornwallis, the well-known biographer whose particular interest was in French history.

Vanessa Sinclair, prompted by Henry, decided to give a large dinner party. Like many at that time she felt that this would probably be the last time she did this for many years to come, perhaps ever.

'I have gathered them all up,' she said to Henry, 'it has been quite an achievement; they dine with us next Thursday.'

She and Henry were in the drawing room sharing a pre-dinner drink.

'Did you remember to invite the de Verdurin girl?' Henry asked her, 'I told you about her. She's staying with Aunt Mary and her mother was a friend of your mother's years ago.'

'Oh Geneviève, yes I did,' Vanessa replied. 'I think I saw her the other day, walking in the park with guess who?'

'I haven't the faintest idea,' he sounded faintly irritated.

'Ralph Cunningham!'

'Oh Ralph, well he would know her family. He has a lot of friends across the Channel.'

Vanessa went over to the window and stood there for a moment, looking down onto the square.

'Are you still definitely joining your father's old regiment if there is war?' she asked him.

There was a small silence and then Henry came over and put his arms around her.

'I think so,' he said, 'but it may lead to more interesting things later on.'

Vanessa moved away from him.

'I don't like the sound of that,' she told him. He took a sip of his drink.

'Everything is dangerous in war,' he told her, 'no matter what you choose to do. Some people die on the way to war without having fired a single shot, look at Rupert Brooke for instance, and others come through the most appalling battles without a scratch. It is just the throw of the dice; and whilst we are on the subject of what we shall do,' he continued, 'I think you should shut this house up and go to Merlinstone with Greville, it would be far safer.'

Vanessa twisted her pearl necklace through her fingers and looked back at him with her long, piercing gaze.

'I can't do that, Henry,' she said, 'I have to be part of it. I shall stay here and get war work, and I shall send Greville to Merlinstone with Nannie.'

Draining his glass, Henry knew they were about to have a heated argument, perhaps even a row. He had not the stomach for it. 'I'll talk to her later,' he thought, and thankfully at that moment Murphy, their Irish butler, came in to tell them dinner was ready and they went into the dining room, leaving their conversation on hold whilst they ate their meal by candle light.

The following Thursday Vanessa waited for her guests. She went into the dining room and admired the long polished table that was laid with the best silver and lace table mats. The branched candlesticks held tall white candles and the guests' names had been written on small white cards and put opposite each place. The heavy curtains had not been drawn; you could glimpse the houses opposite through the branches of the trees in the square. The feeling of late summer washed over Vanessa as she looked, one light went on opposite, it glowed in the window, a pale lemon colour. Surely it can't be time yet to turn on the lights, she thought. Satisfied with the way the table looked she went into the drawing room. Henry was already there, holding up a glass and inspecting the pale gold contents.

'Murphy and I have been doing some wine tasting,' he said. 'Try this, darling, it's champagne, I thought we should have something special this evening for Simon's return from Munich and Claire finishing her school career!'

Vanessa sipped the drink.

'Delicious,' she said, 'how kind of you Henry, this is the very best!'

Tom and Mark Netherfield walked through a heavy shower sharing an umbrella having left their bus in the Brompton Road.

'You know,' said Tom, 'we'll soon have to stop doing this.'

'Doing what?' Mark queried.

'Going everywhere together, people will think we're twins.'

'They probably do already, after all, barely fourteen months divides us,' 'Disgusting really, the energy of our parents.'

'The trouble is,' said Tom, 'we're so useful to the hostesses. They just ring up when they're giving a dinner party and say 'Can I have the pair of you please, that will even us out'.'

'But tonight is different,' Mark told him, 'we are going to be with old friends, the Sinclairs and the Tarnochs - Simon's going to be coming I believe. Soon we'll be up to our universities and we'll be separated.'

Whereupon Tom fell onto one knee in the middle of the pavement with his hand on his heart and declaimed

'Oh my dearest brother, how shall I exist without you?'

Startled passers-by brushed past them and they laughed so strenuously they nearly fell into the gutter.

'It's been a wonderful summer,' gasped Mark when they were once more on their way, 'but soon it will be hard work, or war.'

'No-one works hard at university,' Tom pointed out, 'but war is another matter. By the way are you planning to join Dad's old regiment?'

'Heavens no, I told you it's our boys in blue for me. I want to fly aeroplanes.'

They had arrived at Vanessa's front door. Tom lowered the umbrella.

'Your trousers look a bit odd,' said Mark.

Tom scrubbed his knees vigorously with his handkerchief and then pulled the heavy brass doorbell. Upstairs in the drawing room Vanessa greeted them warmly.

'How lovely you could both come tonight,' she said, 'I thought you might have been Aunt Mary, she is usually the first to arrive.'

Murphy handed them the champagne, gleaming enticingly in the wide, fine glasses that he carried on a silver tray.

'How wonderful!' Tom exclaimed, taking a glass and handing another to Mark.

'This will set us up! We were getting rather gloomy on our way here, contemplating work or war.'

There were more voices in the hall and Mary Tarnoch arrived accompanied by her old friend Sir Malcolm Innes-Hunter. They were swiftly followed by Theresa and Claire, and Simon. He was looking rather thin and pale, Vanessa thought, as she went to embrace him, and though he was smiling he was obviously still shy and a little awkward with them all. This soon wore off once the Netherfield boys greeted him, obviously delighted to see him again. Vanessa's gaze returned to Claire, who was accepting a drink and was standing on her own by the window. She had grown a great deal and resembled their mother, Vanessa thought, with that slightly wild, flyaway look and her hair, although tied back in an effort to appear more sophisticated, escaping from its wide, tortoiseshell clip. Her clothes were somewhat untidy as well - at the back of her skirt there was definitely a large safety pin.

'We have one more guest to come,' Vanessa murmured to Henry, 'she is rather late, I hope she hasn't lost her way.'

Henry went over to the window; there was a taxi outside and he could just see the top of Geneviève's fair head as she went towards the front door.

'She has arrived,' he said, 'we shall soon be able to start dinner.'

When Geneviève entered the drawing room she saw her hostess first; tall and slim in black, moving towards her.

'I am Vanessa,' she said, in her rather deep, husky voice, 'it is so nice to see you Geneviève. Now come, let me introduce you to everyone here.'

She led the girl round the room, stopping at each guest until she came to Henry.

'I know that you have already met,' she said.

Henry smiled, his easy, charming smile.

'Of course we have, at Gloria's ball. I am so glad you could come tonight and we are able to introduce you to all the family.'

Geneviève met his gaze. She gave a faint smile.

'It is so kind of you to invite me,' she replied, her voice cool but not unfriendly. She accepted a glass of champagne and turned towards Theresa, concealing it from Henry as she took an enormous gulp from her glass.

At last they were all seated around the long mahogany table. The candles burned in their silver sconces, giving a soft light, whilst the rest of the room sank back into shadow, save for a few picture lights that dimly lit the large oil paintings that hung at intervals along the walls. The curtains were still pulled back and the evening was turning to dusk. In the square the late summer leaves hung from the trees like lanterns.

'These are the things that will go,' thought Henry, as he dipped a spoon into his golden coloured soup and turned towards his neighbour, 'these memories will be smothered and lost by blood and thunder and noise, and we shall only remember them in our dreams.' Out loud he said to Mary Tarnoch,

'Now tell me about all the good and kind things that you have been doing of late.'

Geneviève had been seated on Henry's left with Tom Netherfield on her other side. She turned to Tom and they started to chat about his forthcoming time at university. Not until they were well into their main course of lamb cutlets and petits pois à la Francaise did she dare look towards Henry. He was waiting for her, smiling and at ease.

'It seems ages since I last saw you,' he said, 'at the Glengower ball.'

She took a sip of her wine and after a brief pause she said

'Yes, quite a lot has happened since then. I am working for Oscar Cornwallis, the historian, helping him to research his new biography on Henri IV of France. My French is quite helpful with this and I am loving my job. He is a fascinating character.'

'Which, Henri IV or Cornwallis?'

'Both,' she replied and at that moment Henry felt a violent pain and a tightening in his stomach and knew this was extreme jealousy. He turned away for a moment to help himself to the pudding that Murphy was handing round.

'And after this book what do you think he will start on?'

She hesitated.

'Well I am probably being indiscreet,' she said, 'but I think he may be considering a military biography next, perhaps about the life of the famous General Tarnoch, who was your wife Vanessa's father, I believe.' Henry laughed.

'How extraordinary!' he said, 'well you are certainly getting to know the right family, if you are to help with that subject. Merlinstone is stuffed with archives but rest assured,' he added, 'my lips are sealed.'

And she knew in that small moment, when he looked at her, that she could trust him.

Further down the table Simon was being plied with questions by Claire and Theresa.

'Did you really see Hitler?' they asked him.

'Oh yes,' he replied, 'he was in Munich several times, making hysterical speeches and drawing the crowds. They worship him, he has become almost God-like to them; I was glad to come home and get away from it all.'

Watching him from across the table Mary Tarnoch thought 'he is such a sensitive boy, too much so for his own comfort. I wish we were not all facing such an uncertain future!' and she sighed.

Malcolm Innes-Hunter who was sitting next to her said

'A penny for them, Mary.' She looked back at him and smiled.

'My thoughts are probably the same as yours tonight,' she replied.

On this particular evening no-one mentioned by name the cloud that hung over the near horizon or the feeling they all had of *fin de siècle*.

There was a small moment before they left the table when Henry said to Geneviève in a low voice,

'Don't leave it too late, will you?'

'What do you mean?' she murmured.

'Your return to your Papa in France. Journeys will become hazardous.'

'Oh I know,' she replied, 'I worry about that. One moment I am lulled into a false sense of security and the next I am in a panic about getting back home.'

'I think there is a little more time, but not much,' Henry told her, and to himself he thought 'I must, oh I simply must, manage to see you again.'

They left the dining room and went into the drawing room. Simon sat down at the piano and started to play and they grouped around him, laughing and singing. The room glowed with colour and was heavy with the scent of lilies and their mood greatly lightened by Simon's playing and Theresa's true, clear voice. It was well after midnight when they all went home, and Vanessa and Henry turned towards their bed. After the dinner party Henry's great problem lay in that there was no pretext under which

he could get in touch with Geneviève. He did not dare ring her in case
Aunt Mary should answer the telephone. In desperation he thought that he
would have to write a note and send it to the house where she worked. He
decided that this imperfect plan was the only course that he could take and
that he would write to her that evening.

It was an unexpectedly stormy day, bursts of sunlight followed very heavy
showers. Henry left his office and went by tube as far as South Kensington
and then decided to walk the rest of the way home. He planned to spend
a short time on the way in the Victoria and Albert Museum to collect his
thoughts and plan what he was going to write to Geneviève. It was dark
inside the great hall of the Museum. He was glad to be away from the
tempestuous day and the noise of the city. He breathed a great sigh of relief
as he strolled through the sculpture rooms. He stood for a few moments
before the massive figure of David, and then turned into the next room
and went towards a glass case where he knew that he would find some
small, sculptured figures. How beautiful it was, he thought, the little torso
of Artemis - but here he broke off his gaze and looked round. He had seen,
reflected in the glass case, the profile of someone he knew. He moved away
from the case and there was Geneviève walking past him towards the door.
He called out softly to her and she turned back, bewildered for a moment
and then she saw him and smiled.

'Henry!' she exclaimed and went towards him; he bent and kissed her
cheek. 'Are you meeting someone here?' she asked.

'Only you,' he replied, 'I quite often wander through these rooms after a
busy day, I find it a soothing thing to do.'

She nodded. 'I too,' she replied, 'it is a fine place for contemplation.'

Talking softly to each other they left the sculpture room and went on to
admire the oriental faience.

After doing this their thoughts turned towards tea.

'I know a good place quite near,' Henry suggested, and they left the
Museum.

Outside the sun had disappeared and a strong wind gusted down the
street. They began to walk along the Brompton Road. There were no
taxis in sight and the rain had started to drive against them in torrents,
accompanied by a brisk shower of hailstorms. Henry took Geneviève's
hand and, pulling her along beside him, he turned into a square that led
them to a churchyard.

'We'll shelter in there,' he said, pointing to the church.

As they ran towards the building they saw that a small door on the side had been left half open, perhaps blown that way by the wind. They ran towards it and Henry pulled Geneviève in and slammed the door. They were both out of breath and laughing. Geneviève's pale hair was dark with water and plastered to her head, her skirt stuck to her legs and rivulets of rain ran off her, making small puddles on the floor. Henry glanced round the small room.

'We're in the vestry,' he said, 'the vicar must have forgotten to close the door! I'll just go and make sure there is no-one in the church.'

Before he went he reached up and unhooked a long black cassock that hung behind the door into the church.

'Put this on,' he told her, 'before you get pneumonia.'

Geneviève obeyed him, pulling off her drenched clothes and bundling them into a shopping bag she had been carrying with her. The black material felt scratchy against her skin and she tried to wring the water from her hair. Henry returned,

'No-one there,' he told her. Then he stood back and surveyed her. She was standing tall and straight and the stiff black material fell in folds around her to the ground.

'I feel like a nun,' she said.

'I hope,' he replied softly, 'that you are not going to behave like one,' and very gently he gathered up her hair and took her face in his hands and kissed her.

Her face was still wet with rain. His kisses moved to her throat, and he said

'Darling, take off that horrible garment.'

She raised her arms and he dragged it off her. Then he took off his own clothes that had not resisted the rain any better than hers and flinging the cassock on the floor he found the surplice and added it.

'That will have to be our bed,' he told her. 'I must say I had not imagined making love to you on a vestry floor.'

'Where had you imagined it happening?' she asked him.

'Oh in a beautiful summer hayfield,' he replied. Leaning against him, feeling his nakedness, she laughed.

'How delightfully English of you,' she said. 'Make love to me, Henry.'

'What else could I possibly be going to do?' he asked her and gently he pushed her down onto the awaiting clerical garments.

'Our sanctified bed,' he whispered, 'as a good Catholic I am surprised you do not remonstrate with me.' She sighed a deep, trembling sigh and in reply she kissed him.

Much later she said, 'We forgot to lock the door.'

'I remembered that,' he replied, 'and then I quite forgot about it. Where did you go to, my darling Geneviève, when we made love?'

'Into a kind of paradise of oblivion, I can't describe it,' she replied. They lay quietly for a while, listening to the rain and the wind against the narrow windows.

Later they were forced to consider the time. They seemed to have been an age in another country. He sat up and looked down on her, thinking how pale her skin was. She looked up at him and smiled.

'You are not going to tell me that you were married in this church, are you?' she said.

'God no,' he replied, 'we were married in Edinburgh, not far from Merlinstone, Vanessa's home.'

'Do you love her?' she asked him. He was silent for a moment, cradling her against him.

Then he said, 'yes, I do I suppose, but I am not in love with her. I don't think that I ever was. We were childhood friends and somehow we drifted into marriage. I thought we had been made for each other, I thought it would all be so easy.'

'And hasn't it been?' she asked.

He sighed, 'oh yes, in some ways too much so. She loves me and we have our little son Greville. But oh God, it is so boring, our marriage!'

She laughed at him. 'You spoilt man!' she said, and he held her even closer.

'Yes, I expect I am,' he replied, 'spoiled, and half alive until now!'

He pulled her up so that she stood beside him, and for a moment they both gazed down at the floor, at the rumpled cassock and the white surplice that was now covered in patches of bright red blood.

Geneviève said 'oh my God!' She closed her eyes and buried her face in his shoulder. 'I am, I mean I was, a virgin. You are the first man I have ever made love to.' He kissed the back of her neck.

'I realised that,' he said; he was laughing. Bending, he gathered up the clothes. 'Give me your shopping bag and I'll take them away and dispose of them. The poor old vicar's robes of office, little will he ever guess what has become of them.'

Geneviève took her clothes from the shopping bag and started to put them on. They were still very damp indeed.

'It must be quickly home for you my darling,' he told her, 'I will have to find you a cab.'

The sun was out again; it fell through the windows onto the dusty floor. Henry dressed and then opening his wallet took out a good number of bank notes and placed them under a candlestick he found on a small table beside the door.

'For some new clerical attire for the poor chap,' he said.

She looked back at him, her mouth quivering, and they both started to laugh. She said

'You know I shall never be quite as happy as this again.'

'Come,' he said gently, his arms around her shoulders as he opened the vestry door.

'Ouch,' he said, 'the world.'

The rain had freshened the air and the wind rushed past them. Wild sunlight splashed the sky and the graveyard shone with sparkling rain drops. They made their way into the streets and the traffic. Henry hailed a taxi which, now the storm was over, were plentiful.

'Will you be alright my darling?' he asked her, 'I wish I could come with you but I had better not appear in front of Aunt Mary and I must get home.'

'I shall be all right,' she replied, 'but when, oh when, shall I see you?'

'Very soon. Now I have your work number I shall ring you.'

'Do I look fairly normal?' she asked him anxiously.

He took her coat collar and straightened it.

'Not bad, considering,' he told her, one eyebrow raised, 'and as beautiful as the moon; now go home and have a hot bath and try to avoid Aunt Mary.'

She was driven away down the streets. He watched her go, his heart ached, he longed to be with her.

When Henry reached home he was intensely relieved to find that the house was empty. The servants were in the basement making preparations for dinner and Vanessa was still out on some mission. He went up the stairs and ran a bath. This was the first time that he had been unfaithful to Vanessa and he was surprised that he felt so little shame or remorse. Instead he just ached for Geneviève. 'She is my moon maiden,' he thought, 'she is so pale.' She had reminded him of a Florentine painting, lying there on the vicar's robes. Whilst he bathed he remembered the first time he had seen her at the Glengowers' ball. Had a chasm of flames opened up between them he would have gone through them and asked her for a dance. He had known then that he had to speak to her, he had to touch her. He closed his eyes and relived the afternoon. Then he got out of the bath hurriedly; he had started to fall asleep and he could hear Vanessa's footsteps on the stairs.

On her return to Montague Square Geneviève was not so fortunate. On opening the front door with her latch key she found Mary in the hall, sorting through her newly-arrived mail. She looked up quickly and on seeing Geneviève she exclaimed

'My dearest girl! What has happened to you?'

'I got caught in a terrible storm and I had no umbrella, and I couldn't for the life of me find a taxi.'

'But that lovely coat!' Mary said, touching her arm, 'it looks like a rag, take it off and I'll hang it in the airing cupboard for you.'

Geneviève moved quickly away. 'Oh no really, Aunt Mary, thank you but I have things in the pocket I must sort out, to do with work you know. I'll go upstairs and have a hot bath' and she hurried towards the stairs. But it was not the coat that had astonished Mary, it was Geneviève's face. Her usually pale cheeks were quite pink and her dark eyes were shining. Her smooth hair was springing free in a wild and not unattractive tangle.

'Oh dear,' she thought, as she made her way to the drawing room with her mail,

'What has she been up to? Have I been negligent? I really think it is high time that she returned to France and her father, especially with this looming threat of war.'

Henry moved through the next few days as if in a dream. If Vanessa noticed any difference in him she put it down to his worries and concerns about the threatened war. Vanessa asked him again what he intended to do.

'It will probably be the army for me to start with,' he said, 'but as I mentioned before I would like to be involved with Ralph's outfit. Nothing in that department is very clear yet.'

Vanessa looked up at him.

'Something much more dangerous, I suppose,' she said, her voice was anxious and cold.

'Darling, I have already told you everything in wartime is dangerous. Have another drink, the other half as they say – I think we need cheering up.'

He picked up the cocktail shaker and took it across to her, shaking it as he went. What a graceful, good-looking man he was she thought, as she watched him fill her glass – he had no idea how deeply she cared for him. He was right, it was stupid to be gloomy on one of the final evenings they would spend together in this house. And then she remembered something she had meant to entertain him with.

She picked up an evening paper she had tossed on to a chair.

'Henry,' she said, 'I simply must read this to you, it is hilarious! It's in our local rag. I was reading it when you came home this evening and I meant to tell you at once, it is so amusing. Now, here it is on the letter page. 'Sir,' she began, spreading the paper out on the piano lid, 'I am compelled to write and recount to you the strange adventure I had the other day which was entirely due to my absent mindedness. I am vicar of St John's Belgravia and the other evening I omitted, on leaving the church after our usual weekday evensong, to close the vestry door. Feeling, the following day, that I may not have fastened it securely, and fearing the strong wind might have loosened it I returned to the church rather late the following evening. I was very anxious indeed when I arrived at the church where I found the vestry door was closed but unlocked. On entering and going over the whole building with great care I was very relieved to find that no plate was missing, and not a single candle either – the only things that had vanished were my cassock and surplice. This led me to ponder on many possibilities. Had a desperate priest, on his way to take an important service, forgotten his own and had nipped in and taken mine instead? Or was it someone who was on his way to some fancy dress party, or a performance of amateur dramatics? And then I noticed something had been placed beneath a small candlestick that always stands on the table beside the door. It was such a large wad of bank notes that I could have replaced my own humble vestments with a Bishop's robes twice over! I want to thank the mysterious intruder and assure him that after replacing my clothing I have given the rest of his generous donation to the church! It is signed, the Reverend Sewell Halsey.'

Henry stood for a moment and stared at Vanessa, expressionless. She waited a second for his laughter and then he flung his head back and produced a peal, which may have sounded slightly false and hysterical, but he managed it. Vanessa folded the paper, relieved at least she had made him laugh. The air had cleared between them, she thought, and for a few moments they had forgotten about the war. Sadly, this proved to be only a temporary truce before they had an argument. Henry, while he ate his consommé soup, wondered why all disagreements and awkward discussions seem to take place during meals, thus managing to ruin them. When the sole with white grapes followed, one of his favourites, he felt that he did not want any. Vanessa had started to work herself up into a fit of indignant rage. He had returned to the subject of her leaving London and closing the house. He knew he would have to mention this again before he left for his army training, and she, as usual, violently disagreed.

'I shall send Greville and Nannie to Merlinstone,' she said, 'and of course

I shall visit them as often as I can, but I shall remain here and work at something that will help the war.'

'Rolling bandages?' he asked her, with a hint of sarcasm in his voice. She glanced down the table at him.

'I think,' she said coldly, 'that I shall go into a munitions factory and find work there, they will need people.'

He paused a moment. The sole was delicious but he could eat no more. He visualised this house, their lovely home crumbling into a mass of rubble as the bombs fell. He thought of the danger there would be in the streets, the fires, the darkness. Softening his tone, he said

'Nessa darling, you must think of Greville. He will need his mother more than ever. After all I might die in battle and it is crazy your having to put yourself in danger when you could be at Merlinstone, safe and sound.'

'It would be disgusting,' she replied, 'I am my father's daughter; I'm not running away.'

No further argument would be of any use. He could see this as he watched her face harden in anger and stubborn determination. After dinner he left her in the drawing room and went to his study where he tried to write some letters. As he sat at his desk, looking out at the dusk-shrouded garden full of birds singing their sad, late summer song he thought of Geneviève.

'I must see you,' he murmured. 'I shall ring you tomorrow, my most precious girl.'

The following day on the third of September, Britain declared war on Germany.

CHAPTER IV

Simon drove north to Merlinstone, for his embarkation leave. He had joined his father's old regiment and after a few weeks of rigorous training he was facing up to leaving the country that he loved. As he drove he thought how strange fate sometimes was. He seemed to have slipped from his youth, shadowed by the effects of the last war and the death of his father, into the prelude of yet another war. Everyone was saying that this one would not last long but deep in his being he knew they were wrong. He felt as he had done before returning to his boarding school, a deep cold fear that it was to be an inevitable nightmare. He wished he could have felt like some of his contemporaries, full of excitement and adventurous anticipation. He could see ambition shining in his sister Vanessa's eyes when she looked at him; he knew that she was picturing him becoming a famous and successful soldier like their father had been. He wanted to say, 'Leave me alone and don't imagine these things. I am an artist, all I want to do is paint and draw.'

He hated to see his mother's sad, proud expression when she looked at him, her precious only son whom she had always loved more than any of her children, going bravely off to war. He did not feel brave and he hated the idea of conflict. He had no wish at all to be covered with military glory. What, he wondered, would his father have thought if he had known his true feelings? General Tarnoch had been an unusual man; with all his brave, military prowess there lay beneath a certain sensitivity. Simon felt that he would have understood.

He drove up the steep road where England becomes Scotland and into the historic and beautiful border country. The evening sky had turned a clear, vivid apricot. He drove down a side turning and turned off the engine. The rolling landscape unfurled before him and distantly the grape-blue hills undulated along the horizon. Simon took out his small sketch book and a stump of a pencil and started to draw. He made small notes telling him the colour of the sky and the hills. Then he wrote 'Last look at the way north' at the bottom of the page and dated it. When he had completed his drawing he sat there for a long time, watching the sky darken. Then he set off once more, and when he eventually reached Merlinstone night had fallen. The great bulk of the house rose before him as he drove up the avenue of lime trees. (The avenue where, years later, he and his nephew Greville would walk and talk together, getting to know each other for the first time.) Now the dark building covered by rays of light from the windows welcomed him home.

The family were all gathered there for their final reunion before they were to be scattered by the war. There were the sisters; Vanessa, Theresa, and Claire, their mother, Violet, Aunt Mary- and Henry, with little Greville. They had all come together to wish Simon Godspeed and eventually a safe return.

'We have planned a large party for tomorrow evening,' Vanessa told him after he had arrived and they were congregating in the library before a late dinner. 'We thought you would like us to ask all the neighbours and people on the estate and the Thompsons (these were the minister and his wife). We have been arranging it all so you won't have anything to worry about.'

'Yes,' he said, 'thank you Nessa, that was most thoughtful of you.' He suddenly felt exhausted and drained by everything.

'Do you think Mother will be all right up here on her own?' he asked his sister.

Vanessa lit a cigarette and inhaled deeply, then she looked at Simon, her eyes narrowing as she blew out the smoke.

'Nannie and Greville will be here,' she said, 'I'm sending them soon to get them out of London and I shall be visiting as often as I can and Claire will be here for a while to help Mother, and then Ishbel will still be cooking – she's too elderly for call up thank heaven.'

Simon raised his eyebrows,

'Aren't you going to leave London, Nessa?' he asked. She tossed back her hair.

'Heavens no!' she said, 'I am going to work in a munitions factory, that is what I am planning to do, and Theresa is joining the Wrens so she'll be down in Portsmouth, apparently. Where are the Netherfields at present?'

'Mark is joining the RAF and Tom the army,' he told her.

'Heaven protect them,' she murmured 'and you too, my darling brother,' and she laid a hand on his shoulder as she said this. 'Henry's going soon,' she said, 'but he can't tell me much about it and I'm worried about Claire,' she confided. 'She's murmuring about war work but she really is far too young and you know how harum scarum she is, she is very difficult to deal with at the moment.'

'She is becoming very pretty,' he replied; he adored his younger sister. At that moment the library door opened and Violet, his mother, came into the room. She had been resting and he thought how frail she looked.

'I heard the car,' she said and came over to kiss him. 'Let us light the fire; these evenings are beginning to get colder.'

He obediently found a match and soon the flames were leaping up, catching the wood and dark pieces of turf that were banked up in the wide hearth. Violet took Simon's hand and quietly held it in both of hers.

'It is so lovely to have you here for a few moments, my darling,' she said.

He smiled back at her and his heart twisted with pain. When they had all gathered in the library they went into the dining room for dinner. Vanessa murmured to Simon as they went in:

'I haven't told Mother yet but we shall soon be expecting a whole lot of children under ten years of age – evacuees, they're coming from Glasgow. I shall have to get in some extra help.'

And before he could reply she went determinedly past him into the dining room where she struck a match and lit the candles that stood on the long table.

That night, before they went to bed, Claire went along in her nightgown to Theresa's bedroom. Her sister was sitting at her dressing table brushing her wiry dark hair. She looked up when Claire came in and put down the brush.

'What is it fair maid?' she asked.

Claire sat down on the bed.

'It's Nessa,' she said. 'I think it is really dreadful of her to leave Mother in charge of all those evacuees. Thirty of them, have you heard about it? They're going to be put into makeshift dormitories in the west wing.'

'I know,' agreed Theresa, 'but what can we do about it?'

'I asked her and she said 'Oh Nannie and Claire will be here and I'll come and go, and Ishbel will love all the fuss; I'm going to find her extra help – that is what she said.'

'I don't think Ishbel will love it!' Claire exclaimed, 'she'll probably pack her bags and leave and then we'll all starve. Anyway, Theresa, I am NOT staying here all the war. I am planning to run away.' Theresa surveyed her sister calmly.

'Where to?' she asked.

'I am going to work as well; I shall be seventeen in December. I'm going to be a nurse. I've found out all about it from Laura Netherfield – she wants to do the same but she can't yet because her sister's still at home and she's got to help her father. He can't cope with everything on his own.'

'I know, poor Laura stuck in that gloomy London house all the war.'

'Perhaps they'll be forced to go to the country. Actually I love the house, it's got such atmosphere.'

'But will nursing really be your thing, Claire?' Theresa asked her doubtfully.

'Yes – I know it would be and I don't just mean rolling bandages. I want to start from the very beginning; I want to be hands on.'

'It will be hands on scrubbing floors to start with I expect,' Theresa told her.

'I don't care, I'll work my way up.'

Claire's eyes were burning with zeal. Theresa had never seen her like this. She was normally rather a dreamy girl, her clothes untidy, hems hanging down and safety pins in various places, riding her horses and forgetting to come home for meals. But, reflected Theresa, there had always been a streak of determination, like the time when she defied her mother and had caught the local bus and gone into Edinburgh to see some unsuitable film with one of the minister's sons, Chisholm she thought his name was, and now he had already gone to join his ship before leaving for Norwegian waters. She sighed and gave her sister a hug.

'Think about the fuss,' she said, 'Nessa will be furious, she'll try and stop you going to London.'

'I know,' said Claire bitterly, 'of course she will. And look at her, abandoning Mother and her son and going to work in a munitions factory! Henry is furious and I must say I don't blame him.'

'We don't want another war here, darling,' Theresa told her, 'let's calm down about it now and go to bed. It's getting late.'

Claire kissed her sister warmly and went back to her room; once in bed she lay for a long time, her eyes closed but without sleeping, making her plans.

The following evening they gave the farewell party for Simon. Everyone who worked at Merlinstone came, both in the house and on the estate, as well as local friends and neighbours. In a way Simon was glad there was such a crowd. He could conceal himself behind the large plates of small sandwiches and sausage rolls and trays of champagne and whisky, which he gladly helped to hand round. Since his father's death and the family's worsening finances there were considerably fewer members of staff.

They had had to say a sad goodbye to many whom they had known since childhood. Ishbel Macrae, their cook, battled on, occasionally helped by a girl from the village called Jessie who was too young to be called up and should really have been at school. It was Ishbel who stopped by Simon on her way back to the kitchen to replenish the plates and asked

'And who is going to be here to look after your Ma when you have gone, Mr Simon? She'll never manage all these evacuees on her own, I know they are bringing their nurses with them but who is going to administrate?'

Simon said, 'Oh goodness, Ishbel, at this moment I am not quite sure. Well Greville is going to be here with Elspeth Gray, his Nannie, and there'll be Claire, and Vanessa will come and go.'

'Miss Claire!' Ishbel snorted, '*she* won't be staying for long. She's got her plans.' Simon stood for a moment, looking at her retreating back as she made her way to the kitchen where Jessie was pulling another batch of sausage rolls out of the oven. It would be useless, he knew, for him to say anything to Claire about remaining at Merlinstone if she had chosen not to. He saw Gloria Glengower advancing, her hair caught back with a large diamond clip.

'Simon,' she exclaimed, 'my very dearest boy.' Her voice was warm and purring, the tone she reserved for young and attractive men. 'This is a sad evening for all the jollity. I do hope you are not too worried about leaving your mother, we shall keep an eye on her, you know.'

'Yes,' he replied, 'I know you will, Gloria.'

The thought of saying goodbye to the frail Violet suddenly filled him with despair and he quickly drank a glass of champagne and felt slightly better. Alastair Thompson, the minister, came up next. He was an old friend and had known Simon since his childhood.

'Well, Simon,' he said, 'all ready to go?' and he put a hand on his arm and drew him towards the window where there was less noise.

'Yes,' Simon replied, 'the day after tomorrow. Haven't you got a drink, Alastair?'

'I'll find one in a moment. So what are your sisters planning?'

Simon told him, finishing by saying 'and Claire is meant to be staying here but I think she may be planning something else.'

Alastair raised his eyebrows. 'I hear the evacuees are coming. Typical of your mother to welcome such an invasion but how on earth are they going to manage? Listen, Simon, I'll keep a close watch on them all and help them if I possibly can and so, I know, will Igrainie.'

Simon said warmly 'I know you will, Alastair. The trouble is Mother has worn herself out. Ever since Father died she has worked so hard trying to keep his charities going and she is always worrying about finances.'

Alastair accepted a glass of whisky, handed to him by Theresa.

'We all love and admire her,' he said, 'she will have great support.'

At that moment someone beckoned to Simon and he had to move away. Alastair watched him go through the crowded room and thought 'he is such a sensitive young man. May God protect him.'

When Simon at last boarded the liner the Franconia, newly painted in her wartime grey, he felt almost relieved. The strain of keeping a stiff upper lip, of smiling when he had felt like howling and beating his fists against the wall was over. He felt almost light-hearted, and there was a strangely festive air about the other young men, many already known to him, who were travelling with him to war. Sometimes he sat a little apart from them, drawing quick sketches of them in his note book and tearing out the pages which he gave them and which made them laugh. At the foot of one page he wrote 'sky blue, sea calm, destination unknown, goodbye England – 1939.'

On his return to London from Merlinstone Henry went into his study and closed the door. Vanessa had gone out and the house was very quiet. Braving whoever might answer (he prayed it would not be her boss) Henry dialled Geneviève's work number. When he heard her voice he said

'My darling! You should have left for France. Can we talk? Are you on your own?'

'Yes,' she replied, 'I am, for a few moments - Oscar has gone out. I know I should have left, there has been a little trouble with my passport and I had to see you before I went; I am so relieved you have called me, Henry! Time has almost run out.'

'I know, I telephoned you as soon as I could; we got back from Merlinstone this morning. Listen, meet me today at Claridges for lunch at one o'clock. Then I have to get back here and pack. I am going up to Catterick first thing tomorrow morning. It's chaos, no-one seems to know where we are heading for after that. Darling, I'm ringing off now, à toute à l'heure.' He replaced the receiver. His palms were damp with anxious sweat.

Geneviève glanced round her bedroom. She was in the middle of packing as few of her possessions as possible. She knew that she would have to manage her luggage herself. Anything left behind she was giving to Mary for one of her charities. She looked at the lovely dress she had worn to the Glengower ball when she had first met Henry and tearing out her useful winter coat she flung it on the charity pile and packed the dress instead. It was madness she knew but she could not part with the sheath of satin that would for ever remind her of that evening.

There would be no leisurely walk down Bond Street to Davies Street today. No admiring of shop windows or enjoyment of the late summer sun. She hurled herself into a taxi and headed straight for the hotel. When she arrived she went into the foyer and saw Henry sitting at a table on the far side. He got up at once and did not kiss her but took her arm and guided her swiftly into the crowded restaurant.

'Are we being very indiscreet?' she murmured.

'For the very first and pray God not the last time I am going to give you a proper lunch,' he replied. 'Anyway everyone goes to the Ritz these days.'

She laughed. They were on the far side of the restaurant by the long windows. Glancing round she was relieved to see that she recognized no-one. Henry, on the other hand, had noticed someone who was seated a few tables away from them.

'An old school friend I haven't seen for years,' he told her, 'he's bound to think we are married so that's all right. And now, Mademoiselle Verdurin, what would you like to drink?'

'A little wine would be lovely,' she replied, 'I daren't risk a cocktail first – I have to keep a clear head. I just cannot believe I'm going so soon.' And to herself she said 'I love you so much that I just cannot bear the thought of leaving you.' To prevent herself from saying this out loud she leaned towards him,

'Did you expect to hear me when you rang?' He looked back at her and saw the fear in her usually implacable gaze.

'I was terrified you might have gone,' he told her, 'and I was equally terrified you might still be there.'

'It is tomorrow Henry, I go tomorrow.' Her stomach dipped with nervous fear as she said this.

'And I shall not be able to help you. Let's not discuss this now, it is too painful. What shall we have to eat? This will probably be the last good meal before you get home, I'll wager, so we must make the most of it.'

The waiter came and took their order and poured out more wine. They held up their glasses.

'This is to our next meeting,' he said, 'and it will happen, Geneviève, eventually.'

They clinked their glasses and drank.

'You are looking so charming,' he told her, lightening their mood, 'very à la mode, I like your hat.' She was wearing a little blue velvet cap with a feather in it that curled round onto her cheek.

'Made by Theresa,' she told him, 'isn't she clever? She really will become a top milliner one day, you'll see.'

But light-hearted banter would not work for them that day. He took her wrist and said

'Darling, about your journey – you have arranged it carefully haven't you? I am so worried about you. I know you intend to stop a night in Paris but please get away from there as soon as you can, the trains will be a nightmare.' She looked at him, suddenly stern.

'I will not discuss it any further,' she said, 'I am getting a train for Dover very early tomorrow with a friend of Papa's who is also going to Paris. I should sail tomorrow night on one of the last crossings. I do not want to discuss it; it will spoil our last moments together.'

She had that steely quality again he had seen in her before and he knew that he could not make her talk about her journey. He understood her feelings. It would have been a bad way to spend their short space of time. They were eating their sorbet. Lunch was nearly over. It was like watching an hour glass and the sands were running too fast, she thought.

'I shall write to you,' he said, 'Somehow I shall get letters to you.'

She said 'oh Henry, do you think we shall be able to meet, I mean before the war has ended?' There was a long silence.

He ordered them coffee before he replied, then he said 'life can have strange twists and turns.'

'Yes,' she agreed. 'By the way I saw that man Ralph Cunningham again the other day; he was walking across the park.' Henry took a sip of the bitter black coffee.

'And did you converse?' he asked, looking at her quizzically with one eyebrow slightly raised.

'Yes,' she replied, 'we had a strange but rather interesting conversation.' Henry looked at her thoughtfully.

'When you get home,' he said, 'you will take great care of yourself; be vigilant, we shall all be living through dangerous times.'

'Yes,' she replied. 'I think I know what you mean, and I am going back to look after Papa.'

'Of course.'

Then he said something that was to come back to her several times on her journey.

'You are a brave girl Geneviève. I think you are probably capable of taking great risks. I repeat - be vigilant.' She nodded. She knew that they had to go.

They left the restaurant and went out into the street. She wanted to cling to him but instead she let him kiss her hand and then her mouth. He opened the taxi door and saw her into it with gentle firmness, then he closed the door and turned away. She had never before seen such torment in his face. She looked out of the rear window and watched him walk away without a backward glance. He was returning to his wife and his son before leaving them tomorrow.

'But I shall see him again,' she told herself, as the taxi rattled away towards Montague Square. 'I shall see him because I know now that Henry belongs to me.'

CHAPTER V

Vanessa sat at her writing table in the library at Merlinstone with her head in her hands. It was late February and the scrapings of snow made the light pale outside and strange and dirty-looking inside the house. So much had happened, she thought, since Simon's party. Their mother had died in October, exactly a month after Simon had left for the war. They buried her in the little graveyard behind the Kirk alongside her husband the General. Although they were greatly saddened the sisters felt relief that she was not going to have to live through the anxiety and carnage of the war. Simon was with his regiment in Palestine and Vanessa knew how deeply grieved he had been by the news. He had felt, he wrote, when he left Merlinstone in September that he would never see her again.

'So here I am,' thought Vanessa, 'at the same time trying not to be here, so to speak.' She was struggling to return to London and continue her war work. There was so much to contend with at Merlinstone. Thirty little evacuees and two nurses were crammed into the west wing. She had found extra help for Ishbel, with great difficulty – one a rather backward boy who had failed his military test and who, poor chap, dropped and broke almost everything he touched. Ishbel got him to work in the scullery peeling vegetables, and scrubbing potatoes and carrots when they came in from the garden, with strict instructions not to touch anything else. The other helper was a very elderly lady from the village who liked to come in and gossip but was quite good at laying the fires and could make an edible rice pudding. Feeding so many children as well as the Tarnoch family was proving to be a great deal of work. Strict rationing had been introduced and they lived mostly on pheasants and rabbits and the occasional chicken.

The children tugged at Vanessa's heart. Such pale faces and some looked mournfully homesick whilst others, the little boys usually, had violent scuffles and had to be dragged out of the avenue with bloody noses. They were supposed to go for walks in a neat crocodile but it seldom worked out that way. Ishbel tried to soothe her:

'Never you worry, Miss Vanessa,' she said – she always called her this in spite of her married status. 'They'll soon settle and enjoy being country bairns, you wait and see.' And Vanessa replied

'But I can't wait, Ishbel, I simply must go back to my work.' And now her next worry was Claire. She had come into the library that morning and announced that she was going to London.

'Where to when you get there?' Vanessa had asked.

'I'm going to stay with Laura Netherfield. I'll need a lift to the station tomorrow.'

'How long are you going for?' Vanessa asked and Claire turned towards her. She was dressed to go out riding.

'I haven't the faintest idea,' she replied.

Vanessa's heart sank. She did not trust her sister. She was her legal guardian, now that their mother had died, and this lasted until she reached the age of twenty-one – she was only sixteen.

'Well, if you won't take me to the station I'll find someone else who will,' had been her parting shot – and now she had gone out riding and Vanessa was left to add this to the pile of worries that were stacking up in her mind and on her desk. She felt like sobbing. Heaving a great sigh she left the library and went into the kitchen to see if she could give Ishbel a hand. When she had plucked and drawn four pheasants she felt a little better. There was a sense of achievement. She was washing her hands under the kitchen tap when she had an idea. It came to her suddenly and her heart lifted. She dried her hands on the roller towel and thought 'Why, oh why, didn't I think of this before,' and without further delay she went back to the library and the telephone.

In London Mary Tarnoch came down the stairs from her bedroom to confront the grey winter's day. Alice, her elderly maid of long and faithful standing, had put her meagre breakfast – tea and a slice of toast – in the drawing room near to the electric fire.

'I think I shall close up the dining room,' Mary thought, as she sat down on the sofa. She pulled the tray towards her and poured out some tea. Whilst she drank she heard a noise in the hall; she got up and went to pick up the letters that had come shooting through the flap in the front door. There were several brown envelopes and a long blue one that looked more interesting addressed to herself in what she always called 'a fine continental hand.' Mary went back to the drawing room and sat down with her tea to read the letter. Inside the envelope were several sheets of thin

blue paper. She took them out and spread them on her knee – they were
from Geneviève. Oh the blessed relief, the girl must have reached home
safely. Months had passed since she left England and Mary had had no word
from her. She had worried about her a great deal and had admired her
courage, the way she had set off for France on such an uncertain journey.
The postmark and the stamps on the envelope were English, she noted, she
must have found a courier to post them for her. Putting on her spectacles
she started to read:

Dearest Mary,

Such a long time it seems since I left England and now I feel so far away from
you all. I have been wondering so much how you are and praying that all is well
with you.

My journey through France was terrible, the worst nightmare I have ever known.
It was not so bad to Paris where I spent one night. I went to my father's apartment
which he hardly ever uses. I found his faithful maid Julie still there looking after
it and terrified out of her wits. The following day together we packed away as
many things as possible. Papa had already been there, she said, and taken away as
much as he could. The paintings had vanished and Julie told me he had ripped up
some floorboards and hidden them beneath, nailing the boards back down again.
Papa had also tried to persuade her to accompany him but she had refused. She
belonged to Paris, she said. She would wait for his return after the war. Eventually
I managed to make her agree to come with me. She said that because of her second
name she was certain they would think her Jewish and she was terrified. The next
day we had to walk to the station with our luggage – for some inexplicable reason
there was suddenly no transport. We took with us some bottles of water and some
sticks of bread which we had sewn into the lining of our coats. The timetables
had all gone crazy and the platform was so crowded you just despaired of ever
getting onto a train. Eventually we managed but we did not get a seat and had to
stand in the corridor for hours. Our journey took us nearly a week. We never knew
where we were going to stop, how we could find our next connection or how long it
was going to take to get there. Eventually, as we got further south things improved
slightly and we were able to buy some fruit from a stall on a station in the Auvergne.
I managed to telephone Papa and let him know an approximate time of our arrival
in Avignon. When we arrived into the station at last we were almost speechless
with exhaustion. And there was Papa, sitting quietly in his big English Bentley,
looking as though it was the most normal thing in the world to be meeting these
unwashed, half starving and exhausted women! We literally fell off the train and
into his arms and Jacques our chauffeur took our meagre luggage and stowed it in

the car. I buried my face in Papa's rough tweed-covered chest that always smells faintly of tobacco and I burst into tears. Julie was crying also, but Papa, bless his heart, burst into roars of laughter. 'Mon dieu, you poor children!' he cried, 'Just look at you both – and is this all the luggage you have with you? We shall have to take you both into the town on another day and fit you out.' We climbed into the car. My exhaustion almost left me, I was so happy to be home. I had forgotten how beautiful it is. On that day of autumn sunshine the houses were glowing yellow ochre and the vineyards had started to turn red – and the calm of it all! The rolling fields of lavender as we drove further north, harvested now and neatly trimmed, the olive trees, a sea of silver, the white roads and the plane trees. I must not go on as I could write for ever about the beauty of Provence. The war has not really reached here yet and although I am not in love with the Vichy government it is possible to lead a fairly normal life. We drove on into the Drôme, through the town of Sault with its high grey walls and terrifyingly steep roads and the ancient little statue of Saint Mark with his sleeping lion that stands at the most dangerous corner – and in the distance the mighty Mont Ventoux. On we went to the beautiful town of Mont Rouge, pasted against the hillside, a cross between both an ancient and a modern painting. Then we drove up into the hills, through the country where the rocks are twisted into extraordinary shapes, and at last the Château Verdurin rose, high above us, growing out of the rocks. As we went beneath the wide archway and into the courtyard everyone came running out to meet us and embrace us. Our old cook Hortense, my Aunt Isabella and my Uncle Herbert, and our gardener who sports a long grey beard and looks like a painting by Cezanne, they were all crying with joy. It was wonderful, Mary, to be back at last in the warm embrace of my family and my country.

But I do miss you all in England, and I miss my work. Please give my love to Theresa and tell her I think of her all dressed up in her smart Wrens' uniform, she must look very glamorous, but I do hope that she will get back to her millinery after the war, she is so talented. I have managed to pack and bring that hat with me she made – the blue velvet one with the curling feather. Dear Mary, perhaps one day you may be able to come and visit us here, my father would love to meet you. You were so very kind to me in England and made me feel so at home.

I am your most affectionate friend
Geneviève

Mary sat some time with the letter in her hands, her tea cooling. Tears had come into her eyes and one fell onto the thin paper, blurring the ink. What a strange girl Geneviève was, she thought. In some ways so cool and distant, and in other ways so passionate. A swift memory came back to her of the day when the girl had come into the front hall drenched with rain; her face had looked so different, so full of life and radiance. Mary sighed and folded the letter. Well, she thought, she is safely back in France now, and that is undoubtedly for the best.

Later that morning, aided by Alice, Mary dragged a tall pair of wooden steps into the drawing room and stood them by the windows. Then she climbed up and with Alice holding steady below she started to stick strips of brown paper in a criss-cross pattern over the glass.

'They will look awful,' she said, 'but we have all been told to do this, so I am following suit.' At that moment they heard the telephone ring in the hall.

'I'll go and answer it, Miss Mary,' Alice said, 'you sit down on the top step for a bit.'

In a moment she returned, 'It's Mrs Henry,' she said.

'Vanessa!' Mary exclaimed, 'I'll go at once.' Wobbling slightly she got down from the ladder.

'Vanessa darling.'

'Aunt Mary,' Vanessa's voice sounded rather faint and far away and the line crackled. 'I'll have to be quick because of the time ration. I'm at Merlinstone and things are not going very well. Claire's gone to stay with Laura Netherfield in London and we so need someone here to watch over the evacuees and their nurses and give Ishbel some moral support; I shall have to leave here soon and go back to my war work. Greville and Nannie are fairly all right but Nannie rubs Ishbel up the wrong way sometimes; we just need someone to keep the peace. Would you ever consider leaving London and coming to stay here during wartime? There are so many things you could help with, we need you terribly. You would be much safer here away from the bombs.'

'Good heavens Vanessa!' Mary sounded very taken aback. 'I really don't know. I shall have to think about it. Listen, dear girl, telephone time will soon be up, I'll ring you later when I have thought it over. I'm flattered, of course, that you think I would be a good remedy.'

'Oh please, oh please Aunt Mary, I beseech you' Vanessa pleaded, 'I'll be waiting for your call,' and with that she rang off.

Later, whilst Mary ate her solitary lunch, a slice of spam, a little salad and a cup of hot Bovril which Alice brought to her again on a tray in the drawing room, she tried to sort things out in her mind. Now that war had come many of her London friends had scattered and much of her charity work had temporarily closed down. What was she going to do here all the war in this tall, cold house? She could see that she would be of far more use at Merlinstone, where she was obviously needed. She felt a little rush of excitement, to be perhaps returning to the home of her childhood. She would work in the vegetable garden, she would pickle and dry and whenever she could lay hands on some sugar she would make jam. She would do everything she could to bring colour into the white faces of those poor little evacuees. There would be her great nephew Greville, as well, and many old friends and neighbours she hadn't seen for years, she would take her bicycle with her, petrol shortage would render it very handy. She would also ask Alice to come with her; she could be of use as well.

Feeling suddenly elated she almost ran to the telephone and dialled the exchange. She listened to it ringing for what seemed a long time and then at the moment of disappointment there was a click and Vanessa answered.

'Listen,' she said, 'I am coming, my dear. I have thought it over and actually it seems the obvious solution to many things, and I will try hard to steer the ship and sort out the problems.'

Vanessa gasped into the receiver 'oh Aunt Mary, that is simply wonderful. I am returning to London soon and we can talk it all over.'

'Splendid, and I will make plans about shutting up this house.'

They ended their conversation on a note of high hope and rejoicing. Mary poured herself out a celebratory glass of dry sherry from the heavy decanter she kept in the sideboard cupboard in the dining room. She felt quite dazed by the suddenness of events. Then she picked up the letter from Geneviève and put it on her writing table. It seemed an age ago when she had read it; her whole world had changed since this morning. Somehow she had not thought of mentioning the letter to Vanessa.

With all that had happened that day Vanessa had not had the time to take Claire to the station to catch the night train to London and had therefore asked Jimmy, the boy who looked after the few horses that remained, helped in the garden and did a hundred other jobs, if he would take her in his blue truck and he had willingly agreed. He was fond of Claire and would enjoy the time away from his many duties. He had been excused military service because he had to look after his invalid mother, his father having died many years ago in the mines. How long this concession would hold good he did not know and tried not to think about it.

It was a fortunate plan for Claire as it meant that Vanessa was not there to see her two heavy suitcases being loaded onto the truck, far more than she would have taken normally for a quick visit to a friend. They said goodbye in the library and were fairly friendly although Claire felt a flicker of guilt when Vanessa said 'see you soon.' Once on the night express to London she started to feel excited. She had not mentioned to anyone except Laura, that the following evening someone called Tony Stanford was coming round to take her out to dinner. She had met him at a party a few weeks before in London, given by a friend of the Netherfields, and their friendship had started at once. He was in the RAF and was stationed somewhere in Wiltshire. She was longing to tell Laura about him, how kind and amusing he had been, they had danced together all evening.

The following morning Claire sleepily left the train and took a taxi to Cheyne Row where the Netherfields lived. Their house was one of the old buildings with a small garden and inside it was reminiscent of William Morris and the Pre-Raphaelites. A relative of the late Mrs Netherfield had owned it; he had been a well-known author and there was a little studio at the end of the garden where he had written all his books. Claire found it a fascinating place, full of shadows and secret landings. Across one there was a small wrought iron gate and beyond this Lionel Netherfield's bedroom and office, the holy of holies Laura called it. Lionel Netherfield's business was soon going to suffer because of the war. He had tried volunteering as a mature naval officer but had been refused on the grounds of his age and his now poor eyesight so he decided to join the ambulance corps who accepted him gladly. He was an intelligent, rather irascible man who suffered deeply from being a widower. His wife had died five years earlier and he had been left with Tom and Mark, his two sons, Laura and a younger daughter called Frances. Miss Taylor, his housekeeper, was the lynch pin that held the house and family together and saved him from going out of his mind. It was she who opened the door to Claire and welcomed her in. She grasped her suitcases and whisked them into the hall as though they held no weight at all. Claire pulled her coat around her; it was colder inside the house than out. In the large front hall stood a long oak refectory table and on the wall above it a large crucifix. Hilda Netherfield had been a devout Roman Catholic. Suddenly there was a shriek and down the stairs rushed Laura.

'Oh Claire, how wonderful!' she cried, 'come down to the kitchen at once and I'll get you some coffee – did you get any breakfast on the train? My, you're looking smart.'

Claire hugged her. 'It's been ages since I've seen you,' she said, 'and so much has happened! I can't wait to tell you all about it.'

The kitchen was a cavernous room, more like somewhere you would normally find in a country house and seldom came across in London. There was a large Aga cooker and sagging basket-work chairs with faded lumpy cushions. They were mostly covered by cats – three of them and one small kitten that peeped out from behind its mother who hardly bothered to open her eyes. Sometimes their purring reached a deafening crescendo. The scrubbed table was so big it would not have fitted into any other house but in this large room it looked a normal size. Everything seemed to have been stacked on it and there a marble slab one end and a chunky butcher's chopping board the other. Laura always said that she had been born on it, as her mother had been very ill at her birth and had had to have an emergency caesarean. On the wall hung the white-faced mahogany bound clock with its deep, friendly tick; and a large sofa stretched along the far wall where Claire had sat down causing one of the cats to spring away with an angry meow.

'Darling,' she said to Laura, who was heating the earthenware coffee pot that stood in a tin of hot water on the Aga. 'I have run away. Nessa doesn't know but I'm not going back to Merlinstone, I am staying in London and I'm going to be a nurse.' Laura looked at her in surprise. 'How have you managed to do that at last?' she asked.

'Well I found out all about it from an old school friend called Vivien Anderson and I've got an interview the day after tomorrow. I do hope I can stay here until I find somewhere else to go. I promise it won't be very long; I shall have to look around the hospital – I don't want to have to travel miles to work.'

'Of course you can stay,' said Laura, 'I'll explain it all to Father, but can't you go to Vanessa's house later on?'

'Hopeless. She wants me to stay at Merlinstone with the evacuees and little Greville and mess about there in a lady-like fashion and I simply will not do that.'

Laura nodded. 'I understand,' she said. 'I do envy you, Claire. I would love to be doing something more positive like nursing, as you know. But I am tied here looking after Dad and Frances. All the other servants have joined up and it's just me and Miss Taylor. We should really close the house and go somewhere safer but Dad flies into a rage whenever I suggest it.'

'You go and take Frances, Laura, but I am bloody well staying here!'

'This is my home and I'm not letting the Huns drive me out.'

Claire laughed at the impression of her father.

'They are talking about evacuating Frances's day school to somewhere in the West Country; I think she may have to go with them and become a boarder.'

The coffee was delicious and Claire drank it thankfully.

'I've brought my ration book with me,' she said, 'I had to steal it from the pile in the kitchen when Ishbel wasn't looking.'

Laura laughed, 'keep it until you are settled,' she said. 'You have to register it wherever you are going to live. We'll be fine – I can still get lots of bread, Father has a friend who runs a bakery and he drops it off here from time to time; he seems to think we are starving.'

Claire told Laura that she was going out with Tony the following evening.

'I'm longing for you to meet him, he's got some leave and he's coming all the way from Wiltshire to take me out.'

'What a quick worker you are!' Laura teased her, 'when you say you have only met him once!'

'I know, it is rather quick, but we got on so well and he is such good company. I just felt grab the moment, it's war time, let's have all the fun we can get.'

At that moment the air raid siren wailed and Miss Taylor came into the kitchen. The cats went back to sleep.

'Do you want to go down to the cellar, girls?' she asked. Laura looked at Claire.

'I can't be bothered,' she said, 'we are more or less in the basement in here.'

'Is there a cellar under here?' asked Claire.

'A huge one,' Laura replied, 'stacked with masses of wine. Father has been collecting it for years. I think this is one of the reasons why he won't leave the house; he just can't face carting it all away with him. We did go down there the other night, there was rather a long raid and we could hear a lot of explosions and Dad went out on ambulance duty but in the end we got so chilled down there we gave up and went to bed.'

After a short while they heard the all clear and Laura took Claire upstairs to show her her bedroom.

'That is the first warning I've heard,' Claire said, as she followed Laura up the stairs. 'It does something funny to one's stomach.'

The following evening Claire put on her only smart dress apart from her one ball gown which she had left behind at Merlinstone. Tonight she wore what she called her 'cocktail outfit,' or her 'little black number'. She felt sophisticated and grown-up. She went into the drawing room to wait for Tony and Laura lit the fire.

'You look wonderful, Claire,' she told her, 'I do hope we don't have a raid tonight.'

'Oh so do I. Think of spending our evening in a shelter or in the

Underground! That would be a terrible anticlimax.'

She went to the long windows and was about to draw back the curtain when Laura said

'Don't! We're not allowed to show a chink of light. It's the blackout and bossy people come round and shine large torches on the houses to make sure we have drawn everything.'

'I do hope Tony will find the house,' Claire said, 'I gave him minute instructions.'

'Of course he will,' said Laura, 'he's a pilot, he must be able to see in the dark.'

And seeing in the dark extremely well Tony arrived at the River House at precisely 7.30 as promised. The doorbell rang and the girls stopped talking. Claire froze. Miss Taylor's footsteps sounded on the hall floor and they heard voices.

'How awful if it was Father,' Laura said, 'come home early. He always forgets his key.'

'Oh don't say that!'

But no, the light, easy sound of a young man's voice came up the stairs and Miss Taylor preceded him.

'Mr Stanford,' she said, 'would you like some drinks brought up Miss Laura?'

'Oh yes please.'

Laura swept up to Tony, taking his hand and drew him towards the fire, and Claire, blushing deeply, accepted his kiss on her cheek.

'This is lovely!' he exclaimed. 'What a wonderful house!'

There was something so easy and charming about Tony that they all relaxed and were soon drinking quite strong cocktails mixed by Laura who hoped that she knew what she was doing.

'I think I have met your brother, is he called Mark?' Tony asked her. 'He's just joined us on the camp. He's great, he makes us all laugh.'

'Yes, he's the eldest, then there's Tom who's joined the army and then myself, and last of all Frances who is in the kitchen doing her homework.'

Claire refused a second drink - Laura really had made stunningly strong ones – and Tony said

'I think we had better go. I've booked us a table at the Diamond Arrow; they have good food and really great dance music.'

No-one mentioned air raids. Laura took them downstairs and opened the front door. There were no stars tonight; it was cold and threatening to be foggy. That was a good sign, she thought. She watched them climb into

Tony's car and drive away and then went back into the house. She could not help feeling a stab of envy. All her friends had disappeared into the war and she wondered how she was ever going to meet someone, confined as she was to this house, looking after her sister and father. She went downstairs and made herself a cup of strong coffee; she was feeling a little dizzy after the cocktails. Then she turned on the radio and listened to the increasingly worrying news.

Claire woke the next morning with mixed emotions and a bad headache. They had had a wonderful evening, and no air raid warnings. She and Tony had danced into the small hours and she had drunk far too much wine and laughed until she ached. Tony was a wonderful raconteur and mimic. When he had finally brought her back to River House, dizzy with drink and happiness, he had put his arms around her for a moment and said,

'Darling Claire. I do hope you will be feeling all right for your interview tomorrow, we have had rather a wild evening.'

'I never should have arranged to go there tomorrow,' she said, 'I must have been mad!' Tony laughed at this.

'It's not like making a hair appointment,' he said, 'those nurse types have to see you when they can, they're always terribly busy.'

'I know, this Sister Fortescue did sound a bit frantic, almost as though she hadn't a moment to consider seeing me at all. I must make a good impression. I shall tie my hair back and wear a hideous felt hat I still have from my school days.'

'Darling, I must go back now, it's a long drive to Wiltshire. When shall we be able to meet again?'

'I do hope very, very soon,' she whispered, putting her arms around his neck. He kissed her and then turned quickly away. Claire let herself into the house, closing the door softly behind her and by the light of her small torch made her way up to bed.

The morning light was grey and yet piercing. She rubbed her head – aspirin, she thought, and then to splash her face with cold water. She dressed quickly. Just a little makeup, she decided, otherwise she would look too young. She patted some foundation cream around her eyes, trying to hide the heavy shadows. Then she dragged back her hair, pinned it down with hair grips, and put on her felt hat. For a moment her mouth quivered, if only Tony could see her now, he would have howled with laughter.

Downstairs in the kitchen Miss Taylor gave her some breakfast. Laura had taken Frances to school; she had left a note telling Claire that she would see her that evening and wishing her luck. Refusing any food Claire swallowed some coffee and blowing a kiss to Miss Taylor she left for her interview.

'So, Miss Tarnoch, sit down please.'

A tall, dour-looking woman wearing a brown linen uniform stood behind her desk, sorting through some papers with large, capable hands. She looked at Claire rather narrowly through a pair of rimless spectacles and Claire, terrified, obeyed and sat down on the hard little chair opposite her. Her headache was still there but her night of dancing with Tony had left her floating on a cloud of blissful unreality, the remnants of which were rapidly fading. The woman sat down with a crackle of brown linen and Claire clasped her hands together in her lap and tried to look grown-up and responsible. The felt hat shaded her face and, she hoped, her hangover. The woman put down her papers and picked up her pen.

'I am Sister Fortescue,' she told her, 'recruiting. And you, I think, are Claire Rosabella Tarnoch.'

'Yes,' murmured Claire.

'Good. I run this section of the London Red Cross. I gather from your application form that you are seventeen.'

'Yes,' lied Claire.

Sister Fortescue raised her eyebrows very slightly, 'And you have had no previous nursing experience.'

'Only what I did at home. I helped look after my mother. She died last year.'

A pause. There were no words of condolence from Sister Fortescue.

'And your London address, please, Miss Tarnoch?'

'Well, I'm staying with a friend called Laura Netherfield at the moment, her home is in London; but if I get a nursing job I would like to find somewhere that is nearer to the hospital perhaps,' she continued, apprehensively, 'I thought maybe you might know of some accommodation?'

'I see, it isn't easy you know, but I'll make a note of it. We may have some nurses wishing to share.'

Her tone was perhaps a shade warmer. Claire said 'oh thank you, thank you,' with too much warmth.

Sister Fortescue put down her pen, sat back in her chair and appraised Claire with cool, grey eyes. She saw a very young girl in a ridiculously ugly hat that did not look as though it could belong to her. She was leaning forward, there were dark stains beneath her eyes and she was clutching her handbag to her chest as if afraid of losing it. But there was something about the slant of her high cheekbones, and the determination of her mouth, that told you fortitude lay beneath her impulsive youthfulness. If she was anything, Sister Fortescue was a shrewd judge of character. She knew that this girl would become a nurse whether she accepted her or not. She would go onto the battlefield itself, if necessary, so perhaps she had better save her from doing this.

'I could send you to join a group of young women who are rolling bandages,' she mused, 'but I think you could be of greater use than that to us. I shall send you instead to work in one of our new hospital units. We have taken over Launceston House near to the White City, and we are expecting our first batch of wounded to arrive there any time now. You can start your training there; it will be telescoped considerably from the usual routine and it will be hard work and very unglamorous.'

'That is what I am expecting it to be,' Claire replied, quietly. Sister Fortescue smiled for the first time, a thin, almost cynical smile.

'You will have to work hard,' she repeated, 'we simply do not tolerate anything less. You will be with some fellow Red Cross and also some Queen Alexandra's nurses. It will be a test of your stamina, I advise very few late nights.'

Was that because of the dark stains under her eyes? Claire wondered. Sister Fortescue handed her a slim sheaf of papers.

'Complete and sign them when you get home,' she said. 'I'll let Matron know that you will be arriving on Monday morning at 8.30 sharp. That will give you this weekend to organize yourself.' She sounded a shade warmer.

'The address of the hospital and other details are in the forms. They will provide you with your uniform at the hospital. I shall have to say goodbye, others are waiting, so good luck Miss Tarnoch.'

They shook hands and with an odd mixture of triumph and apprehension Claire left the room.

That evening, back in River House, Claire regaled Laura and Frances with the story of her interview. Mr Netherfield had come home and was in the kitchen demanding some tea as Miss Taylor was out. Whilst Laura put the old black kettle on the Aga, he said to Claire:

'So you're going nursing are you? Excellent idea, we must all join forces and do war work. Laura can't do much when she's running this house and looking after Frances but I told her she could knit scarves for the troops.'

Laura made a face behind his back and Claire thought how nice it was to be commended for a change.

'Don't count on it, Dad,' she said. 'I may pack you and Frances off to the country and join the Wrens.' Later she said to Claire 'I've had a letter from

Tom – he's hating the army.'

'I wish I had heard from Simon,' Claire replied, 'it's ages since I have. One feels so cut off from them all.'

When she went upstairs to her room that evening she wrote a letter to Tony. She wondered how Vanessa would take her news now that it was a certainty that she had left home for good. She felt a sharp twinge of guilt, 'I shall have to write and ask her forgiveness,' she thought, 'but not quite yet. I'll wait until I am part of the nursing scene, she might get in touch with Sister Fortescue.'

She still had visions of being dragged, screaming and kicking, back to Merlinstone. Her new-found freedom had given her wings. In spite of the war, she felt buoyed up by an inexplicable happiness.

CHAPTER VI

On Saturdays Geneviève drove her ramshackle little car to the market in Mont Rouge. It was her favourite day of the week when she could escape the chateau where she was starting to feel confined. In spite of being busy running the whole establishment and seeing to the needs of her elderly relatives and her father, she missed her work in London and her English friends and most of all, with a gnawing ache, she missed Henry. Sometimes she took her father's horse and rode as far as she dared over the wild country. He hated her doing this and would stand in the courtyard under the large walnut tree that grew there, waiting for her return. One evening, when she had been sitting with her father in the dining room, waiting for Aunt Isabella and her Uncle Hubert to join them, he suddenly said to her in a quiet tone,

'We shall have resistance here you know, eventually.'

'Yes, I do know,' she replied steadily. 'Back in England a man called Ralph Cunningham discussed this with me once.'

'Oh yes, Cunningham,' her father said thoughtfully. 'I have heard of him. Well, when the movement gets its act together I shall assist it.'

'And so shall I, Papa,' she replied.

'Only the other day,' he continued, 'a young man came to see me. He wanted to discuss many things. We must be very careful with these people, with strangers, and even with those we know. I know this boy slightly, his name is Paul. He comes from a good, reliable family who have a small business the other side of Brantes. He was in a great hurry to start creating groups and organizing people to meet the men when they drop here from across the channel. I warned him to bide his time and said that I would get in touch with him later. I shall need a password. How, otherwise, shall I ever know that anyone is entirely genuine? If you are to be involved, Geneviève, you must take great care.'

'Of course I shall, Papa.'

They had been speaking very quietly and when they heard the footsteps of her aunt and uncle coming along the passage they changed the subject of their conversation. 'Ah!' her uncle had cried, 'all alone in the candlelight! We are sorry to have kept you waiting.'

And Aunt Isabella added 'we are late but now quick, we need the soup, we must not keep the wonderful Hortense waiting in the kitchen,' and seizing the little hand bell she rang it with all her might.

Now, on her way to the market, Geneviève remembered her father's words that evening. The rough, narrow road twisted its way through the hills and she had to drive with care. The whole place swarmed with animals and people. There were carts pulled by moth-eaten old horses, there were trucks full of anxious-looking sheep and small groups of beautiful goats bounding their way along, their coats the colour of caramel. Many cars followed, jerking and hooting, and men walked behind their geese bellowing and waving their sticks, telling everyone to get out of the way. Geneviève was resigned to this, she knew better than to try to hurry. Through the open car window drifted the smell of animals and cigarette smoke along with the scent of lavender and herbs, the aromatic air of the Drôme. When at last she reached the town, she parked her car near to a church and gathered up her rush baskets. She set off through the streets, glad that she was wearing her fine wool coat now that an autumn freshness tinged the air – although by midday it would become quite warm. She wore a blue linen dress under her coat and her fair hair was tied back under a small flower-strewn scarf, peasant style. In the clear light she looked dazzling and people turned to stare at her as she went by. Many old friends saw her and welcomed her back and she smiled and waved.

'Bonjour, Mademoiselle Geneviève,' they called 'bonjour Jacques, bonjour Monsieur Fournier, bonjour, bonjour!'

She reached the large market square where the stalls groaned with pumpkins and marrows, and peppers of all colours. There were pots of honey and great bunches of lavender and herbs. The houses on the far side of the square were built along the flank of a hill which, in its turn, was clasped by another higher hill on the summit of which perched the ruins of a mediaeval castle. On the other side of the square two bridges spanned a river in which only a trickle of water now ran after the long, hot summer. As she went through the market Geneviève noticed there were more strangers around than usual. She made her way to the cheese stall where she found Bertrand, a handsome, burly man with a wide smile and skin burnt a dark copper by the sun. He was delighted to see her.

'You have been away for so long!' he exclaimed, taking her hand, 'but now I think you will have to stay.'

'I shall have to,' she replied with a smile. 'Bertrand, who are all these strangers?' she asked him, nodding in the direction of a worried-looking woman who looked distinctly Parisian in a smart black coat, and who was anxiously counting the change in her purse.

'Ah,' he replied, 'she must have come from the north, from Paris I expect. They are fleeing the invasions.'

'There is something very sad about this,' Geneviève replied, 'being like refugees in your own country. Where are the Pendique family? They always had the stall next to yours.'

Bertrand nodded, 'yes, they had planned to go to America, they have relatives there, but at the last moment the grandmother, old Madame Rosa Pendique, fell ill and they had to delay. I think they may have gone by now but Thomas, their younger son, the one with red hair, he is going to England he hopes. He plans to leave tomorrow.'

'Where is he now?' she asked. She knew Thomas; he was a promising musician and a friend of her childhood days.

'He may be up at their house. It is right on the edge of the town near the Durance Bridge.'

'I would so like to say au revoir to him, Bertrand.'

'Wait a moment, I will have a word with Maria and I will come with you.'

He went over to his wife who was wrapping a large piece of golden-coloured cheese in green paper for a customer. She nodded and smiled and blew a kiss to Geneviève. Bertrand returned and said

'I have her permission! But first we will have a little cup of coffee in the Café de l'Eglise.'

'That good old café,' Geneviève replied, 'it has been there for better or for worse, all my life.'

It was no use suggesting they should hurry, in case Thomas should decide to be on his way, and have gone by the time they reached his house - this was not the Provencal way of doing things.

Once they were seated at a small table under the plane trees, outside the café that was humming with activity with waiters dashing in and out, Geneviève felt in the pocket of her coat.

'Bertrand,' she said, 'I have two letters with me for friends in England that I was going to send. Perhaps Thomas could take them for me instead?'

'We will ask him,' Bertrand agreed. He was delighted to be with the beautiful Geneviève de Verdurin whom everyone admired, and he leaned back in his chair and smiled as he saluted passers-by.

'But,' Geneviève continued, 'do you think he will ever get there? He has left it so late.'

'He is travelling with a little orchestra,' Bertrand replied. 'They were booked to give a performance in England ages ago, in London I think. The arts are still able to move about.'

'I do hope so,' she replied, doubtfully. Everyone appeared so laid back and calm about things in this part of France. Could they really be so blind?

As if reading her thoughts Bertrand continued 'Life goes on the same here, as you must have seen since you arrived home, war or no war, but people are nervous and there is a different atmosphere.'

'Yes,' Geneviève agreed, sipping her café au lait. 'That woman we just saw in the smart clothes, she looked so exhausted and worried and there is a whole group of people sitting at a table over there reading newspapers. They just do not belong.'

At that moment the church bells exploded into a wild cacophony of sound that nearly blew them across the square.

'The feast of Saint Antony!' Bertrand shouted, 'come, it is time we went and found Thomas.'

A cloud of pigeons that had flown out of the bell tower in alarm now whirled and turned in the sky above the square and then returned. Still throbbing with the noise Geneviève followed Bertrand up a steep, narrow road until, out of breath, they arrived at a long street that ran the length of the escarpment of rock. The houses here were tall and slim and painted in pale ochre yellow, some dark to almost orange, others pale or bright and glowing, the colour of the sun. At the end of the street they stopped at the last house and knocked on the grey wooden door. A few moments of silence followed and then a voice shouted in French

'Who's there?'

'It's Bertrand, Thomas, I'm with Geneviève de Verdurin.'

The door opened instantly and a tall young man stood there with a mop of curly auburn hair and a pale, intelligent face.

'Ah!' he cried, 'come in,' and he bent over Geneviève's hand and kissed it.

They went into a dark, cool room; the shutters were closed but Thomas pushed one open at once. The room was bare save for one small table and four chairs.

'Please sit down,' Thomas waved his hands. 'I am afraid everything we owned has been packed away or sold. Now, what will you drink?'

Geneviève shook her head but Thomas said 'yes, yes, a little wine for us all, for this is my goodbye to you.'

He whisked out of the room and came back with three glasses and a dusty green bottle and poured out the dark red wine.

'From my Aunt Corrine's vineyard,' he said, holding his own glass up to the light so that he could admire the colour.

'I am so sad that your parents have already left,' Geneviève told him, 'I shall miss their beautiful stall in the market.' Sylvie Pendique, Thomas's mother, was famous for her embroidery and lace.

'Yes,' sighed Thomas, 'they have been gone a few weeks now. It has been a terrible uprooting and I only hope that they will be happy. America is such a different place. They went with this rich family who were customers of my mother's. My grandmother was really too old to go but she would not leave them, and they took almost nothing with them. When I said to my grandmother what would she do without her life-long collection of belongings she said she still had her golden casket.'

'What did she mean?' asked Bertrand.

'She meant that she still had her memories. They lie in a golden casket in her mind and she can take them out and look at them whenever she wishes. She said it is one advantage of being old. When we are young there is just a scattering of memories on the floor of the casket, but as we age they pile up and up.'

Geneviève smiled as he said this and thought how true this was. Her casket was full of memories of Henry.

'You have not gone with them, Thomas,' she said.

'No, I cannot endure the idea of America and I was due to go to England anyway with the orchestra. Things could get very bad here, for people like me and my family. It does not show in our name but we have Jewish blood. They are bound to find that out. There are harsh opinions in the town, particularly in the Mairie.'

He lowered his voice when he said this and looked towards the door.

'I am not going by the usual route,' he added, 'my friends have other ways of crossing the channel.'

Thomas sighed and refilled their glasses.

'We are full of nostalgia we French,' he continued, 'we love our region, our homes, our way of life. Someday I know that I shall return.'

They were silent for a moment and then Geneviève took the letters out of her pocket.

'Would you take these for me, Thomas, and post them when you get to

England?' she said.

He smiled. 'Enchanté, Mademoiselle, you must have great faith in my reaching the British shores.'

'They will be your talisman,' she replied, 'they will bring you good luck.'

He took them from her. 'I shall deliver them with the help of God,' he replied, 'they will go into the first post box I can find on the other side of La Manche.'

'We must go now,' Bertrand exclaimed, 'Maria will kill me – leaving her to man the stall for so long. Goodbye, my dear Thomas.'

The two men embraced, and Thomas kissed Geneviève's hand and then her cheek.

'God speed,' she whispered. Feeling choked, they left him standing in the doorway, one hand raised in a farewell salute.

Later Geneviève, laden with fruit and a fresh chicken she had bought from the butcher's stall, drove back through the mountains to the chateau. The world was painted a rich gold in the autumn light, but a bank of dark clouds was gathering towards the west.

'Tomorrow we shall probably have rain,' she thought, 'the strangest summer of my life is nearly over.'

CHAPTER VII

Claire was so tired that she seemed to have lost all feeling in her body. Her head throbbed and halfway through her long day she longed to tear off her cap, her starched collar and her hideous black wool stockings and throw herself down onto a bed. When she had first arrived the hospital had been quiet but now the wounded were pouring in; sometimes there were not enough beds and they had to prepare makeshift ones in the cold conservatory where the roof leaked when it rained and the paraffin stoves smelt terrible. The men who were beyond hope of any recovery were put here, it seemed both practical and inhumane.

Late in the evening Claire was at last allowed to stop work. She made her way slowly back through the streets to the room she shared with Vivien, a fellow nurse slightly older than herself, whom she had been at school with. It had been hard to find somewhere affordable but at least their room which was above a large estate agent's office, was fairly near to the underground when there was a raid. It also had a small kitchen attached to it with a Baby Belling cooker that sat on a table beside the sink. This was a great luxury and they could brew up their suppers before they fell into a deep sleep. On this particular evening Claire lay down on her bed, too exhausted even to accept a mug of cocoa Vivien had thoughtfully offered her. She kept hearing Vanessa's voice saying 'You'll never stick to nursing, you'll find it far too hard.' She clenched her teeth angrily. Well, she would stick to it! She would show Vanessa what she was really made of. To give her due her sister had been conciliatory when she had realised that Claire had really left home and carried out her threat to nurse. She had written to her telling her she was always welcome to come and stay in her house.

'At least you would be tolerably warm and as well fed as is possible these days,' she had written. But Claire, whilst she had thanked her, had refused. She did not wish to return to Vanessa's world of privileged luxury. It would have been terrible to have stepped out of that environment each day into the world of the hospital. And also there was Tony to be considered. She couldn't have asked him to that house where he would have had to face Vanessa's inevitable disapproval.

Now she lay thinking of him, wishing she could see him again. His cheeky grin would have cheered her, and more than his amusing personality there was the feeling that with him she was safe and secure. Vivien came back into their room carrying a glass.

'Come on,' she said, 'this is whisky kept for dire moments of exhaustion and stress. You look as though you need it.'

'Oh darling you are kind! Have we got enough?'

'Yes, I'll try and squeeze another bottle out of our coupons once we've done our weekly shop. We've had this one for ages.'

Claire sat up on the bed and had a sip of the precious peat-brown liquid. It sent a fiery warmth down her throat and into her stomach. The world started to look less grim.

'Wonderful what a little firewater does for a girl,' she said. 'What sort of a day have you had, Viv?'

'Rather terrible. Matron was livid because there were not enough beds. Not really our fault. We had to put two perfectly healthy chaps into the conservatory. They're supposed to be getting some more tomorrow. We are at maximum intake now. I just pray we don't get a whole lot more wounded before next week.'

Claire pulled on her dressing gown.

'Foggy tonight,' she said, peeping out from behind the blackout curtain. 'With any luck there won't be a raid. I could do with some sleep. Viv, I want to confide in you.'

Vivien sat down on her own bed obediently.

'What about?' she asked. 'I hope you are not contemplating an end to your nursing career.'

'Of course I'm not. It's about Tony. He has asked me to go down to Wiltshire in two weeks' time. He's got some leave and we have both been asked to stay at a place called Rainscombe Hall by someone he knows. Anthea Harding is her name, I think. Anyway she lives there with her children.'

'How wonderful!' Vivien exclaimed, 'I really am envious.'

'I know, but will I ever be able to go? It's not my weekend off.' 'You haven't had any leave for ages, Claire. You must have a break; you are looking terribly pale. You'll just have to ask Matron.'

'Oh, how terrifying! She is such a monster. Couldn't I ask Sister Berwick?'

'You could try her first, but she'll only send you to see the boss.'

'Well I must see Tony,' Claire replied, 'I will have to make them give me permission.'

The next morning Claire left for work – dry-mouthed and nauseous with apprehension and hope. Her hands shook and she kept dropping things.

'Nurse, what on earth is wrong with you today?' This came from the staff nurse, as a bowl full of dressings spun out of Claire's hand and rolled over the floor.

'I am so sorry. I'll clear it up at once;' a cross look from the nurse and a grin from the man who lay stretched on the bed beside them, awaiting the dressings.

'Had a late night, nurse?' he asked her, with a wink.

She turned away, her cheeks pink with irritation. On and on the morning went – bedpans, mugs of Bovril, cups of tea, dressings, bandages, thermometers. 'Yes, I really will write a letter for you later on today if I possibly can'; 'Yes, I'll stop by before I go off duty tonight'; 'Yes, yes, yes, I will, I will try', supposing, she thought, 'supposing I suddenly screamed No! I won't! I simply will not do one more thing!'

At last it was four o'clock in the afternoon. Outside the cold grey sky was full of sleety rain. Claire set off down the long passage to Matron's room. There was a pane of frosted glass in the door and behind it a light dimly showed. She could see the faint image of a high, puckered white cap – the tremendous badge of office. Few people approached this room without having made an appointment first. Claire had forgotten to do this but now, on remembering, she did not turn back. She knocked lightly and a sharp 'come in!' responded. She turned the handle and there she was, the Dragon of all Dragons, seated behind her desk, her ample bosom covered in white and adorned with a watch that hung from a gold pin, and all about her wrists, her neck, in fact everywhere it seemed, there were starched white frills. She looked surprised.

'I was not expecting you, Nurse Tarnoch,' she said. 'You have no appointment with me today.'

Claire stood before her: 'I am sorry, I know, there wasn't time.'

'Well, sit down then.' She jerked her head towards the chair.

Claire sank down, her throat had almost seized up with fear. She drew in a very long, deep breath.

'I've come to ask if I may have a little leave the weekend after next.'

The words suddenly came rushing out, tumbling over each other. Matron put down her cup of tea she had been drinking. She consulted the little watch pinned on her bosom before her gaze went to Claire who sat rigid, staring at her. Then, incredibly, she smiled – a nice, almost normal smile.

She said 'yes, Nurse, I think you are due for a break. It will do you a lot of good.' Oh God, Claire felt tears pricking behind her eyes, she simply must not cry. She lifted her chin a little.

'Would from Friday until Sunday night be all right, Matron? I have been asked to go to the West Country.' Matron smoothed her spotless cuffs.

'You need not return to us until the Tuesday, Nurse. You need a good, long weekend.'

Had it been so very obvious, her exhaustion, she wondered?

'Oh thank you so very much, I'll be back on the dot on Tuesday morning.'

'I know you will,' Matron replied. 'You are a good and a hard worker. You have your faults, of course, but you are training up well. Now off you go and enjoy yourself.'

She smiled again, briskly but kindly, and opened a ledger. Claire left the room in a daze. Had this really happened, she wondered, as she skimmed down the passage. They were pleased with her? She felt incredibly happy and she was going away, she would see Tony! All her exhaustion had left her. She arrived back in the ward, trying not to smile too broadly, and went at once to find the young soldier who needed a letter written to his mother.

'But what am I going to wear?' Claire was standing in their bedroom, her wardrobe spread around her. Vivien came in from the kitchen with a saucepan in her hand. It was her turn to make supper and their store cupboard had only been able to offer up baked beans.

'They're fine,' Vivien told her, 'ballerinas live on them.'

She was a mine of strange pieces of information. Claire held up a pair of trousers, 'slacks' they called them, and a short ginger-coloured jacket known as a bum freezer.

'They are so unglamorous,' she wailed. 'I simply must have something else. I haven't had any new clothes for years.'

Theresa had given her an evening dress which she never wore herself – it was pretty with sequins sewn around the neck. She could take that with her but what to wear during the day? And oh for a new lipstick, and some exotic scent!

'Tony won't mind,' Vivien comforted her, 'he just wants to see you.'

But the ginger jacket was rather frightful, she thought, perhaps Claire could wear an orange and green scarf to smarten it up a bit.

'I can't,' said Claire, 'I hate it.' She rummaged in a drawer. 'I have got some clothes coupons, Viv. Here they are, I'm going to blow them, let's go on our day off and lay siege to the West End.'

They went together to Oxford Street, taking the tube with Claire intent on spending most of her wages and all her coupons. She felt delightfully extravagant and wild. It was a cold, dry day and wrapped in their old winter coats, their gas masks slung over their shoulders, they wished they had been wearing something more elegant as they entered Selfridge's. Even in wartime this seemed to the girls like fairy land.

'It smells so wonderful,' said Claire, 'oh the luxury of it, Viv! And we'll go to the restaurant for tea later on.'

They went to the ladies' fashion department where Claire tried on a great many clothes and discarded them all. The elderly assistant was kind and patient and Vivien sat down on a gilded chair and waited for Claire to emerge from the fitting room. At last, after many outfits had been tried and discarded, Claire appeared in a beautiful amethyst jacket with a skirt to match. She twirled in front of Vivien, and was about to say 'no good, I don't like the sleeves' when the assistant said

'That looks really wonderful on you, Madam,' and Vivien agreed.

Claire stopped in front of the long mirror once more and to her friend's great relief said

'Yes, perhaps you are right. Anyway I am exhausted. This one is the winner,' and with a wide smile she clapped her hands and sped back into the fitting room.

They watched the amethyst-coloured outfit being swathed in tissue paper and then packed into a smart cardboard box with Selfridge's written on it in tall black letters.

'I would like to buy so much more,' Claire sighed, 'but this has cleaned me out. Let's go and have a really huge tea, then we needn't bother about supper.'

The train for Bath left from Paddington Station at 4 pm. Tony had promised to meet her there and together they would drive to Rainscombe and meet Anthea Harding who had asked them to stay. Anthea had befriended Tony along with many other young men on the airbase and had been kind to them, often asking them to the house for drinks and entertainment of some kind. Her husband was away in Palestine with his regiment and she had a busy time running a mobile canteen which she drove to the camp to provide the airmen and all who worked there with tea and cigarettes. Claire felt sure that she would like her but at the same time she was feeling a little apprehensive about their first encounter. She was wearing her new amethyst-coloured outfit and had her least terrible old coat slung over her shoulders. She wore short, fur-lined boots and a chic little beret on her head.

'Not too bad,' she thought, making one more check in the mirror before she left. 'Not quite Parisian chic but it will have to do.'

There was no heating on the train. Claire wrapped her coat around her and was relieved to find a seat. For once the train did not seem to be overcrowded. The posters in the carriages had ceased being welcoming and pretty. Instead there were notices warning the travellers that 'Careless talk costs lives,' and to 'Guard your tongue.' The other passengers in her carriage were all elderly and buried in their newspapers and books. Claire settled back in her seat. She knew that she must count the stations carefully as they made their stops. The place names had all been removed and there would soon be little light. Bath was the fourth stop.

It was strange to be slipping through a darkening land where towns lay so silently with hardly a light pricking the oncoming darkness. The journey seemed to take a long time and when at last she felt the train slow for the fourth stop she took her case down from the rack and peered anxiously out of the window. She could only just make out the faces on the busy platform. Praying she would see Tony she got out of the train. Then she gave a small scream for someone had thrown their arms around her and was hugging her against their chest. It was Tony, and he was laughing.

'Claire, darling! Don't look so scared; here let me take your case, you're losing your gas mask, I'll take that as well.' He slipped it off her shoulder. 'The car is just outside. I had to borrow one as mine is in dock – a friend has lent me his terribly smart Ferrari.'

'I thought I might not find you,' she gasped, as he hurried her out of the station.

'Well, I would have found you,' he replied, 'even if you had gone to the moon.' They found the car, gleaming and sleek, waiting outside the station entrance.

'Goodness how dashing it looks!' said Claire, 'We'll have to be terribly careful.'

'It goes tremendously fast,' he replied. 'It is so kind of Alan to lend it – you'll meet him at the dance.'

'What dance?' she asked, alarmed.

'Oh don't be scared, it's just a little hop Anthea is giving with her rather super radiogram. She often does this, to cheer up the lonely bachelors. Sometimes she plays the piano as well. It always finishes at a respectable hour so that we can all get enough sleep.'

'That sounds wonderful, Tony!'

He looked sideways at her profile, her high cheekbones and small, retroussé nose, and her smile that started taut and then broadened into a delightful grin.

'You are looking wonderful,' he said, 'although I can hardly see you in this darkened land,' and spoken by him the words sounded truthful and not falsely flattering as so many men could be. This was the quality she recognized in Tony the first time she met him. He was as honest as the day.

They drove out of Bath into the country.

'A pity we couldn't really see the city,' he said, 'it is so beautiful.'

After they had gone a few miles they climbed a long hill at the top of which they passed a group of tall stones standing by the roadside.

'That old cromlech is where Wiltshire, Gloucestershire and Somerset all meet,' he told her, and he slowed the car so that they could see it. Claire wound down the window. An owl hooted and a cold little wind blew in their faces.

'I have so missed this in London,' she said, 'the country things.'

'Our camp is over to the right,' he told her, 'we are very nearly at the house. Poor Anthea, they came and built a huge fighter command right outside her gates, but she is very good about it. She has a lot of our aircraft tethered in her fields in camouflaged hangars.'

They drove through a small hamlet and down another road and then, there they were - the tall iron gates and Stone Lodge leading to a long avenue of beech trees, the imposing entrance to Rainscombe Hall. The gates were open and they drove on and up the long drive. The house rose before them behind a large mown lawn. Claire just caught sight of the grey stone walls and the long sash windows before Tony switched off the car lights. Getting out, they went to the door and pulled the rusty iron doorbell. Then they waited.

'Do you think it worked?' she whispered.

'Yes it does, it rings in the back part of the house and in the old days Anthea said the butler answered it. Now it is Iris the maid who is rather slow because of bad legs or Nannie who may not have heard it, or Anthea herself.'

A few moments later there was the sound of a handle being turned, and the door swung open to reveal a tall woman with shoulder-length dark hair and two friendly dogs that were pushing against her. She grabbed their collars and looking up laughing at Tony and Claire

'Come in, come in. These boys want to go out and hunt rabbits but I don't want to be calling them back all night,' she said.

Once she had banished the dogs to their baskets she turned and said

'You must be Claire, how lovely to meet you; Tony has told me all about you. Goodness your hands are cold, come into the fire, and Tony, dearest, you as well' and she gave him a light kiss.

They followed her through a large front hall and then into a panelled room which was obviously a library, at the end of which was a concealed door. Anthea pressed a small catch and the door swung open and they went into the most beautiful room Claire had ever seen. It was coloured pale green and lit by two large, sparkling chandeliers. Opposite them, in a wide hearth and below a white and green marble mantelpiece, burned the most welcoming fire. Deep, comfortable sofas and chairs were drawn up into which Tony and Claire were ordered to collapse.

'And now,' said Anthea, 'tea or a drink? I'll go and ask Iris, our last remaining pair of hands, to bring us something.'

But she need not have worried as Iris herself had appeared in her best black dress, wearing a starched white cap and apron, to obey their requests.

'We are having a little party tomorrow night, Claire,' Anthea explained, 'I expect Tony has told you about it. Nothing grand, just a few boys and their girlfriends in from the camp.'

'Is drunken Bob coming?' Tony asked her teasingly.

Anthea laughed, 'he did rather overdo it last time, I gave him a lecture and he has promised to behave,' she replied.

They all laughed and Claire felt less shy, she liked Anthea. At that moment the concealed door clicked and the handle twisted but it did not open.

'That must be Lucy,' Anthea said, 'my youngest one; she can never get the hang of it.'

She went over and opened the door to reveal two little girls who came into the room together. They had long, dark hair like their mother and were dressed in green kilted skirts and coral-coloured Shetland jerseys. Charmian, the eldest, followed by Lucy, went over to Claire and Tony and politely shook hands. They both stared at Claire until Anthea looked at them with raised eyebrows and they turned away and blushed. Charmian said to Tony

'You promised you would play spillikins last time you were here.'

'Oh,' Anthea remonstrated, 'I'm not sure about this evening.'

But Tony interrupted her, 'I would love a game, come along girls, Claire would you like to play?'

But Claire could see that they wanted him to themselves so she smiled and shook her head.

Left alone together, when Tony and the girls had gone into the library, Anthea threw another log on the fire and offered Claire another drink.

'How wicked! Just a very small one,' Claire replied. 'It is so wonderful to be here, Anthea, I can't tell you what a joy it is to be in a civilized house as beautiful as this!'

'But you have a lovely home,' Anthea replied, 'called Merlinstone in Scotland. Tony told me about it, he said he had never been there but you often describe it.'

'Oh yes,' Claire replied, 'but since father died it belongs to Simon now, and one day he will live there I hope. At the moment I am in London sharing a bedroom and a kitchen with a friend who is nursing as well. It is just heaven to get away into this atmosphere.'

'I know, we are lucky, but I do miss Oliver. I have to deal with it all now and it does get exhausting, running the farm and the forestry and the house. We have forty evacuees arriving soon, they are all blind, poor little things, and they are coming down from London.'

Anthea handed Claire her glass and sat down on a low stool in front of the fire.

'I wonder what it will be like, everything, after the war.' She continued 'we are all changing. I think you are wonderful to do nursing Claire, doesn't it tear the heart out of you?'

'Yes it does, and it is exhausting! But in many ways it is such rewarding work. My sister Vanessa thought that I would never stick to it but she is wrong, I shall, I am determined to.'

'Well you are going to have a good rest tonight,' Anthea told her. 'I have given you the azalea room. It is quiet and looks out over the garden. You will sleep well in there.'

After a while they went into the library where Tony and the sisters were sitting on the floor playing their game, the spillikins scattered on a board in front of them. Claire and Anthea sat down to watch. Claire saw Charmian laugh at her sister's concentrated face and wobbly hand; as she turned towards Tony to share her laughter she caught her expression and thought 'Oh dear!' For on the child's face was a look of shy adoration; it made Claire's heart lurch to see this on anyone so young. 'She loves him!' she thought. For the flicker of a moment Charmian looked up and Claire quickly averted her glance, but the child knew she had been observed and her cheeks flamed. She shook her hair forward to hide them and went on watching Lucy's game. In spite of her wobbly hand Lucy won. She pranced round the room excitedly and Anthea said that it was time for them to go to bed. There were cries of 'No it can't be!' and 'Just one more game!' Then there was a tap at the door and Nannie arrived to tell them to hurry up as she had a lot to do and it was time for their supper. Tony promised them he would come back soon so that he could win the next game and they left waving as they went. Later, standing in the old nursery beside the tall fireguard, brushing her hair Charmian said

'Do you think Tony's going to marry this Claire person, Luce?' Lucy stopped brushing her own hair and considered.

'Because,' Charmian continued, 'he can't – I want to marry Tony when I grow up.'

'People don't get married in wartime,' Lucy said sagely.

'Of course they do, look at Cousin Louise. She married last month in London. Mummy told me all about it.'

'Well, Louise is old,' replied Lucy, as if this settled the whole matter. 'Maybe she married because she was lonely. I'm sure Claire isn't lonely. She works in a hospital with masses of wounded soldiers!'

'Do you like Claire?' Charmian asked. Lucy considered again and then she said 'yes, I think I do.'

Later, as they climbed into their beds Lucy said,

'Of course Tony may get killed. Lots of airmen do, then neither of you will be able to marry him,' and with that discomforting announcement she was very soon asleep.

On Monday, their last day, Claire and Tony went for a walk in the woods. Anthea watched them set off from the drawing room windows, laughing together.

'So young,' she thought, 'they are still children really. What, I wonder, will become of them?'

The couple were full of a shining confidence. The sun had come out in a thin, wintry way and in spite of a late night the evening before, Claire felt refreshed and rested.

'You look quite different today,' Tony told her; 'no shadows under your eyes. I hardly recognize you, Nurse Claire.'

They crossed the fields and went into a wood where they climbed down a steep bank to a stream below.

'Anthea tells me wild lilies of the valley grow here in May,' Tony told her, 'and there is a mass of pink spindle berry.'

'Perhaps,' said Claire 'she just might ask us to stay again in the summer. I can imagine how wonderful it must be.'

'And she also says she has heard the nightingale here,' he continued.

'It must be Paradise,' she replied, and he looked at her and said

'But it is that now, darling Claire, to be here with you. Will you marry me?'

She nearly burst out laughing but his face had become serious and he held her by the elbows.

'Must I go down on one knee?' he asked. 'It's terribly wet, the ground, and I have only one decent pair of trousers.'

'Darling Tony, of course I will marry you.'

After he had kissed her she said 'I suppose it is a rare thing, to marry the first man who asks you. But I know that I would never want anyone else.'

'Perhaps we are a reincarnation,' he replied. 'Perhaps I asked you in another life and a wicked stepmother drove us apart!'

On their way back to the house Claire said

'We shall have to keep this a secret for the moment, Tony. My sister Vanessa is my legal guardian, she will never give her consent.'

'I don't care about anyone or anything,' he replied. 'I just know that we must marry.'

As they walked over the wintry fields they made their plans.

Two weeks later when Claire had returned to work and Tony was flying Spitfires once again, Theresa, trim in her Wren's uniform, got off the tube and found her way up the stairs onto the cold London streets. For a moment she paused and surveyed the scene before her; it had been snowing and this seemed to accentuate the devastation. A long line of buildings had been blown to pieces by the bombing and there was a dark, jagged gash running the length of the pavement. At the end were a few shabby little shops still intact and clinging together defiantly. People were hurrying by in a surprisingly normal way.

Theresa took a scrap of paper out of her pocket and studied the directions that Claire had given her. They described the way to the British restaurant, which was based in a church hall where they could have a cup of tea and a good talk. 'A confidential tête-à- tête,' Claire had written. Theresa wondered what the confidence could be about. She turned left out of the station and walked towards a church spire she could see poking up behind some buildings. The hall was a little further on and was larger than Theresa had expected. She pushed open the door and found herself in a dimly lit room full of factory workers, elderly men, and cigarette smoke. A long counter ran the length of the room at the far side and all around her were metal tables and chairs. Theresa scanned the crowd for her sister and then suddenly she saw her, sitting alone at a table at the back of the hall - she was reading something. As she made her way towards her, pushing past the tables with care, Theresa was struck by her sister's appearance. No untidy clothes or dishevelled hair now! There sat a young nurse in a smart grey cloak, her hair pulled smoothly back and coiled at the back of her head in a snood, her handbag and her gas mask placed neatly on the table before her.

'Claire, darling!' Theresa said.

Claire jumped up, cramming the letter into her pocket. They hugged and then sat down laughing.

'How wonderful, I haven't seen you for so long!' Theresa exclaimed. 'You are looking lovely, darling, but you have grown so thin!'

Claire had taken off her cloak and had revealed her slim waist, which was clasped by her nurse's webbing belt.

'It's all the hard work,' she replied, 'scrubbing those bloody floors! But I'm over that now and onto better things. You look awe-inspiring, Theresa, in that uniform! I feel I should salute!'

Theresa put out her tongue and took off her navy blue overcoat.

'It's amazingly warm in here,' she said, and she picked up the stained menu card from the table. 'What shall we have, two cups of tea and some daisy cakes?'

'I am afraid that is about all we'll get, unless we have baked beans,' Claire replied.

'I'll go for the cakes I think; stay there, I'll get them,' Theresa told her.

When she came back she carried a tray with two chipped mugs full of tea. There was powdered milk and a plate of very small buns that were supposed to be cakes.

'Not a hint of a daisy about them,' said Theresa, 'except perhaps their size. Have you heard lately from Simon, Claire?'

'Yes, Nessa sent me a letter the other day. It was really meant for all of us. I've brought it for you in my bag. He sounds fine, he's painting a bit and doing a lot of drawing.'

'And Nessa, have you seen her lately?'

'Well, I have seen her, but quite a long time ago now. She was well but she still isn't best pleased with me, you know.'

'No, I thought not. I spoke to her quite recently. She seems to be working hard in the munitions factory and worrying because she hadn't heard from Henry recently. But you know Nessa, I think she expects to get a letter from him every week!'

Theresa leaned forward and took hold of Claire's hand.

'Darling, you are all right aren't you? This nursing life really is going well for you?'

'Oh yes,' Claire looked back at her sister steadily. 'It really is all right. It kind of becomes your life. I thought I might never cope to start with, but somehow one does. It is a tremendous challenge – and those boys, I can't tell you how brave they are!' Her voice started to break and she took a gulp of tea. Theresa wondered what the confidence Claire said she wished to share was going to be. She did not like to be the first to mention it. Claire put down her cup and took in a deep breath. Then she said,

'The thing is, Theresa, I am drugged to bits on that great narcotic, love.'

'Aha!' Theresa thought, 'so that is it!'

'Go on,' she said.

'He's called Tony,' continued Claire, 'Tony Stanford and I admit I haven't known him for very long. I met him at a party that was given a few months ago by one of my school friends. He's in the RAF and stationed in Wiltshire. We are going to get married.'

She paused and watched Theresa's face, waiting for alarm or horror or at least surprise but her sister registered none of these. Instead she said

'I thought it would be something like this, your secret. You haven't got to marry, or anything like that have you, darling?'

'Of course not!' Claire laughed, 'you sound positively Victorian, dear sister.'

'Well you know quite well that I'm not! Describe him to me.'

'Better than that, I have a photograph.'

Claire produced a snap of Tony, wearing his flying jacket, which she had taken on the day that he had proposed to her. Theresa looked at it and smiled.

'He looks like a naughty school boy,' she said.

'There's much more to him than that,' Claire replied 'but he is tremendous fun to be with. You really will like him, Theresa.'

'And he is over fourteen years of age?'

'Don't tease, darling, we are so in love. No-one apart from you and Vivien, my friend I share with, knows about this and Nessa simply must not find out, she is such a snob. Apart from thinking me far too young she would never approve of my marrying an orphaned stranger I have only just met! She would do everything she could to stop us.'

Theresa nodded sadly. She knew that Claire was right about this.

'Nessa is very conventional in many ways,' she said, 'but in this case you could hardly blame her. You are taking a big risk if you do this, Claire!'

'Everything is a risk in war,' Claire replied. 'I am entirely certain about Tony. I know that I love him and that he is a good man. If you could see the amount of poor boys I have to help in hospital when they write to their sweethearts begging them to wait for them to recover, it is pathetic. Some of them will never walk again although they refuse to believe this; and others are so badly burned their girls won't be able to recognize them. I want to marry Tony because I know I shall never meet another man like him; I want to marry him before he is shot to bits out of the sky,' Claire's eyes had suddenly filled with tears.

Theresa took her hand.

'I see exactly how you must feel,' she said, 'let's have a bit more tea,' and she picked up the tray.

When she returned Claire had dried her eyes and was smiling again.

'Thank you for understanding,' she said 'now I must tell you our plans. We are going to get married in the little church you passed on your way here, the one that belongs to this hall. The vicar is lovely, I've met him. He's very old and doesn't seem surprised by anything.' Theresa could not help laughing at this. 'He gave me some forms and I have forged Nessa's signature - as she is my guardian I had to do this, and also said I am eighteen. Will God ever forgive me, do you think?'

'You've faked Vanessa's signature,' Theresa said slowly, 'I wonder if they could send you to prison for that.'

'No-one is ever going to know,' Claire replied. 'Everyone is far too busy with the war.'

'Nessa will have to know one day but by then you'll be married so there will be nothing that she can do.'

'No, I suppose not, but our names will be on the church register. Still, as you say, who is going to bother to look? We've booked the church for the 28th of March, it's a good long way ahead, so you must be able to come to it.'

'I shall have to come,' Theresa replied, 'although I shall not be able to give the real reason for my absence.'

The café was emptying at last; girls in overalls, their hair pinned up under headscarves, were dragging on their coats. Occasionally a soldier came in and was greeted with cheerful cries of 'Got a day off from Jerry, have you?' as they made their way to the counter.

'I must go,' Theresa murmured, 'it's time I caught my train. Let me know how plans are going - oh, and what about a dress?'

'I want a real wedding dress,' Claire replied. 'I'm not going to go all wartime in a trim little suit. I'm going to swear Laura Netherfield to secrecy and see if she can help me. She might have an old lace bedspread put away somewhere. I want to look like a real bride.'

They left the steamy café and went out into the cold street. For a moment they clung together before they parted, Theresa to catch her train and Claire to report for night duty at the hospital.

On the day of Claire and Tony's wedding it tried to snow again. In spite of it being late March, the weather suddenly switched back to winter and a few flakes were falling when Theresa arrived early at the church to find the rector already there. Theresa was feeling torn by guilt; she kept thinking of her sister Vanessa and how upset she would be if she had known what was happening. But what else can I do? She asked herself, as she settled quietly in a pew and bent her head in prayer. Claire would have married Tony in spite of them all, just as she had left home and became a nurse. Once she was determined to do something, nothing could stop her. The church was dark and cold, and Theresa wished heartily that the whole thing was over with and they could be in the Great Northern Hotel where Tony had booked a table for lunch. She could dimly make out the ugly Victorian windows and the few commemorative plaques on the walls. 'William Gaiger of Westminster 1832,' she read. Perhaps once it had been thronged with an enthusiastic Victorian congregation. There were some meagre white flowers on the altar and three lilies in a tall vase beside the pulpit. The rector had decided to light the altar candles and was doing this with a trembling hand. He was wearing a red velvet robe edged with gold. Nice of him, Theresa thought, to bother to dress up. When he had lit the last candle he turned and saw her sitting there. He came carefully down the altar steps and made his way towards her.

'Good morning,' he said politely. 'My name is the Reverend Clive Carter. Are you by any chance part of the wedding party?'

He was exceedingly elderly, she thought, and had a kindly face.

'This is to be a very small affair, I gather. Wartime weddings so often are, I find.'

She nodded nervously. 'I am Claire's sister,' she said. The rector pondered on this for a moment but made no comment.

'Miss Moordew is coming to play a little organ for us, I'm glad to say. It's not one of her knitting Saturdays. Do sit down again, I must attend to a few more details.'

He made his way to the lectern where he started to turn the pages of a large Bible, putting in a few paper markers as he went. There was a faint click of the vestry door and a small woman came into the church carrying some sheets of music. She wore a brown felt hat with an alarmingly long pheasant's feather in it – Miss Moordew, Theresa presumed. She went to the organ and scrambled up onto a pile of cushions that had been placed there and continued to sort through her music. Theresa wondered which hymns Claire and Tony had chosen. A few moments later the west door opened and two men came into the church. Theresa recognized Tony at once from the photograph Claire had shown her. He looked young and slim and smart in his uniform. The man with him was dark-haired and slightly older. She left her pew and went to meet them.

'I'm Theresa, Claire's sister,' she said, taking his hand.

Tony smiled his impish smile. 'This is my best man,' he said, 'Michael Hankinson. Mike, this is Theresa Tarnoch.'

Then Tony whispered 'it's freezing in here; I hope Claire doesn't catch pneumonia.'

A few more people arrived - Anthea from Wiltshire in a warm-looking red coat and velvet hat, and Laura Netherfield who was wearing trailing, ethnic-looking clothes and a hat with violets in it. After some further whispered conversation the rector came over and asked who was giving the bride away.

Theresa said bravely 'I am!'

'Then I think you had better move to the west door,' the rector told her, 'and best man and bridegroom here, on the right, and ladies do take a seat in one of the front pews.'

Theresa went outside and stood at the top of the church steps. The sky had lightened a little and no more snowflakes fell. How grey and sad London looked, she thought. At that moment a taxi drew up and she saw Claire's excited face. She was helped out by Vivien, and she looked so lovely that Theresa caught her breath. Laura had found an old lace bedspread that had belonged to her grandmother and she had cut it up and made Claire a perfect dress. It clung to her slim figure and had long, elegant sleeves. Her hair was pinned back and two cream-coloured flowers nestled in the nape of her neck. She carried a small ivory-backed prayer book. Theresa took her arm and felt her trembling.

'It's ok,' she whispered, 'everyone is here.'

Followed by Vivien they went into the church whilst Miss Moordew thumped out *Praise My Soul the King of Heaven* as loudly as she could.

'We are nearly there,' Theresa thought. They had reached the 'any just cause or impediment' moment which she was looking forward to getting over with when the air raid siren went, piercing the quiet of the church. There was a very brief pause, the rector's bushy white eyebrows twitched, but he continued with 'why these two persons' etc. and after a moment or two Claire and Tony took their vows and were declared man and wife. They were about to go into the registry office when there were several very loud explosions. Theresa wondered if they should lie down under the pews. The church seemed to quiver and somewhere they heard the sound of glass falling.

'One of those hideous windows,' she thought, 'I hope they replace it with clear glass.' The rector jerked his head and they followed him into the registry office.

'I think we should remain in here for a little while,' he said, 'until the all clear sounds. There are no windows to fall on us and we could get under the table. It has a marble top. I think it once belonged to a fishmonger's shop.'

No-one seemed inclined to follow this advice. After a while the all clear sounded and Miss Moordew returned to the organ and the wedding march rang out through the little church. Claire and Tony walked down the aisle followed by their small party of guests. Theresa sighed with relief. Thank heavens, she thought, that is over with and we are still alive; and they are looking so happy together. No-one dared to look around as they left the church for the damage that must have been caused by the bombs. Claire heard later that the café had been demolished in the next door street where she and Theresa had so recently met. Luckily no-one had been there as it had been closed on that Saturday.

The Wedding Breakfast – it had to be called this although it was lunch time – took place in a private room in the Great Northern Hotel. Claire and Tony were catching the night train to Edinburgh where they were spending their four day honeymoon. The management of the Great Northern Hotel had done them proud and a large vase of spring flowers stood on a table by the window. The menu was as good as it could be in the days of rationing and, as Tony said, 'considering this was not exactly the Ritz!'

Years later Theresa looked back at the photographs she had taken that day with her humble box camera: Claire in her going away clothes, the amethyst outfit she had bought in Selfridges and a pretty hat that she, Theresa, had managed to make for her –and Tony, so young looking with confetti still clinging to his uniform. It had been, she thought in retrospect, one of the happiest days of the long, dark war.

A few weeks after Claire's wedding Vanessa returned home one evening after a long and tiring day's work at the factory. She was glad that it was April at last and London was leaping into spring. War or no war the trees were budding and the birds had started to sing. Her heart had been heavy of late, she had not heard from Henry or Simon for over a month. She worried greatly about both of them. She would make herself a pot of strong tea when she got home and listen to the news on her radio in the kitchen, the only fairly warm room in the house. She stopped on her way and bought an evening newspaper and then hurried on. It was getting towards dusk and she had forgotten to bring her torch. Once home she went down the basement steps and let herself in through the back door. In the kitchen her spirits rose a little. She pulled down the blackout blinds, closed the curtains and turned on the lights. Marcus, the ginger cat, jumped off his chair and circled around her legs, purring. Vanessa changed her mind – no tea this evening, it was too late, she would pour herself a precious whisky and water. Sitting in the comfortable kitchen chair that sagged and creaked but still accommodated any who sat there, her cat on her lap and her drink beside her on the table, Vanessa unfolded the evening paper. At first the tall black letters on the second page meant nothing to her, and then, in a flash, she understood. *'Famous hero General of the First World War's daughter, Claire Tarnoch, elopes and marries in secret her fighter pilot lover,'* she read. Vanessa continued to read in disbelief; she felt certain it must have been invented by the press. She read it through twice and then, throwing the paper on to the floor, she buried her face in her hands. How on earth could Claire have done this? And who was this boy orphan Tony whom she had married? And, far more terrible than anything else, why had Theresa failed to tell her anything about it?

'I can't believe it!' She moaned, 'I simply cannot believe it.'

Marcus, irritated by her grief, jumped off her lap and stalked towards, the cat flap, and delights that were offered by the night outside.

Vanessa sat there for a long time. She helped herself to some more whisky, and returned to her chair. She was starting to feel drunk; tears welled up and spurted down her cheeks. The pain of both her sisters' disloyalty and secrecy cut her heart, and not having Henry to say all this to, not even Simon whom she felt would have been sympathetic to her grief, there was no-one to tell it all to, or be comforted by. After a moment or two of drunken misery she got up and went unsteadily to the telephone and dialled the exchange. By a miracle Theresa answered the telephone.

'Nessa!' she sounded alarmed, 'is everything all right?'

'No! It's not!' Vanessa's voice shook at the other end of the line; Theresa quailed. Vanessa suddenly became cold and collected. 'You are to come and see me here as soon as possible,' she said, 'you owe it to me. I must talk to you about Claire and this boy Tony and this idiotic marriage. It is all over the evening papers – I can hardly believe that it is true.' A short pause. Theresa said

'It is true, Vanessa, and I will come and see you as soon as I can and tell you everything; there will not be time on this call.' A few moments later they were cut off.

Vanessa replaced the receiver and went to the drawer in the kitchen table. She pulled it open and took out a pen, paper, envelopes and stamps. She sat down and wrote to Claire, jabbing the paper with the nib as she wrote. She covered six sides, and then signed it, simply, your sister Vanessa. She did not read it through. In the letter she poured out her grief and rage. She also wrote that she did not wish to see her sister again. After sealing the letter she wrote to Simon telling him all that had happened. It was a loving letter. 'You are the only loyal relation I have left,' she wrote. When she had finished she grabbed her coat and her torch and rushed out into the night to the post box at the end of the square. A fire watcher saluted her as she went by but she did not notice him. 'Had one or two, that one,' he thought, as he watched her weave her way down the street. Vanessa pushed the letters into the box and waited to hear them land with a little plop, then she turned and walked back home. The search lights were raking the dark sky.

'There is no-one,' she thought, 'no-one anywhere who can help me get through tonight.'

Simon, in the North African desert, received the letter from Vanessa on the day before he was captured by the Germans and taken prisoner of war. In spite of not being cut out as an ideal soldier, he was quite enjoying himself. One of his few complaints would have been that he did not have enough time to paint. When he read Vanessa's letter he was filled with sadness. Had Claire really found it necessary to be so deceitful? Surely, he reasoned, if she had only gone to Vanessa and confronted her. At that moment he remembered the tall, commanding figure of his elder sister, and wondered if he would have had the courage to do this had he been in Claire's shoes. He pictured Claire as he had last seen her at his farewell party at Merlinstone, very young in a white dress, her hair tied in a ribbon behind her head like a child's. She had come a long way in a relatively short space of time. She had recently sent him a small snapshot of herself in her uniform. Nurse Claire, a face that was confident and calm but with a glint in her eyes and an upward turn of her curly mouth that belied her spirit.

An attractive young woman and no longer the harum scarum girl he used to know. His reverie was broken by Tom Netherfield coming into the mess. Simon hailed him, waving his letter.

'News from home,' he said.

'Good news?'

'Well, mixed – depends on how you look at it. My sister Claire has eloped with a young airman and they have secretly married. Vanessa is furious.'

Tom whistled his surprise. 'Dark horse, that one,' he said, 'I remember her; she seemed almost a child at that dinner party Vanessa and Henry gave just before war was declared. Who is the lucky guy?'

'A Tony Stanford; orphan, I am told. He flies Spitfires.'

'Not a very good candidate for life insurance then. Funnily enough I think Mark has mentioned him. They're stationed together somewhere in Wiltshire. Like a drink?'

'We're over the yard arm, so let us have one and toast them.'

And with that they both went to the bar and clinked their glasses together.

The following night Simon was captured and interned by the Germans as prisoner of war. As liaison officer he had obeyed an order to seek out the New Zealand Brigade. Advancing in his Crusader tank, and assured that the route forward had been cleared of the enemy, he drove straight into a German trap. Many years later he learned that his senior officer had got his map references wrong, hence his failure to turn up at the appointed venue and no armour came to save him. Simon never confided his whole range of feelings to anyone after his capture, although Claire and Theresa could have guessed what they might have been. Although he knew that he would probably have to face much suffering, even death as a captive, he had been liberated at last from the burden of feeling that he had to justify being his famous father's son. Later, greatly weakened and seriously ill with dysentery, he could not even attempt to escape. He was also frozen with cold as he had left behind his warm coat when starting on his ill-fated mission. In spite of all this he had time now to be what he wanted to be, an artist, and this gave him the strength and determination to live. Later, Theresa and Vanessa managed to send him art materials through the Red Cross and although too weak and ill to use them he lay on his uncomfortable pallet and dreamed of what he would create when he was well again.

Theresa did indeed obey Vanessa's summons. Sacrificing a precious day's leave she took an early train from Portsmouth to London. Now she sat in her sister's kitchen waiting for her to make some tea. It seemed these days that nothing could be accomplished without this beverage and Vanessa had hoarded a great amount of it in her kitchen cupboard along with soap and candles. To begin with she was very cool, cold you could have said, towards Theresa, but as the morning wore on she thawed a little. They were both shocked by the news about Simon.

'He'll escape, of course,' Vanessa said, confidently, picturing her brother glad in a heroic cloud of glory, bravely returning to the front. Theresa did not reply. She doubted Simon had the strength after his prolonged illness to even contemplate an escape.

'He'll hate being incarcerated,' she said, 'we must send him some art materials; perhaps the Red Cross can help.'

Vanessa poured hot water onto the tea leaves.

'We'll wrap a scarf I have knitted around them,' she replied. There was rather a long silence. Theresa sipped her tea.

'It is like straw,' she thought, 'perhaps she is being economical.'

'About Claire and the wedding,' she began bravely.

Vanessa sat back in her chair, her long, elegant legs crossed, her dark eyes trained on Theresa in a disconcerting manner; it was hard to tell what she was really thinking.

'I know it was wrong of me not to tell you about it, Nessa, but it would have been useless for you to have intervened, somehow Claire would have married Tony even if it had come down to Gretna Green.'

'It was totally illegal to have forged my signature,' Vanessa replied, 'she could go to prison for that and their marriage could be declared invalid.'

Theresa nodded. 'I know. Claire would just say 'it is valid in the eyes of God' and that would be that.'

'And this Tony man, what would he say?' Vanessa demanded.

'He would stand by her, he adores her, they are really in love.'

'Love!' Vanessa exclaimed – a terrible wave of jealousy suddenly choked her. Where was the love in her own life? Where was Henry whom she longed to be held and comforted by but whose passion, and she had never admitted this to anyone, always failed in some odd way to equal her own?

'Got a cigarette?' she asked her sister. Theresa took a cigarette out of her bag and handed it to her, followed by the click of a little gold lighter.

'That's nice,' Vanessa said, 'where did you get it from? It looks like real gold.'

Theresa blushed. 'Someone gave it to me, a guy I know who is half Lebanese.'

'Quite a gift!' Vanessa sounded arch and slightly acidic. 'Anyway,' she continued, 'I have written to Claire and told her that I never want to see her again, and as for Tony, I definitely do not ever wish to meet him.' Theresa was shocked by this announcement.

'I don't expect you'll get the chance,' she replied. 'He flies Spitfires, you know. Oh Nessa, that is a sad and harsh thing to have done. One day, when this rotten war is over, you'll regret it.'

'Well, I can't help that, I've done it. She has been swept out of my life and I relinquish any guardian rights I may have had. She is a married woman and must stand on her own feet.'

'She'll do that all right,' Theresa replied.

Soon after this conversation Theresa left. She kissed her sister warmly, promising to meet up with her as soon as she could. She knew that she had not been entirely forgiven but at least she had not been told to clear out of her life for ever. Vanessa closed the door and bent down to pick up the post that lay on the hall floor. Flicking through the letters she found, with a great leap of joy, that there was one from Henry at last.

A considerable time after having had her meeting with her sister, Theresa discovered what was puzzling everyone – how on earth the story of Claire's marriage had leaked out to the press. One of her friends was married to the editor of the newspaper and told her how it had all happened. A short while after the wedding, two young journalists were wandering through London on a rainy afternoon trying to find some news that might cheer up their editor; he had complained he was sick and tired of printing nothing but war news and felt his public needed a break as well.

'For God's sake find something juicy,' he had said, 'some scandal involving high society; our readers need a change.'

Disconsolately they were wandering the rainy streets complaining to each other about the difficulty of suddenly finding a titbit that would excite the exhausted readers who were pulverized by bombing and bad news. Passing by the little church where Claire and Tony had married one of them said

'I'm going in there to find some dirt.'

The other looked incredulous.

'Are you raving mad?' he asked, and rather angrily followed his friend into the church. At least, he thought, it would be a short reprieve from the rain. His friend went into the registry office and flicked through the register whilst he himself wandered around, reading the notices on the wall. 'Please close the door firmly and always remember to lock,' one said and another read 'Miss Moordew choir practice Thursday six pm.' This was a memo left lying on the marble-topped table. Neither led him to believe a great discovery of scandal would be found here when his fellow journalist gave a loud whoop;

'Look at this!' he cried. 'The great General's daughter has married! I bet this is a runaway wedding; we haven't heard about any engagement. She probably forged the signature of her guardian. I'm going to get hold of my sister – she'll know if Claire Tarnoch is officially married or not. I can't wait to ask her!'

And, delighted, they rushed out of the church. After much probing they found out that Claire was not known to have married, and Vanessa, when questioned on this at a small party she had been to in Highgate, had said

'No! She most certainly has not married; she is a nurse,' as though this would prevent her sister from leading any other kind of normal life. Armed with every piece of information they could find they joyfully wrote their article. The editor was delighted and the story went into print.

'Just shows how useful despair can be sometimes,' Reg, the elder of the two, remarked. 'It can drive you to find the most astonishing success.'

CHAPTER VIII

Henry Sinclair leaned his head against the hard wall of the plane and closed his eyes. The thrumming of the engine pierced his brain and numbed him. A half sleep came over him and he drifted in and out of dreams. When someone shouted in his ear he jumped. It was the co-pilot.

'We'll be fifteen minutes now, are you prepared?' he asked. Henry shook himself.

'Yes, perfectly,' he shouted back.

The other man smiled and went back to the cockpit. He felt a rush of excitement. The aircraft started to lose height and he could see France in the moonlight below, and the wild country of the Drôme stretching beneath them. A few moments later the pilot shouted, 'Ready for the drop?'

He shouted back 'Ready.'

The door opened and he got in position; a massive rush of cold air hit him and he loosened his grip and away he went into the moonlit sky. He pulled the cord and his parachute opened above him. It was a perfect night. He glided down in widening circles, landing eventually at the far side of a small plateau, near to a small wood of scrub oak trees. This was a much smoother landing than the last one he had done when he had badly sprained his ankle. He grabbed his parachute and pushed it into the pack on his back; two figures had appeared on the edge of the wood. He recognized them and crawled towards them, only getting to his feet when he reached the trees. An elderly man and a boy were waiting for him. He gave the password and they responded.

Henry said, in French, 'I am making contacts. The plane has gone on towards Sault with some ammunition.'

The man replied, 'Yes, they are expecting it and you are to go to the Château Verdurin. They will tell you there who you are to contact next.'

'Thank you, Gaston. Thank you for meeting me.'

He shook the man's hand and then the boy's. They spoke very quietly and the trees concealed them.

Gaston said 'You know where it is you have to go? You have a map?'

'In my head.'

'Then we must go. Come, Antoine.'

He turned to the boy and then back to Henry.

'Au revoir,' he said, 'may you be lucky,' and they disappeared into the trees.

Henry stood motionless for a moment and then breathed in deeply. He longed for, but did not light, a cigarette. He removed his wrist watch, turned it over and flicked open the back, which revealed a small compass. When he had got his bearings he went through his directions methodically. He had memorised them many times. The only time he had ever set eyes on the Château Verdurin he had seen it from the road that lay below it. Tonight he had to find his way overland, through a maze of scrub and rock. There would be stiff hills to climb. He had hidden his parachute in his rucksack. He was wearing the clothes of a French labourer and now – to complete his disguise – he pulled on a blue woollen cap. If questioned he was a farmer from the other side of the Drôme on his way to visit his family. He had perfected the local patois as well as he could and he cut a stout staff from the scrub oak before he set off. He must hurry before the moonlight went; there was only an hour or so left. He felt so light-hearted he could have burst into song but instead he whistled a French ditty under his breath. The rocks really were enormous; they towered around him making eerie shapes and casting rich, black shadows in the moonlight. He seemed to have walked for a long time and got nowhere when suddenly he came to a high ridge of land where he stopped. Below him the rocks and red earth fell away; he was standing on the edge of a steep escarpment. Way below he saw a road snaking its way westwards, and beyond this, high on the crest of another ridge he could see the dark shape of the Château heaving up against the sky. That was it – with a rush of relief and excitement he recognized it. The Château Verdurin where his love Geneviève waited for him, the pale maiden of fairy tales, guarded by a dragon perhaps, he thought, laughing to himself, a dragon he would have to slay before he seized her and kissed her and kissed her. But now the problem was how to descend the escarpment between him and the road. He was forced to walk quite a long way along the ridge before he found a narrow sheep track and sliding, slipping and cursing, he made his descent.

At the bottom of the escarpment, bruised and bleeding and out of breath, he paused. The land was less steep now before he reached the road.

Ah! he thought, great to feel the smooth tarmac under his feet at last. He followed the road up a steep hill where it branched out. The part that bore left became a rough track whilst the other way would have led him on westwards towards a small town named Brantes. He took the road that climbed steeply up and then arrived at last at some tall iron gates that were open and beyond a wide courtyard in the middle of which grew a tree; and here were the old walls of the chateau, he touched one as he went by. 'I am here at last', he thought. He went to the large wooden door and prayed that this also would open. It was a beautiful Provencal doorway, the wood faded to almost silver by age. He turned the heavy iron handle and pushed and the door swung open, and he went on into a wide hallway. The room was circular, and the walls were ochre coloured. Ancient weapons were hanging on them as well as threadbare tapestries. A staircase swept down into the hall with shallow stone steps that also looked a great age. There was the smell of wood smoke mixed with scented geranium.

Henry wondered whether he should climb the stairway. He was debating this when he heard the sound of soft, slippered footsteps and he had an odd moment of fear. Here she was at last, her thick, pale hair spread over her shoulders, her dark eyes searching for his face. She came towards him with her arms held out, and she said with a small sob in her voice,

'I have dreamt of this for so long.'

And he pulled her into his arms and replied 'So have I.'

They stood together quietly for a while and then she leaned back and looked at him and laughed.

'It suits you,' she said, 'the Bohemian look!'

'Is that what you would call it?' he replied.

He continued to hold her close to him; their hearts beat against each other like two agitated drums. Then he said,

'Come, take me into the house, we have so little time.'

She led him from the hall through several rooms and then down a long, dimly-lit passage at the end of which she opened a door and drew him into a cavernous kitchen.

'We are safe in here,' she said, 'no-one can hear us. My aunt and uncle's rooms are at the other end of the chateau and Papa is away for a few days.'

Henry sat down on a carved, pine seat and looked about him. It was a wonderful room, he thought. The walls were painted a pale terracotta, one side of the room was almost obscured by a vast dresser that was laden with every kind of china plate and jug and hooks from which hung a great variety of kitchen implements. There were bunches of herbs and a large green, glass jar stood on the kitchen table full of cornichons.

'How wonderful,' he said, 'it's an Aladdin's cave.'

She smiled at him her secret, obscure smile.

'I sit in here when I write to you,' she said. Then she took his hands and rolled up his shirt sleeves.

'You are terribly cut and scratched; I will bathe them in witch hazel for you but now I think we both need a drink.'

She picked up a bottle that was standing on the dresser.

'Whisky?' she asked him.

He raised an eyebrow and laughed at her.

'How bloody marvellous and very unfrench of you; I expected local wine!'

'That would be very like syrup of figs,' she replied. 'Papa gets his wine from Burgundy. He has a cellar full of wonderful vintages. But this is a better pick-me-up after a long journey. Even a French woman can realize that!'

He raised his glass to her.

'Come here,' he said and she obeyed and sat down beside him, and gazed at him whilst he spoke to her, looking as he did so at her throat, her pale skin, that he had remembered so many times when he had been alone and thinking of her. She listened to him intently. He took her hands and examined her wrists, the narrowness of them and the little blue veins.

'So, that is it,' he concluded, 'I haven't got long, my darling, you must give me the messages and then I shall have to leave very early tomorrow. I shall be able to spend one more night here on my return, probably in about a week if I am lucky.'

'But of course,' she replied, 'I shall be waiting for you.'

Later, after they had made love on the wide comfortable sofa, Geneviève murmured,

'I should have taken you to my room, but I couldn't wait.'

'Neither could I,' he replied, 'and I love it in here, it is like a wonderful cave. It is in tradition to make love to you in strange places! Do you remember the vestry?'

'How could I ever forget that funny little room and you throwing the vicar's holy raiment onto the floor for our bed!'

'And that letter in the evening paper,' he said.

She sighed. 'It seems such a long while ago,' she said, 'and so much has happened! Claire has married and Theresa is marching about in her navy blue uniform. Her letters have made me laugh so much.'

It was long after midnight when she took him upstairs to her room. He followed her through a labyrinth of passageways and then up a narrow flight of stairs to her bedroom. The walls were covered in an ancient paper that had a curious pattern of stars and shells. The bed looked inviting, the fine linen sheets turned back and a bolster supported large pillows that were edged with old lace. Before he could start to undress Geneviève put her hand on his arm.

'Listen,' she said, 'before we sleep come with me a moment; there is something I must show to you.' He followed her out of the room.

*

Simon's world had both contracted and expanded. To begin with he had been kept in solitary confinement, locked up behind the grim walls of the mediaeval castle which was his prison. Later he was allowed to share his time with some fellow prisoners who, like him, were of special interest to the enemy being the sons of distinguished politicians or, as he was, the British military elite. In spite of most of them being strangers to him Simon came to enjoy their company. Obligingly several of them sat for him and allowed him to paint their portraits. He used as much time as possible to draw and paint; it was the one thing that made his incarceration bearable. They were all unsure whether the fact they had been selected to form an elite hostage group meant that they would eventually be killed, or whether they were being accorded protection. It was an uncomfortable feeling with which to live. Still very weak from dysentery, Simon would sometimes fling himself down and fall into an exhausted sleep.

One of the friends who cheered him up was a young officer called Marian Grant. His mother was Polish and he made Simon laugh. He spent much time dwelling on the beautiful girls he had known and the present terrible lack of them.

'How shall we feel when we get home and see them all again?' he demanded. 'We will seem like gauche old school boys, they will have to educate us all over again!'

He regaled them all with stories of the wild parties he had held in his mother's old home in Poland where they tossed back the vodka and then dashed their glasses to the ground and danced to a band made up of gypsy fiddlers and a blind old man who played an accordion. This description of those parties made the London ones look decidedly lacklustre, Simon thought. He painted a portrait of Marian that hangs at Merlinstone to this day. He is looking back over his shoulder and smiling. Later he was to attempt a daring escape which failed. He was recaptured just as he reached the border with Holland. They marched him off and by the dawn light they shot him. For some time after this Simon was cast into near despair. He would lie for hours on his bed and travel back in his memory to Merlinstone, his only solace, just as he had done when he had been homesick at school. In his mind, he was beside the river, watching it rush and gurgle through the woods, his fishing rod in his hand. He saw the dark line of the hills against the pale sky and a whirl of rooks flying in a spiral over the house. He was completely there, as though his astral body had left his earthly one behind. He walked up to the house, and went through the hall, the room they called The Museum where his father's memorabilia was on display. And then in his imagination Marian would have come and shaken him gently by the shoulder.

'Come back Simon,' he used to say, 'We are making something you might almost call tea.'

And he would see his friend's humorous, glinting eyes looking down at him with kindness. And now he had gone – and who knows where his soul had travelled to; back to Poland, perhaps, and the land of his own childhood?

A short while after Marian's execution Simon fell asleep one night and had a strangely vivid dream. He was back at Merlinstone again, and this time in the garden. He realised in his dream that it must be spring. The blue muscari was out and the daffodils were shaking their heads in the breeze. Then he saw a tall figure coming towards him and he recognised his sister Vanessa. She was wearing black and she stood there silently, her long eyes were filled with tears. Suddenly he saw another figure in the distance at first, half running towards them. For a moment she came and stood beside Vanessa. She was a young girl and a stranger to him. She was wearing a blue dress and she was laughing. Then, just as he was about to greet them, the figures vanished, as they so often do in dreams, and he woke up. For a moment he expected to see the two figures still standing before him. Then he realised where he was and he sat up and looked around the room. His companions were all sleeping. Very quietly he left his bed and padded to the window – the scene outside was eerie. Searchlights combed the building and the courtyard below. They lingered on the windows of the castle, the frames of which were all painted a brilliant white, to make any necessary marksmanship easier to carry out. After a moment Simon drew back and returned to his bed. Lying on his back he closed his eyes and remembered his dream. The light that had flooded it had seemed to come from the girl.

She herself was radiant. After a long time, just before dawn, he fell asleep.

CHAPTER IX

Ralph Cunningham sat at his large desk in his office in London wrapped in thought. The frail spring sunlight was trying to penetrate the heavily taped windows behind him, and almost failed to do so: little slices of light managed to creep in, making a delicate fretwork pattern on the opposite wall. Ralph stared at the telephone that crouched before him, at the cooling cup of tea and the formidable pile of papers he had not yet read. Then he leaned forward and pressed a red button on his telephone. A few moments later a tall, thin young man tapped lightly on his door and came in, looking apprehensive.

'Yes sir?' he said.

'Oh, Philip, sit down a moment.'

The young man obeyed. He carried a file and his slender hands trembled slightly. He found Ralph Cunningham a somewhat daunting superior. Ralph took a sip of cold tea and studied the young man for a moment.

'A trifle timid,' he thought 'but intelligent and discreet. Not a bad lad at all. I must try not to bark at him so often.'

Out loud he said 'Mrs Sinclair, Vanessa Sinclair, I have decided to go and see her myself. I do not want her to receive the usual notification.'

'Yes sir, of course.'

'So,' Ralph continued, 'please see that someone gets hold of her and tells her I am coming on urgent business.' He flicked a piece of paper over to Philip. 'This is her home number. Let me know her reply as soon as possible.'

'Thank you, sir.'

He hurried out, ducking his head to avoid the lintel above the doorway, clutching his file. Ralph sat back and drew in a long, deep breath. This was a bad business, a very bad business. Someone had blundered; and in many ways it puzzled him.

Henry Sinclair had been an excellent officer. Of course, he ruminated, it could have been something incredibly small, something totally unavoidable that had caused Henry to lose his life. In this game things were like that. Everything could be oiled and polished and planned and then thump, you had tripped over the smallest detail and those bloody murderers had shot you or had you incarcerated. Poor Vanessa, and poor Greville, their young son – he did not look forward to telling her. He turned his mind resolutely to the business of the day.

Later that evening Ralph took a taxi to Vanessa's house; a light spring rain was falling. He went up the steps to her shiny front door and pressed the bell. To his surprise it was opened by Theresa. He took her hand and said

'My dear, I have come to see your sister. How nice to find you here.'

Theresa led him into the hall.

'We have such sad news,' she said, 'my sister Claire's new husband did not return from a mission the other night. He was doing that awful low flying and they think he was probably shot down and died in the sea.'

'Oh my dear,' Ralph stood very still in front of her. 'This is dreadful news. Poor little Claire, I know they were only recently married. I read about it not long ago, in that ghastly rag.'

Theresa said, 'Yes.' She was biting her lip and trying not to cry.

'This is bad,' said Ralph, 'this is very bad, for I come with the most unwelcome news for your sister.'

He put his arms round Theresa's shoulders, 'Come with me, my dear. Perhaps it would be a good thing if you are with her when I tell her.'

They climbed the dark green carpeted stairs. How many times, he thought, have I dined here? Such happy evenings, Henry and Vanessa were wonderful hosts. They went into the drawing room. Vanessa was standing in front of the fireplace. She was still in her working clothes.

She said 'Good evening Ralph, I know what you are going to tell me.'

Ralph took hold of both her hands. 'I hope no-one else has told you,' he said, 'I wanted to myself.'

'No,' she replied, 'no-one has told me, but I know that Henry is dead.'

Then she sat down on the sofa.

She said, 'Theresa, could you get me a glass of water – and you, Ralph?'

'Nothing for me,' he replied.

He sat down beside her and Theresa went to get Vanessa's glass.

'We should know more later,' he told her. 'What we do know now is that Henry was taken away and executed. He was on a mission to France, in the area of the Drôme. I am afraid that I am not at liberty to tell you any more at present, but as soon as I possibly can I will.'

'Thank you, Ralph,' she replied. She sat staring in front of her, clasping her glass of water. 'It is kind of you to come and tell me yourself. I know how busy you are.'

'My dear,' he replied, 'it is the very least I could do for a friend. I wish to God I could be more explicit. There are so many reasons why this could have happened. So much in this game hinges on luck – and it is a very dangerous game.'

'I know,' she replied, her husky voice barely above a whisper. 'I know that Ralph, and Henry loved playing it.' There was a hint of irony in her words.

Ralph said 'It is a wretched business; and about your other loss, poor Claire losing her new young husband. I really am so sorry to hear about that.' Vanessa did not reply. 'Anyway,' Ralph continued, 'How is your little chap Greville?'

'He is at Merlinstone with Aunt Mary. I shall have to go there soon and tell him.'

'And you have news of Simon?'

'Yes, we do, and thank heaven he, at least, is still alive.' Ralph stood up.

'I shall have to go,' he told her, 'I have a meeting later on this evening. If there is ever anything that I can do for you my dear, let me know.'

'Thank you again,' she replied, 'you are a good friend.'

She went with him down the stairs and into the hall. He turned in the doorway and he kissed her and then hurried out into the London evening.

Sitting back in the taxi he heaved a heavy sigh and closed his eyes. She had been so brave, he thought, a true daughter of the General. There was something about Henry Sinclair's death that troubled him deeply. He knew that he had stayed with the de Verdurins at their chateau and they would never have let him down. But someone had blundered. He had a sudden, vivid memory of seeing Henry lunching with the de Verdurin girl in Claridge's, just before her return to France. He had been on the other side of the restaurant with two colleagues and they had not noticed him. Henry should have spotted him, perhaps he did and thought better of coming over to his table.

'One thing I am certain of,' thought Ralph. 'Vanessa must never discover where her husband was staying during those two nights in France.'

Back again in his office Ralph pressed the red button once more on his telephone. Most of the staff had gone home but he knew that one or two would still be there. This time a young woman appeared.

Ralph said 'Ah Angela, can you get Mr Mather to come in if he is still in his office.'

'Yes sir, he is sir.'

'Good.'

Ralph sat back in his chair and lit a large cigar. Dick Mather was sound, and the right chap with whom to talk over these sad and puzzling events.

∗

Mary Tarnoch walked down the long lime avenue at Merlinstone with her nephew at her side. Spring had come at last to the north. High above them on the branches of the trees the rooks were building their nests. Greville had grown a great deal during the years and now he almost reached Mary's shoulder. He went daily to a small school nearby but he would soon be leaving for his big boarding school, a thought Mary did not altogether like; she knew that she was going to miss him. Today he seemed lost in deep thought. It would have been his father's birthday and he was remembering the time when his mother had told him that he might never see Henry again. That is what grown-ups always did, he thought, underestimate a child's perception. He had known that he would never see his father; he realised that he had died in France, although his mother had tried to leave it that he was simply missing. To Greville, Henry was a heroic figure, he could never be replaced. He remembered Vanessa coming upstairs to tell him. He had already been put to bed and he was reading. Vanessa had sat down at the end of his bed and he had watched her thin, handsome face and thought how sad she looked. There had been something discomforting about her. He had not wanted to hug or console her. He just sat there and listened and wondered why grown-ups were so stupid. Of course father was dead – why did she put a question mark to it? When she had gone he had not been able to sleep. He had lay there feeling miserable. The musky scent she wore only seemed to increase his sorrow.

Now Mary looked sideways at him. She did not like to break his thoughts but she worried about him.

'He was very brave, your father,' was all she said and she squeezed his hand.

He was grateful. He loved his aunt – she was sensible and left things alone. They came to the end of the avenue and took the winding road that led up to the village. They were on their way to have tea with the minister, Alastair Thompson, at the Manse. He was an old friend of the Tarnoch family; Greville loved to visit him. Although the Thompson children were all grown-up and away, now, fighting in the war he was allowed to go into their old playroom where a great many of their youthful possessions were still kept, including a wonderful train set. One of the best things about the visit would be the tea that Alastair's wife Igrainie always managed to produce in spite of the rationing.

The minister came to the door to welcome them in. He took Mary's coat and then shepherded them into the sitting room where a peat fire burned in a wide, old-fashioned hearth.

'Sit down, sit down!' he said, 'and you, young man, off to the trains I expect!'

Greville smiled and slipped willingly out of the room. Mary settled herself in a comfortable chair by the fire and Alastair sat opposite her and lit his pipe. They were old friends and he knew she would not mind him smoking, although Igrainie might tut a bit and open the casement window.

'And how is the whole family?' Alastair enquired.

'Well enough on the whole I think,' Mary replied. 'It would have been Henry's thirty-second birthday today, had he been alive.'

'And Greville knows this?' Alastair asked.

'Oh yes, he has been very quiet all day but he has mentioned it to me. He adored his father; Henry is a hero to him.'

'And Vanessa?' he asked.

'She is heartbroken. I don't think that she will ever marry again. She has thrown herself into her war work.'

'And how is Claire?' he asked tentatively, 'Poor little Claire – married one moment and widowed the next.'

Mary smiled proudly. 'She is amazing. She has kept her chin up and has carried on at the hospital where, I hear, they think a great deal of her. Who could have ever dreamt this of harum scarum Claire!'

'And now we come to Simon,' Alastair said. 'He has a very special place in my heart.'

'Ah, that does give rise to much conjecture,' Mary replied. 'I worry a great deal about Simon. There is one advantage in his present circumstances; he does get far more time to paint. We try to send him as much art equipment as possible through the Red Cross. He has had many recurrences of that miserable dysentery that so weakened him and must hate the claustrophobic atmosphere, not to mention the fear that surrounds him. He never complains.'

Alastair nodded and pressed some more tobacco into his pipe.

'I often pray for Simon,' he said thoughtfully.

A few moments later Igrainie came in and called them into the kitchen for tea, where Greville joined them, and they stood whilst Alastair said grace. It was very difficult not to fall on what lay before them, Greville thought, tucking his hands under his thighs so as not to grab a large scone and a dollop of Flora's wild raspberry jam. After listening to the news of the three Thompson boys, all of it good, they started on the tea and Mary and Greville feasted unashamedly.

Later, Mary, wrapping her scarf around her neck, turned to the Thompsons and exclaimed

'The news is better.'

And quite spontaneously they stood in a circle and joined hands whilst Alastair said a short prayer for peace. Mary and Greville left and walked back to Merlinstone with lighter hearts.

CHAPTER X

1956

Gloria Glengower came through the French windows that opened onto the south facing terrace of the castle. She was wearing a pair of fashionable, wide-framed sunglasses; a double strand of pearls with a large diamond clasp encircled her neck. She had not aged greatly during the war years. Her blonde hair was lightly streaked with silver and she wore it in a fashionable bob, and her famous smile still held its brilliance. The Duke, who was prodding at a dandelion with his thumbstick way below her at the foot of a flight of wide stone steps, had not noticed her sudden appearance. She was waving a letter in her hand.

'Arnold!' she called to him.

He looked up. She did not bother to summon him very often these days. Even from a distance he could detect her agitation.

'I have had a letter from Geneviève!' she shouted. 'You know, the de Verdurin girl. She was here years ago staying at Merlinstone. She wants her daughter Elizabeth to visit us!'

He could hardly hear her. He was growing rather deaf and he climbed up the steps towards her followed by his faithful retriever Emily. Gloria drew him back through the French windows into the castle. Her cheeks were flushed pink and her eyes were sparkling.

'Who is this girl?' he asked her.

'Oh, really Arnold,' Gloria replied impatiently, 'Surely you remember Geneviève de Verdurin! She took London by storm – everyone knew her. Her mother was a friend of the old Tarnochs. Anyway she went back to her family home in France for the war years and married some Frenchman called de Saint André, I can't recall his first name, and they have a daughter called Elizabeth who is coming to study singing in London. They want her to visit us and I would love to meet her. I was such an admirer of Geneviève. We can introduce her to Simon – he really needs to get to know some girls.'

'Ah,' the Duke replied, thoughtfully. Then he remarked 'to study singing in London! Why not in Paris, or in Rome?'

'Apparently the great teacher Helen Gilder has forsaken Europe and has set up an academy here. I imagine it must be a great opportunity for the girl. I shall certainly reply and invite her here; perhaps to our hunt ball in the autumn – what do you think?

We shall be having a house party for that anyway.'

'Yes,' he replied, 'that probably would be a good idea. By the way where is Thomas? I can't find him anywhere in the gardens and the dandelion family are getting their teeth into the lawn below the terrace. He must do something about them before they seed.'

But Gloria's mind was racing away on her plans for a house party.

'I'll write back to Geneviève at once,' she said. 'Our hunt ball is always early-ish, October 27th this year, I think. We'll have our usual big dinner party. I'll invite Theresa Tarnoch to stay. What is her name now? She married that funny little Middle European with lots of money and property in the Argentine and her hat shop is doing wonderfully, I hear. Everyone who is anyone was wearing something designed by her at Ascot this year.'

But Arnold had stopped listening; instead he looked up at the clock and having decided that he could decently do so, he went into the dining room and poured himself a glass of Madeira.

Gloria went into her small sitting room, she called it her 'boudoir', and sat down at her writing table. The walls of the room were lined with pale blue satin damask and a frieze of gold cherubs and garlands ran beneath the ceiling. The whole room resembled a gilded cage. Seizing her pen Gloria wrote to Geneviève, telling her that she would be enchanted to have her daughter to stay. After doing this she decided to make a list of the other people whom she would ask and another list of suitable locals she would summon to her dinner party before the hunt ball. She never for a single moment imagined that anyone would refuse her invitations. At the top of her dinner party list she wrote Simon Tarnoch. He was the only questionable one. Simon very seldom went to parties. Would she be able to persuade him she wondered? She had a great weakness for Simon, and had done a good deal to help him rehabilitate after his return from being a prisoner of war. He had been through a painful time but he was improving and his paintings had started to cause interest and attention in the art world. Gloria had bought a painting by him quite recently. It was of the river that flowed through the woods at Merlinstone; fairly abstract in its approach. Gloria had experienced a twinge of pride when she hung it in one of the rooms in the castle. She had felt dashingly modern in her choice, but it would do her an injustice to assume that the sorrow in the painting had been lost on her. She felt it intensely, and hoped that in some way she had helped to lighten Simon's mood.

Now, seated in her boudoir, she resolved that she must somehow manage to get him to accept her invitation. She wanted him to meet Elizabeth de Saint André whom, she had heard, was enchanting. Her mind went back to the last party she and Arnold had given in their house in London. It seemed so long ago. She had sat out in the garden sharing a drink with Ralph Cunningham. 'That old fox,' she always called him, although he was somewhat younger than she. What a deliciously warm summer night that had been, smelling of syringa and jasmine. They had watched Geneviève de Verdurin go by accompanied by Henry Sinclair. Ralph, she remembered, had commented on the girl's strange beauty. How tragic it was to think of Henry's death! Gloria stopped compiling her list and, taking another sheet of thick ivory-coloured writing paper, started a letter to Ralph.

'You had better accept,' she wrote, 'before you are too old to get here, and I am too old to tease you!' Although younger than herself he had always seemed venerable.

'I wonder,' thought Gloria, finally rising from her seat and carrying her letters into the large, circular hallway, 'I wonder what Elizabeth de Saint André is really like. I really cannot wait to meet her.'

It was a fine day in early September. Simon came in from riding for a bite of late lunch. He had asked Jessie to leave him a sandwich in the dining room as he had breakfasted lightly and it was her afternoon off. Jessie, although she deeply disapproved of snacks, had done so and he found a ham sandwich waiting for him laid between two plates. He poured himself a glass of beer that he found in the kitchen fridge and took both of these into the library.

Mary Tarnoch, his aunt, still lived at Merlinstone. Somehow she had never left since the war had ended; she had become part of the fabric of the house, and he was content that she should be so. Today she had eaten earlier and gone out to see what extra work there was to be done in the garden. He caught sight of her staking some dahlias from one of the library windows. Harrison, the gardener, was chatting to her, whilst he dug over a bed for potato planting. It was a breezy day. The sun skidded in and out of the clouds and the rooks rose, cawing loudly. Late roses scattered their petals over the lawn and away in the distance the hills were a misty, hyacinth blue, a sign that it was unlikely to rain. Simon finished his sandwich and started to climb the stairs to his studio. He was due to have an exhibition in

Edinburgh before Christmas and there was much work to be done. His foot was hardly on the bottom step of the staircase when the telephone rang. He was tempted to ignore it but gave way to mild curiosity. He returned to the library to answer it. A voice said,

'Hello, is that Simon?'

'Gloria!' He sank down into a chair.

'Darling boy, how are you, I haven't seen you for ages. I know you must be working hard for your show.'

He laughed, 'Well, I'm trying to, Gloria,' he replied.

'Listen,' she continued, 'I am giving a lovely big dinner party in October for the hunt ball. You simply must come to it, Simon. Theresa is coming up to stay.'

There was a long pause.

'Simon?'

'Yes, I'm still here.'

'Well, you will say yes, won't you? I really need you.'

Her voice held her purring, pleading tone. Simon sighed.

'The thing is, Gloria, I am so busy with this show coming up, and all the other things – farm I can't afford, garden that gets out of control, horses.....'

'Yes, yes I know,' she replied, 'but this will only be one evening, and I have someone coming whom I need help with. She is from France and called Elizabeth de Saint André. Her mother was called Geneviève de Verdurin, do you remember her before the war? She stayed in London with your Aunt Mary. Her family were friends of your father and mother.'

Gloria's voice was both honeyed and commanding. He felt trapped.

'I – oh well, all right Gloria. When is it? 27th October, I'll put it in my diary.'

'Wonderful!' Now her voice was velvety and warm with triumph. 'And don't you dare duck out; I'll send you a 'pour memoire'. We must all be kind to La Petite Elizabeth.'

As Simon made his way once more to his studio, he thought 'Gloria never changes.' He went into the large room that beckoned, the room in which years later Olivia would write her biography but which now was empty save for easels and paints and the smell of turpentine. He pulled on his painting smock and going over to an easel he surveyed his latest work. He was fairly pleased with the way things were going. Quite soon he had forgotten about the forthcoming party and Elizabeth de Saint André as he became immersed in his work.

A few days before the dinner party was due to take place and the hunt ball, Simon caught up with Mary whom he had hardly seen for several days, coming into the front hall. She was carrying a large basket of apples.

'I should have come in the kitchen way,' she gasped, putting the basket down on the large, circular table. 'But these are so heavy. Aren't they beautiful? I am going to make some chutney with them if Jessie will allow me to, and all sorts of other things.' Simon peered into the basket.

'What a lot you've picked!' he said. 'Here, I'll take this basket into the kitchen for you.'

He swung it over his arm and she followed him.

'They're windfalls,' she said, 'and almost all of them are useable. It's better not to let them rot into the ground.'

Simon put the basket on the large, scrubbed top table.

'I meant to tell you I'll be out Saturday night,' he said, 'Gloria is dragging me over for dinner before the hunt ball.'

'But that is wonderful. What fun!'

Mary clasped her hands. In her opinion Simon did not go out nearly enough. He was always refusing invitations and making excuses.

'You should do this far more often,' she told him. He knew that she was right but he hated being social. Now he looked at her with an almost angry expression.

'I really cannot imagine why I accepted this!' he complained, 'I hate hunt balls.'

'And dinner parties?' she asked him, her head slightly on one side.

'Yes, almost all dinner parties,' he replied, 'except for very few, perhaps at someone like my sister Theresa's house. She always has interesting guests. This one I am doubtful about. Gloria is really giving it for some girl she will have staying – she is from France, Elizabeth de Saint André she is called. Apparently years ago her mother Geneviève stayed with you, Aunt Mary.'

'Geneviève!' Mary looked startled for a moment, then she smiled.

'Ah yes, she certainly did. She was fascinating. I called her the Moon Maiden; and so this Elizabeth is her daughter – how very interesting. I haven't heard from her for years. She must have married.'

'A Monsieur de Saint André apparently,' Simon replied.

'She used to write me wonderful letters from France at the beginning of the war,' Mary said, 'then they stopped coming. Things became too tricky, I suppose.'

'I think I met her once,' Simon said thoughtfully, 'at one of Nessa and Henry's dinner parties. I had just got back from Munich; it was probably the last one they ever gave. You were there Aunt Mary, and I remember a tall girl, very pale and fair with dark eyes, a strange mixture.'

'Yes,' Mary replied, 'people either thought her beautiful or simply rather strange. She was an intelligent girl; she had just come down with a good degree from Cambridge University. I wonder,' she continued, 'what this Elizabeth is like.'

'She is training to be a singer, apparently.'

'That sounds interesting,' and Mary started to sort the apples into groups.

*

When eventually the evening of the hunt ball arrived the autumn, weather had also made an appearance. A chill wind blew the lime tree leaves across the lawns and the sky darkened with rain, but as yet no frost had come to slaughter the dahlias. Simon found that his deep unwillingness to socialise had returned. He did not wish to go out anywhere; all he wanted to do was to shut himself away in his studio. His exhibition was due to open in mid-November and he was working every hour of the day. He looked at his watch – it was time he went and changed for the evening ahead. Later, wearing his white tie and his hunt evening coat, he went into the hall. Mary arrived from the direction of the kitchen.

'You are looking very smart,' she said, 'I do hope that you have a good time.'

He looked at her and made a face.

'I really don't want to go.'

She smiled and did not reply. He looked so distinguished in those clothes, she thought, what affect would he have on this young French girl? Of course he was a deal older than she must be, an important point to be taken into consideration. But hadn't Violet Tarnoch, Simon's mother, been many years younger than her husband? And what a love match that had been. Simon picked up a large torch from the hall table and went to get out the dirty old Land Rover. Mary sighed as she watched him drive away down the lime avenue. She wished he had taken the shiny and fairly new car that waited patiently in the garage and he only used for long journeys. Simon loved his Land Rover – he found it comforting. The back was piled with canvases and paints, and the odd fishing rod. The seats were covered in dog hairs and a dented basketwork creel with a broken webbing strap was chucked on top of a rolled-up tartan rug. He started up the engine that gave a throaty rattle and made his way towards Glengower Castle.

Gloria waited for her guests in a pleasurable state of excited anticipation, unlike her husband who would far rather have had a quiet evening chatting to one or two of his cronies from the House of Lords over an excellent bottle of port. Gloria, on the other hand, liked to swim with a great tide of guests, so to speak, washing up on the shore with whoever took her fancy. Eventually her husband shouted to her from the drawing room

'For heaven's sake, Gloria, come and sit down a moment and relax. They won't be here for ages. You've inspected the dining table a thousand times.'

Gloria turned back from the door; 'I know,' she said, 'I just wanted to make sure that Gunthorpe had remembered to put enough ashtrays around; people can be so careless and things may get a bit rowdy later on. The band are all downstairs with the kitchen staff. I hope they've put them in the servants' hall or Mrs Mullins will go mad!'

'Mullins is quite capable of controlling everyone,' the Duke replied.

Mrs Mullins was their cook, and the Duke had great respect for her. It secretly amused him that at times she even daunted Gloria.

'A pity Vanessa and Greville couldn't come,' she observed as she went back into the drawing room, watching her reflection in the mirror that gleamed in its Chinese Chippendale frame. She tucked back a strand of hair. She was wearing her large pearl and diamond earrings.

'They are both in Ireland, visiting some of Violet Tarnoch's dotty relations.'

'I thought her family came from Cornwall,' replied the Duke.

'Some of them did, and they are even dottier.'

Shortly after this conversation Gunthorpe the butler appeared and announced Simon. Gloria swooped forward with an exclamation of pleasure. Now she could relax.

'Simon dear, come in! What will you drink? Whisky? Champagne?'

'Champagne please, Gloria,' he kissed her and shook hands with the Duke. Then he looked around the room.

'How awful!' he said, 'I'm early, and I thought I was going to be late!'

The Duke smiled, he was fond of Simon. He liked his shyness.

'Very good of you to come to this jamboree; I know you are busy at home,' he said.

'Gloria says your exhibition is coming up in November.'

'Yes it is,' Simon replied, relaxing. 'There is always a bit of a panic beforehand.'

The dinner party had started to arrive. Guests who were staying in the castle were the last to join them; this included Theresa and her husband Franz. She gave her brother a warm kiss. She was looking pretty, he thought, in an emerald green velvet dress. Ralph Cunningham came and introduced himself.

'Don't expect you remember me,' he said, 'I know most of your family. How is your sister Vanessa these days?'

Simon told him, and then he asked, 'And how is Claire? I haven't seen her for many years.' Simon smiled.

'Well you may find it hard to believe but she is now matron of a big teaching hospital in London, the harum scarum Claire! She is married to a surgeon and she has a daughter called Olivia, my niece. I think she is very happy.'

'I am so glad to hear this,' said Ralph. 'People can be surprising,' he added rather inconsequentially. 'I gather we are really here tonight to meet a Mademoiselle Elizabeth de Saint André,' he continued, 'who is going to be launched into British society, poor girl, by Gloria's hunt ball!' Simon looked around the now crowded room.

'Is she here?' he asked.

'I am not certain,' Ralph replied, 'I have not met her yet – I arrived here rather late.'

At that moment, as he spoke, Gloria went to the doorway and greeted someone. Simon watched her and knew at once that this was Elizabeth. Her fair hair sprang back from her face and reminded him of flames. She moved like a dancer. She was wearing a blue dress that floated out around her to the floor. Simon felt suddenly faint with shock. He put his hand on a table that was near to him to steady himself. He had seen this girl before. Suddenly he was back in the cold room where he had slept with his fellow prisoners. He had dreamt one night of Vanessa, a curiously vivid dream, he had never forgotten it. Someone else had been in the dream and had stood beside his sister, then they had both vanished. The following day Henry Sinclair had been shot by the Gestapo. And now, walking with Gloria towards him was the girl in the dream. Gloria introduced her slowly and carefully to every guest. He heard her say

'This is Simon Tarnoch; he lives in a house called Merlinstone and his family knew your mother and your grandparents. Simon, here is Elizabeth de Saint André.'

She shook his hand and looked up at him. Her blue eyes were both wide and tilted. They reminded him of the eyes you might see in Greek sculpture. They were brimming with laughter.

'I have heard of you,' she said, she had quite a marked French accent, 'from my mother. She so enjoyed her time in London when she was young.'

'You are seated next to Simon at dinner,' Gloria said, 'so I am moving you on now to meet the rest of my guests.'

They continued to circle the room. Gloria is treating her like royalty, Simon thought. Poor girl, she seemed rather shy, except he had seen the mirth in her eyes, and hoped she would be able to let it bubble over later on. This evening must be an ordeal for her. At last Gunthorpe arrived to tell them dinner was ready and they all obediently headed for the dining room.

The table groaned with silver and white damask. Flowers were bunched around the tall candles. Elizabeth, pressing her starched napkin across her lap, looked sideways at Simon and smiled rather shyly. He was wonderfully romantic-looking, she thought, rather like Prince André in *War and Peace*. She felt more than a little in awe of him. Simon had managed to down another glass of champagne and was feeling slightly better.

'Now,' he thought, 'I must try and make polite conversation. Instead of which I would like to say to her '*I have seen you once before in a dream and you are the most beautiful girl I have ever met. You are radiant, like the sun. Come to Merlinstone tomorrow or I shall die a thousand deaths.*' Instead he said

'So you have come from Provence. It is a wonderful place, I have painted there.'

'In the steps of the Impressionists?' she queried. He laughed at this.

'Well I like to think I am more in the steps of Cezanne, or Braque.' They talked for some time, easily and happily until he had to turn to the lady on his left who was a much heavier task. Later, when he turned back to Elizabeth, he said

'Listen, come and visit me and my Aunt Mary at Merlinstone tomorrow, she would love to meet you and I can show you some work I have done.'

Instinctively she knew that he was seldom so impulsive. He laid his hand gently for a moment on her wrist. She blushed and quickly looked away.

'I would love to come,' she said. As she started on her chocolate mousse she thought 'I cannot imagine kissing him and anyway, what a stupid thought. I must seem just a young, inexperienced student in his eyes.' Innocent Elizabeth! How could she know that Simon longed to hold her, and there was no-one to whisper to him a warning, '*Turn back now, or you will be burned by the fire.*'

'I shall organize that,' he said, 'you shall come over to me tomorrow, perhaps Ralph Cunningham could come as well and bring you.'

Eventually they left the dining room and drifted from there to the ballroom where enthusiastic couples were already dancing to the loud music of the band. Quite a few guests, mainly men, were standing in the passageway around the bar. Simon found Ralph Cunningham there with a glass of whisky in his hand, conversing with a man whom Gloria had invited and who was rumoured to be her lover. He had dark hair and a bright complexion. Simon went up to Ralph and he asked

'Would you be able to come and have some lunch at Merlinstone tomorrow? And bring Elizabeth de Saint André with you; my Aunt Mary so wants to see her.'

Ralph smiled, his little grey eyes curling up under his eyebrows until they almost disappeared.

'That is most kind of you Simon,' he said, 'I will of course bring the fair Elizabeth. I expect Gloria can spare us for an hour or two.'

'Damn the old fox,' Simon thought, 'he always sees through everything.' Out loud he said 'That would be wonderful – shall we say one o'clock-ish?'

Ralph winked, 'I'll give you a call to confirm,' he replied.

They danced the last waltz together. Round the ballroom they flew, everything spinning past, the family portraits, red-faced farmers, pale-faced London guests, they all became a huge whirl. When they stopped, Elizabeth flung herself down on a sofa, laughing.

'That was wonderful!' she gasped.

When he finally said goodnight he reminded her that Ralph was bringing her over for lunch the next day.

'I shall so look forward to it,' she replied.

He hadn't stayed out so late for ages, he thought, as he went out into the cold night to find the Land Rover. He hummed the tune of the waltz all the way back to Merlinstone.

Back in the castle the Duke opened one of the long windows and let his dog out for a bedtime run. Everyone had gone to bed except Ralph Cunningham and even he was on his way now that his cronies had all disappeared. Gunthorpe locked the heavy front doors with an ancient key. Gloria paused a moment in her boudoir to glance at her reflection in the small mirror that hung above her boulle writing table. She pushed a lock of hair back into place. She too had had a wild last waltz. It had been a good evening, she thought, as hunt balls go. Not too much rowdy drunkenness, although one or two young men had returned home somewhat the worse for wear.

She smiled at her reflection in the mirror. What a success it had appeared to be, Simon's meeting with Elizabeth! She remembered seeing them flying round the ballroom to the waltz, obviously enjoying themselves. Gloria left her boudoir and went into the drawing room. Ralph Cunningham was still there; he had been talking with Arnold.

'Oh, dear hostess,' he said, 'I was just coming to find you to say goodnight and thank you for a lovely evening before I hit my pillow.'

He took her hand and kissed it, as he always did.

'I am invited to Merlinstone tomorrow. Is that all right with you? I am to take the fair Elizabeth with me; Simon has invited us to lunch, subject to your approval.' Gloria smiled.

'Of course I approve,' she said 'I shall be on the golf course and the rest of the party can amuse themselves. We have all been asked over to the Raddingtons tomorrow evening for dinner and various entertainments.' He looked at her and lifted his finger, half-jokingly severe.

'Now Gloria,' he said, 'she is far, far too young for him. You could be making a big mistake.'

She raised her eyebrows, 'Do you really think so?' she replied, 'I am rather surprised, Ralph, that you say this. What about Simon's mother Violet, and the General? The age gap there was enormous, far greater than this.'

'I cannot understand why you didn't introduce her to Greville,' Ralph said.

'Oh Greville,' her voice trailed away vaguely, 'he is in Ireland with Vanessa, they couldn't come to the ball.'

Gloria had never been very fond of Vanessa, although Henry, Greville's father, had always been one of her favourites. The boy looked like his mother, she thought, handsome it was true, but somehow lacking his father's charm. The Duke came in from the garden with his dog and closed the French windows.

'Lovely night now,' he said, 'beautiful moon.'

'People can be affected by a full moon, they say,' Ralph observed, and bowing slightly to them both he went to bed.

Coming downstairs the following morning Mary Tarnoch was surprised to find Simon already up, finishing his breakfast.

'I expected you to have a lie in this morning,' she said, helping herself to some porridge.

'Oh no,' he replied, 'I have already been out for a ride, Aunt Mary. Ralph Cunningham is coming over today; he's bringing Elizabeth de Saint André for lunch. Can Jessie rustle up something do you think?'

'Oh, how wonderful!' Mary exclaimed, 'I am longing to meet her and so nice to see Ralph, but I had better quickly go and tell Jessie.'

Jessie was well able to deal with any last minute requests.

'That's fine, Miss Mary,' she said. 'I have a big fowl I can roast and I will make a fine tart; there are a lot of apples in the store room.'

Her eyes were sparkling with interest, but she enquired no further about the guests.

The rest of the morning was spent in a flurry of preparation. Simon helped Mary pick the last of the dahlias and they filled large vases with them and put them in the library and the hall. Simon opened some bottles of good red wine he found in the cellar and stood up a bottle of port for Ralph. He was thankful to be busy. He had started to feel foolishly nervous at the thought of entertaining Elizabeth. When at last they heard the wheels of the car both he and Mary rushed to the front door. Ralph was helping Elizabeth out of his highly polished Rover. She stood for a moment and looked up at the house. Then she came towards them and Simon kissed her cheek and introduced her to Mary.

'Come inside both of you,' he said, 'lunch is nearly ready.'

'It is so wonderful, this house!' Elizabeth exclaimed, 'So strong-looking and well, you know, I think the word in English is fortified.'

Leading her through the museum she stopped again and Ralph laughed when she surveyed the glass vitrines in the museum and exclaimed

'Mais, c'est comme *Les Invalides!*'

'It is all in memory of my father,' Simon told her, 'come into the library and have a drink.'

They gathered round the fireplace and sipped glasses of dry sherry. Mary had hardly spoken but now she told Elizabeth how she had known her mother Geneviève before the war. Whilst she spoke she thought, 'What a fascinating girl she is. She is fair but much more golden than her mother and her blue eyes are quite different as well, she must have a Northern father. Geneviève's eyes were so dark; they were the only thing about her that belied her Provencal heritage. I used to call her the Moon Maiden, but this girl is definitely the sun.' Out loud she said

'So you are training to be a singer?'

Simon was pouring some more sherry into their glasses.

'Yes,' Elizabeth replied, 'I have always wanted to do this and I am very lucky to have got a place in Madame's academy. It is terribly hard work, and the discipline you have to keep – mon Dieu – you have no idea! No late nights, no smoking and very little drinking! Everything possible you have to do to protect your precious voice.'

'Terrible,' Ralph observed, 'I couldn't do it!'

After they had eaten lunch Ralph returned to the library to have a chat with Mary while Simon took Elizabeth for a tour of the house. They went first into the museum. 'And is all this in memory to your Papa?' she asked.

'I know he was famous, my mother told me.'

'Yes,' he said. 'We'll pass by all this quickly, it may bore you.'

'Oh no!' she replied, 'It will not do that. Please explain carefully to me – it is history.'

Obediently he led her round the glass cases and she followed him, listening in silence. Finally she stopped in front of a large group of photographs.

'They were amazing, those generals,' she said, 'they look so strange to us now sitting there on their horses with their moustaches and their plumed hats. And yet, if you think of it, it was not really all that long ago.'

'Yes,' he agreed, 'and this was my mother Violet; that really does look old-fashioned today.' Elizabeth examined the faded brown photograph.

'She was beautiful,' she said, 'I think you look like her, you have her bones.'

They finished the museum and went up the wide staircase where the walls were crammed with paintings.

'Stop!' she said. 'You must let me look – which ones are yours?'

He pointed them out to her and then they came to a gap on the wall where a painting had obviously hung.

'What happened to that one?' she asked.

'Gloria Glengower has it,' he replied. 'She wanted to buy it from me.'

'Ah!' Elizabeth exclaimed, 'Is it of a river? Rather abstract and done in pale colours?'

'Yes,' he replied.

'I have seen it,' she replied. 'I was looking at it this morning in the castle. I saw the signature so I knew it was yours. It interested me - there is something sad about it.' He looked at her and smiled but did not reply and she followed him up the staircase.

He thought to himself 'One day I shall take you to my river and we will walk together along the banks and listen to the rushing tumble when we get to the waterfall.' Elizabeth followed him through a door then up a steep, narrow staircase until they reached another small door which Simon unlocked with a key he had in his pocket. They were suddenly standing outside behind a stone parapet, from which they could see for miles over the woods and the fields to the hills in the distance. Between the dark, bending branches of the trees that were still partially covered in leaves you could see flashes of the river.

'This is where they came to in the old days,' he said, 'to keep a watch on the beacons that were lit all the way along the border between Scotland and England to warn the Borderers that English raiders were coming.'

She leaned against the stone parapet and gazed at the rolling countryside and she knew that she would always remember this moment and the tales he was telling her.

On their way back to the library Elizabeth stopped to look at a photograph of a young man that stood in a frame on a small table.

'Who is this?' she asked. Simon looked over her shoulder.

'That is Greville,' he said, 'my nephew, my sister Vanessa's son.'

She studied it for a moment and making no comment she followed him into the library. Ralph got up when they came in.

'Done the family history then?' he said to Elizabeth with a wink. 'We must be getting back to the castle, my dear Simon, Gloria is marshalling us together to go out somewhere this evening, and I think we shall all need a rest before we go.'

Mary watched Simon handing Elizabeth her coat. 'He is falling in love,' she thought. 'I do hope it will be returned.'

Ralph and Elizabeth went to the Rover and getting in they waved and called out their thanks again, and then they drove away down the lime avenue. When they went back in the house, it seemed very quiet. Simon made his way to the kitchen to congratulate Jessie on the lunch and then returned to his studio. Mary picked up her knitting; she needed to think. It had been such a surprise, meeting Elizabeth. 'She is a lovely girl,' she thought, 'I do hope and pray she does not break his heart.'

*

That year the winter in the north came in, tearing the gentle, golden autumn to shreds and shocking them all with early snow and freezing wind. Some of the rooms at Merlinstone were uncomfortably draughty. Simon shut himself into his studio, pushing an old bolster against the door to keep out the cold. His exhibition in early November had been more of a success than he had expected. He had sold a good number of paintings and there had been a flattering review in one of the English papers. In spite of this he felt empty and oddly depressed, as though his fountain of creativity had ceased and there was only a tiny trickle left. He knew this was not an uncommon symptom after several years' hard work but he hated feeling so aimless and defeated. Mary Tarnoch wrapped herself in a number of shapeless cardigans under her voluminous old Loden coat and busied herself with many winter tasks. She made rose hip syrup to keep away colds and several Christmas puddings. She gilded fir cones she had collected for decorations and sorted out her collection of dried seed heads and plants which she would take and arrange in the church, and all the time she worried about Simon. He hardly spoke when they met, and he seemed remote and depressed. All the hope she had treasured that he might have met a girl he could fall in love with was gone. He never mentioned Elizabeth or her visit to Merlinstone. He did not try to visit London. He had withdrawn into himself and she did not like to ask him why. Had Elizabeth seen the admiration in his eyes and had subsequently fled? Mary wondered. 'Don't be so ridiculous,' she told herself, 'He is just having his post exhibition blues, he'll get out of it.'

Christmas drew nearer and Mary put her decorations in a large basket and made her way to the church. It was Monday, and she hoped to have stolen a march on the other ladies who came in from the village with their candles and bunches of holly to decorate their appointed areas in the church. She liked to be alone when she did her part which was to make a garland for the front and then to crown it with a large arrangement of whatever she had managed to find. She crept in through the west door; the church seemed empty. Then, with a start of surprise, she saw that Alastair Thompson was standing in front of the lectern wearing a bemused expression.

'Ah Mary!' he exclaimed, 'Thank heavens it's you. Rhona Innes has put so much holly round the lectern I won't be able to read the lesson.'

He indicated the wreath with an impatient gesture. Mary laughed and replied soothingly with a conspiratorial glint in her eye.

'I'll snip some of it off with my secateurs,' she said, 'no-one will notice if I am careful.'

'A brilliant idea!' he replied, 'I sometimes think that being a minister or anything else to do with the church would be an excellent training for an aspiring diplomat. You have to be so careful.'

He peered into her basket. 'Wonderful!' he said, 'You are a clever lady. All those beautiful seed heads and what sensational chrysanthemums. I was hoping that you would bring some of those.'

Mary clipped the holly round the lectern with care and then went into the vestry to find a vase for her flowers. When she returned Alastair was leafing through the large Bible.

'Something different for the Second Lesson,' he murmured, 'something surprising to wake them all up. Are you expecting many at Merlinstone for Christmas, Mary?'

'Vanessa is coming,' Mary replied, 'and so are Theresa and Franz and their little boy Louis, so we shall be quite a few. Jessie will have someone to help her in the kitchen and we may have to find one more for a bit of extra help – I think she has a relative who will come in. I am glad we shall be so many, it will be good for Simon to have them there.'

'Ah!' Alastair looked at her thoughtfully. 'Igrainie said she ran into him the other day in Melrose. She said he was looking rather pale, she thought – and was, well, a little remote.'

Mary stood back from the font and inspected her garland, it was sagging a little. She tweaked it and tied in another chrysanthemum head.

'Yes,' she replied slowly, 'well, in confidence Alastair, I am worried about him.' She stopped arranging her flowers for a moment and sat down at the end of one of the pews.

'You know we had a visit from a certain Mademoiselle Elizabeth de Saint André a little while ago?'

'Yes, I met her with Duchess Gloria one Sunday.'

'Of course. Well, Simon was smitten by her. I am certain he was – he never spoke of it but his whole mood lightened. For a short while he was a different man. But nothing has happened; he has never met up with her again and he appears to have made no effort to see her. Of course she is years younger than he is but she seemed to greatly enjoy his company. I can't understand it. He shuts himself away in his studio and when he does come out of there he hardly speaks.'

Alastair stood in the aisle and stroked his chin thoughtfully. Then he said 'Perhaps he, not she, has taken fright. Perhaps he feels that he is indeed far too old for her and has decided to drop out of her life before things have gone too far.'

Mary nodded. 'It could be something like that,' she said, 'he does lack confidence.'

'Can't you encourage him to take a trip down to London, to visit one of his sisters for a change of scene? And then you can drop into his mind that he might like to visit this young lady as well?'

'You are quite a schemer, Alastair!' Mary laughed. 'But yes, I might try and do something like that.'

'Did she take a shine to him?' Alastair asked.

Mary was gathering up her baskets.

'She appeared so delighted with everything,' Mary replied, 'meeting Simon, being in Scotland, it was hard to dissemble. She is a radiant girl, like sunlight, and the effect she has on other people is extraordinary. I don't think she realises how beautiful she is. Of course she is, as I said, very young.'

'Well, unions are made in heaven, so they say,' Alastair replied, 'and one imagines they are made regardless of age.'

They left the church together. It had grown dark and snowflakes eddied in the wind. Mary said goodbye and hurried back to Merlinstone.

Later that evening, as she was about to sit down in the dining room and start her supper, Simon, as usual, was nowhere to been seen, when he suddenly appeared and joined her. He had changed out of his working overalls and wore an old but elegant velvet jacket and, Mary noted, he had shaved. He was smiling and as he sat down he handed her a large white envelope.

'Open it!' he said, 'I've got one too!'

She slit it open with her knife and pulled out an invitation card. Elizabeth de Saint André was giving a recital of songs at the Wigmore Hall in March.

'Shall you go?' he demanded.

'Sadly I don't think I'll be able to,' she said, 'how kind of her to invite me. I promised I would help Gloria Glengower with her Spring Fair. But you will go I hope?'

There was a pause. Simon had picked up his soup spoon.

'Of course I shall!' he said, 'I'll most certainly go.'

She could feel the lightness of his mood and his excitement.

'Quite an event for her,' he said, 'to sing in the Wigmore Hall!'

So everything had started to be all right, and in time for Christmas as well – she could hardly believe it. Later that evening when she was drawing her bedroom curtains against the wintry world outside she heard music. Simon was playing the piano. He hasn't done this for ages, she thought. She opened her bedroom door and listened to the music welling up from below.

The Wigmore Hall was crowded and Simon had to push his way through to find his seat. Once he had found it he sat down and looked around, wondering if he would see anyone he knew. Vanessa was away in Italy and he had no idea of the whereabouts of Greville but then, with a start of pleasure, he saw his sister Theresa arrive with her husband Franz. How smart she looked, he thought. She was wearing something violet coloured and her thick dark hair was combed back to display her large diamond and amethyst earrings. Very much the fashionable milliner, she was one of the top names in London now. Simon was immensely proud of her, rather to Vanessa's irritation. People recognized her as she went by and whispered

'Look, there are the Kaminskis – he has made a fortune, you know, but then so has she.'

In spite of all this Theresa was still the warm, down to earth sister he loved, unchanged by money and success. She came towards him and sat down in the neighbouring seat.

'We are together!' she said, 'How lovely,' and gave him a kiss.

Franz followed her and shook hands. 'Did you arrange it?' he asked her.

'No,' she replied, 'it was a happy coincidence,' but he wondered if she had said anything to Elizabeth.

'This is so exciting,' she continued, opening her programme. 'They must think a great deal of her to let her have a recital here so soon, although I hear she had been training for quite some time in Paris and it was her teacher there who recommended she should come over here to the academy. In fact I think she found her a place. I knew her mother so well, years ago – Geneviève de Verdurin, do you remember her Simon?'

'Only vaguely,' he replied, 'I think that I met her once.'

The lights dimmed and all eyes turned towards the stage that was brightly lit. A tall, thin young man stood bowing to them behind whom stood a grand piano. They listened obediently whilst he played his piece. Next came a pause for coughing and whispered conversation and this was followed by a quartet. Elizabeth was the last to perform. Simon wondered if she was feeling nervous. He enjoyed the quartet but could not really concentrate. There was an enthusiastic clapping, a short encore and the musicians left. Once more they settled down and a man came in with a large sheaf of music who was to accompany Elizabeth. He arranged these on the piano and then waited. A few moments later she arrived, wearing a simple white dress, her hair a halo of brightness around her face. She stood very straight and still beside the piano. Simon closed his eyes and listened. As she sang he went back to Merlinstone. He was walking with her down to the river. Her beautiful, wild young voice took him there and then away towards the hills; they were riding together, and although she had finished her first song he continued with their ride. Theresa nudged him gently, and he opened his eyes. Elizabeth sang another two songs and then bowed shyly to the audience and smiled. There was enthusiastic applause.

'Encore, encore!' came the cries.

She sang again several songs, and then left the stage.

'Wonderful!' Theresa exclaimed. 'Her voice has such an unusual quality, don't you think Simon? She will go far.'

'Yes,' he replied, and thought to himself 'This is the trouble. She will go far and how shall I ever capture her? She is heading for the Royal Opera House, for La Scala, for many more. She will probably travel miles in a blaze of triumph.'

He stood up and said that he would meet them later for dinner. The little concert was over. He left the main hall and walked round the building where he found a small, open door. Some musicians were coming out, talking and laughing, wrapping warm scarves around their necks. He stopped one of them and said,

'I've come to see Elizabeth de Saint André, is she there?'

The young man he addressed looked rather startled.

'Yes – I think she will be coming down soon,' he said, 'we are all leaving now.' After a short time Elizabeth appeared, wearing an old winter coat over her white dress; she carried a limp bunch of early spring flowers.

'Simon!' she exclaimed, when she saw him, 'You came! How wonderful, I wondered if you would.'

'Of course I did,' he replied, 'How could I miss it? You sing beautifully.'

He kissed her cheek. 'Listen, can you meet me for lunch tomorrow? I want to take you to Ma Belle Amie, it's a restaurant owned by a friend of mine and it's rather good.'

Elizabeth's eyes danced with pleasure.

'Oh, what a treat that would be! We have such disgusting food at the academy, you have no idea! I expect I can get out of their clutches for once, providing I don't spend too long. I'll say a very important impresario has asked me and it is vital I go for my career!'

'I'll come round and pick you up at 12.45.' he said, 'You really were wonderful tonight, Elizabeth!' She blushed a little.

'I am glad you enjoyed it,' she replied, then she turned to go and he watched her speed down the street, waving her little bouquet of flowers. As he turned to find a taxi he thought, 'I should have sent her a big bunch of red roses. I wonder who gave her those – some young admirer, I expect. I feel positively Proustian in my suspicious jealousy.'

The following day Simon called for Elizabeth at the academy. She was waiting for him outside the door. Every moment she could spare that morning had been spent in getting ready. She wore her only smart coat that came from Paris. When Simon commented on it she laughed and said

'It was Dior's new look, a year or so ago now. You must have heard of it, Simon!' she teased him.

She had combed back her hair, striving for sophistication, and on her head she wore a small white hat, trimmed with a dark blue ribbon. She had even remembered her gloves. When they arrived at the restaurant she was in a state of excitement. She had never been taken anywhere so distinguished-looking in London before. They were greeted with warmth by the head waiter who obviously knew Simon well, and who guided them to a table where they could sit side by side on the banquette. The restaurant was quite large and filled with the hum of conversation.

'Will you drink wine?' Simon asked her.

'Well, perhaps a glass,' she replied. 'We are not really supposed to but this is such a treat day for me.'

She studied the menu that was laid before her. 'What wonderful food!' she exclaimed.

'My friend is a clever chap,' Simon replied and, raising his glass to her, he said 'To the Prima Donna Assoluta, are you going to make singing your life's work, Elizabeth? You would be crazy not to.'

A great deal hung on her reply to this seemingly innocent question. But the fates were standing there silent, invisible, waiting for her answer. Elizabeth surprised herself when she said

'I am not entirely certain. I probably will.'

As she said this an image of the signorina swept into her mind; she was looking at her with a slight smile and her eyebrows raised.

'Only probably, Elizabeth,' she heard her say, 'what is all this?'

But Simon was delighted by her words – there was still a glimpse of hope for him.

'I see,' he said, 'you are thinking things over. Well, at your age there is still plenty of time.'

At that moment Gilpin Rathbone, the owner of the restaurant, came up to their table. He had seen them come in earlier and was discreetly intrigued. Who, he wondered, was this beautiful girl with Simon? Usually he came here with one of his sisters or a male friend.

Simon said 'Gilpin! I must introduce you to Elizabeth de Saint André.'

Gilpin bowed to Elizabeth. He cut a stately figure in his dark coat, high white shirt collar and knotted silk cravat. Above this his face was wreathed in smiles. He has quite a florid complexion, Elizabeth thought, which goes well with the atmosphere of excellent food and drink.

'I hope you are dining well,' he said, 'We are quite busy today, and a bit of a panic as the Princess has just called and wants her favourite table; she'll be here any moment now.'

'Then you must hurry away,' Simon replied, laughing at him. 'We'll catch up another time.'

'How grand,' Elizabeth exclaimed, when Gilpin had moved away into the crowded room, 'the Princess coming here; I have seen photographs of her in the papers.'

'Oh, she goes everywhere,' Simon replied, 'she could just as easily have turned up in a Lyons Corner House, it's all part of her attitude towards 'discovering life!' and now,' he continued, 'when we have had some coffee I am taking you to visit my sister Theresa in her hat shop.'

In her showroom in Knightsbridge, Theresa was finding it hard to concentrate on her demanding customers. She tried not to glance out of the window too often as she went backwards and forwards to find more hats, and sending her assistant Anna to search in the stockroom. Lucinda Lloyd-Radcliffe, the wife of a well-known racehorse trainer, was seated in front of a mirror whilst Theresa and her assistant, Anna, showed her the summer collection. On the other side of the room, trying to read a newspaper, sat Jack MacVicar, Lucinda's lover, who had obediently accompanied her and was now feeling both embarrassed and bored. Theresa knew him slightly and was trying not to catch his eye as she whisked by with yet another creation wrapped in yards of rustling tissue paper. She was longing for Simon and Elizabeth to arrive, at the same time praying that they would be a little late.

Lucinda Lloyd-Radcliffe was a strange-looking woman. Beautiful in a pale ethereal way; she had light red hair and heavy-lidded green eyes. Her air of languid vagueness could be deceptive. Now, as she gazed at herself in the mirror and adjusted the wide blue tulle hat she said, quite sharply,

'Jack, what do you think of this one?'

Jack MacVicar dutifully lowered his paper.

'It's good,' he said, nervously, 'is it for the Derby?'

'No, Ascot of course,' she replied. 'I shall have to find something with a smaller brim for Derby Day. Theresa, have you anything in a lovely green?'

She removed the blue tulle hat and laid it on the chair beside her. Did she want that one or not? Theresa wondered as Anna sped away to search for a green hat. It was getting very warm in the salon. The spring sun poured in through the window and the room had become so crowded with hats it looked like a flower garden. A green model arrived and was gently placed on Lucinda's head by Anna.

Theresa, looking down the street once more, saw Simon and Elizabeth advancing.

She whispered 'I won't be a moment,' to Anna and flew to the door to let them in. 'So wonderful to see you both,' she said as she kissed them. Then she whispered,

'Come in and look around. I've got rather a tricky customer at the moment but she should have finished soon.' They entered the salon nervously; Anna was returning with a pile of black hats. Lucinda had just remembered she had a memorial service to attend.

'Can you take over for a few moments?' Theresa murmured to her, and then, turning to Elizabeth she said, 'Now, I'll take you round and show you everything and Simon, come too if you want.'

They followed her, admiring all the creations on their stands and trying not to look too often towards Jack MacVicar who was still behind his newspaper.

'He must know it off by heart now, poor man,' Theresa thought.

She stopped suddenly and picked up a wide-brimmed, simple straw hat threaded with a long, blue satin ribbon.

'Sit down, Elizabeth,' she commanded.

The girl obeyed and Theresa placed the hat on her head. It was the perfect thing, Elizabeth thought, for a hot summer day in the garden or an idle picnic in a hayfield. She gasped as she looked at her reflection.

'It is beautiful,' she said.

Lucinda Lloyd-Radcliffe watched with narrowed eyes.

'That is Simon Tarnoch, Theresa's brother,' she thought, 'I haven't seen him for years. I wonder who the girl can be?'

There they sat, for a moment, the two women – one so young and lovely in her simple straw hat, the other sophisticated and a great deal older in a black hat adorned with bows, sequins and a veil. The difference between them was almost painful. Elizabeth caught Lucinda's eye in the mirror and gave her a shy smile. Lucinda returned it, almost, then she said

'I'll take this one Theresa, the blue tulle and the green. Jack, we must go, or we'll never make the cinema.'

There was a whirl and a bustle, Jack MacVicar stood up and folded his paper. In a few moments three large bandboxes appeared, smartly striped in black and white.

'Oh, have them sent round Theresa dear, will you?' Lucinda demanded, and tossing her a smile she took Jack's arm and they left the shop. Theresa sank onto the chair.

'Thank heavens that is over!' she exclaimed, 'She has been here for hours, and that poor man having to wait.'

Anna came up, 'She has ordered three others to follow,' she said, 'we shall have to have them made up – a white straw for Wimbledon and two more for Ascot.' Theresa picked up the simple straw.

'Pack this up please, Anna, I am giving it to Elizabeth.'

'Oh Theresa!'

'You look wonderful in it – the simplicity suits you – and you can wear it anywhere, anytime when the sun is out!'

'Oh thank you!' Elizabeth sounded overwhelmed.

When they had left, Theresa watched them go from the bay window - Elizabeth, skipping along, swinging her bandbox from its black, braided string, looking up at Simon and laughing.

'What a beautiful child,' she thought, 'but oh dear, I do hope she does not break my brother's heart.'

CHAPTER XI

Summer came to the north with unusual enthusiasm. The grass at Merlinstone grew tall and lacy with wild flowers. Two figures walked together along the avenue, deep in conversation they went up and down under the lime trees. One was Simon and the other Greville Sinclair, Vanessa's son and Simon's nephew. They were getting to know one another. There was, perhaps, a family likeness between them. Greville was a little taller than his uncle; both had dark hair but were you to confront them and speak to them you would notice the differences. Simon's long eyes were dark while Greville's hazel, and there was a kind of arrogance about him his uncle did not possess. Women found him attractive. There was a dangerous quality to him, the feeling he may risk too much. He could resort to a bruising sarcasm. None of this was in evidence today for Greville was being both charmed and charming. He had always, hitherto and for some reason or other, been unable to visit Merlinstone where he spent so much time as a boy. Now he came to stay and taken a much-needed holiday in order to do so. He worked as a foreign correspondent for a well-known newspaper and he was doing well. You could almost say that he was becoming 'a name'.

Greville was surprised, on that day under the lime trees, at how easily his uncle told him of his time as prisoner of war. He had always heard that he did not like to discuss those days. Eventually they headed back towards the house when they saw Mary standing in the doorway calling out to them that lunch was ready. As they neared her Simon said, 'Oh I don't think I have mentioned it. I have asked someone called Elizabeth de Saint André to stay. She is studying music – singing, to be precise, in London and she is due a holiday. Have you ever met her?' Greville was surprised that his uncle had not mentioned this before.

'No, I haven't,' he replied, 'but Aunt Theresa has told me about her.'

As they reached the front door Mary announced,

'Jessie is doing a spinach soufflé, we are practising our skills so we can show off to Elizabeth - the French are so wonderful in the kitchen.'

Mary was keeping her disquiet about their guest to herself. She had been expecting Elizabeth to stay for some time; Simon had told her that she had been invited, after which Greville had called and invited himself. 'Three will be a crowd,' she thought to herself. 'But I suppose Simon had to say yes. Such a pity Greville could not have chosen another time.'

Later that day, when he was upstairs in his bedroom, Greville stood by the window and looked towards the hills. He had hardly ever visited Merlinstone since he had lived here during the war. It was like coming back home again. Aunt Mary was always the same; she was one of those people who appeared ageless. He supposed she had been moderately young during the war, she had just seemed older because of her prematurely white hair and her rather strange clothes, and he, of course, had been a small child. He loved her more than any of his mature relations and certainly more than he did his mother. She was kind with just a hint of steel behind her warmth that belied her determination. Simon was a new discovery; Greville had always been rather in awe of his uncle, the little he had seen of him, but now he seemed more like a contemporary. What a pity he had had to invite this girl Elizabeth. Greville wondered if there was anything between them or was he just being hospitable. It would have been far better, he thought, if they could have been on their own and able to discuss their family and all the many things he wanted to talk about. He left his bedroom and wandered in and out of the rooms, remembering many things about his youth. He spent a long time admiring Simon's paintings that were hanging on the stairs. He ended in front of the portrait of his grandmother, Violet, by Sargent. What a beautiful woman she must have been, he thought. He wished so much that he had known her. This house was where he belonged, far more than in his father's home in Hampshire. He took in a long, deep breath; it smelt of scented wood and peat smoke and the cold, clear air of Scotland. 'Yes, this is home to me,' he thought, 'although it is not my home.'

'We will meet Elizabeth tomorrow,' Simon said, when they had congregated later before dinner. 'I thought we might go to Berwick, Greville, it will make a shorter journey for her and it will be a lovely drive back here; we can show her some of our country.'

Greville agreed that was a good idea, but he could not help feeling slightly resentful at the thought of this girl arriving. He was so enjoying his time alone with Mary and Simon.

The following day they left early for Berwick in Simon's old Land Rover, much to Mary's disapproval.

'You should take your other car!' she told Simon reproachfully, but Simon, as usual, ignored this advice.

It was another fine day. When they arrived at last at the small station it looked welcoming with its hanging baskets full of flowers. A few people were gathered on the platform and Simon and Greville strolled along to find a bench where they sat down and waited for the London train. Simon was feeling both excited and apprehensive and Greville only slightly curious. He felt the whole thing was rather a waste of time and they could have been back at Merlinstone fishing for salmon in the river that ran through the woods. The signals clunked and Simon said 'It's coming!'

The station master came onto the platform and the express from London came gliding in. A good many people piled out onto the platform and Simon made his way through the crowd. Greville stayed behind and watched. He saw Simon stop and there, in the distance, he saw a girl with gold-coloured hair that shone in the sunlight. She was wearing a grey skirt and a little white and grey jacket.

'Chic,' he thought. She looked happy and animated. Simon picked up her suitcase and brought her to Greville.

'This is my nephew,' he said; they shook hands. Her eyes were set in a curious way, he noticed, they were large and there was a slight slant to them. They reminded him of a Greek sculpture and they were arrestingly blue. As they walked out of the station to find the Land Rover he asked her if she had been to Scotland before.

'Oh yes,' she replied; her French accent was quite strong. 'I had a wonderful visit last year and I have longed to return.'

'You speak good English,' he told her; she blushed a little.

'We speak it a lot at home,' she replied, 'my father is half British.'

They piled into the Land Rover, Greville in the back. Its shabby familiarity affected them and made them relaxed and in a holiday mood. Elizabeth talked excitedly to Simon.

'I've been let out of school!' she said. 'You don't know how wonderful it is to be here!' Her mood affected them all.

Simon thought, 'Why was I ever worried about entertaining her? She will fit in with everything. I am so happy, I cannot quite believe this is happening.'

When Elizabeth arrived at Merlinstone everything came alive. It reminded Simon of his childhood days when his mother and father were there, and his sisters; there had been a vigour and colour to those days.

Now it was warm enough to leave doors and windows wide open, a thing rare in the north. Their days shaped themselves into a rough pattern. They took Elizabeth out riding, one on each side of her on a pair of hunters and Elizabeth between them on a large pony called Hortensia. They rode to the hills and picnicked by a small loch and were eaten by midges. Aunt Mary found a bottle of citronella which they applied liberally to keep the midges away, without much success. Elizabeth would always remember that time at Merlinstone whenever she smelt lemons. They took her down to the river and on reaching a wide clearing in the trees they taught her to fish, and they played croquet on the lawn in the rose garden. Mary heard their laughter as she went to and fro, and their voices as they chatted, seeming in perfect harmony.

Simon remarked once, 'I ought to ask some people to meet you both, I suppose,' and Elizabeth replied

'But why do that? We are all so happy as we are.'

Alastair Thompson, returning from the church and on his way back to the Manse, saw them run across the road on their way to the village, two men and the fair young girl, they each held one of her arms and they were swinging her up in the air; they were all laughing. He watched them, smiling to himself until they were out of sight.

'Oh to be young again,' he thought, and wished he had not got to spend the evening at the session.

One evening they went down to the river. Simon took his fishing rod and Greville and Elizabeth sat together on the bank and watched him. Simon's line spun out like a strand of silk over the water, and Greville and Elizabeth conversed in low voices.

It was then that Greville turned suddenly to Elizabeth and said, 'You will come and see us in London, won't you? I am there quite often and I know that my mother would love to meet you.'

As he said this he gently took hold of her wrist. At this moment Simon lifted his rod from the water and turned to speak to them. Greville held her wrist for only the briefest moment, and Elizabeth turned away from him, but Simon saw and was filled with a terrible anxiety. He reeled in his line and called

'Nothing this evening I'm afraid, let's go back and have a pre-dinner drink.' His voice was easy, and he strolled away towards the house, followed by his labrador, Othello. Elizabeth and Greville jumped up from the bank and followed them.

Later, whilst he changed for dinner into casual but slightly more presentable clothes, Simon spoke sternly to his reflection in his dressing table mirror.

'It was nothing,' he told himself, 'it was just a small, friendly gesture and I am making far too much of it. But I must speak to Elizabeth; I can't let this drift on for ever, knowing that I am deeply and profoundly in love with her and not telling her about it! I haven't even kissed her, and I long to, oh how I long to.'

He hated his cowardice – he wanted to say to her

'Marry me and I will love you and help you for the rest of my life. Go off and sing if you must but please come back to me, I shall always be here for you. There will never be anyone like you again in my life!'

He realised that he was being totally unreasonable, expecting her to do this for him but perhaps, just perhaps, she would change her mind and give up her career and marry him instead. He could offer her a home, and children, and endless devoted love! And the house would stay alive and not die again as he knew it would once she had left it.

In her room Elizabeth too was looking into her mirror. She saw a young girl in a white dress with wide, horrified eyes.

'What can I do?' she whispered to her reflection. 'When he held my wrist for that moment I knew, I just knew. It was like a great bolt of electricity.'

For a brief moment she wanted to run away, to leave the house and everyone in it and run as far and fast as she possibly could. Instead she went down the stairs to the library. Simon handed her a glass of wine and she joined in the general conversation with Mary and Greville.

Mary said, 'It would be lovely if you could sing for us a little after dinner, Elizabeth. I have been longing to ask you if you would.'

She nodded. 'I would be delighted,' she replied. And to herself she thought 'And what can I sing that will not lead us into dangerous territory for what is there to sing about other than love?'

Normality returned; their lives followed the same pattern but with an even greater intensity. Time was running out and the holiday that had stretched before them had now developed a hazy and unwelcome end. Still there was no rain, and still the sun shone, and still Simon had failed to speak to Elizabeth of his love for her. He had rehearsed again and again what he was going to say to her and had always been unable to find the right time in which to say it.

'If only,' he thought, disliking his disloyalty, 'if only Greville would go away for just one day.'

Late in the afternoon Simon took his rod and went down to the river.

Elizabeth was in the garden helping Mary to do some weeding; it was hot – Mary wore a white linen hat with a floppy brim.

'I usually wear it in Italy,' she told Elizabeth, 'I hardly ever need it here. This is an unusually good summer. We had one other like this, it was the first summer of the war.'

'It makes me think of home,' Elizabeth said.

Later, when they went back into the house Mary said, 'I shall leave you for a little, I am going into the village. Will you be happy on your own for a while?'

'Of course I will,' Elizabeth replied, 'I must practise. Can I use the piano in the library if I am not disturbing anyone?'

'You know you can.'

Mary left her and Elizabeth set out her music and lifted the lid of the piano, settling herself on the seat. At first she felt self-conscious, the house was so still and quiet, but then she relaxed and sang with less constraint. Whilst she practised she looked up at the portrait that hung above the piano. It was an oil painting of the Tarnoch children. Vanessa stood in the middle, on either side of her were Claire and Theresa and Simon was at the end. He was clasping a small black dog. They gazed out of the heavy gold frame, Vanessa very proud-looking she thought, the artist had caught her almost scornful look, her head was flung back. Theresa, the only member of the family she had met besides Simon looked serene, and Claire intrigued her. Her pale oval face was different to the others and Elizabeth noticed her small, determined mouth. She sighed and sang the scale again; she had not practised enough lately. She must try and make up time. Ah! ah! ah! Up and up the scale she went once more. Greville walked softly into the hall and smiled. Should he disturb her, he wondered? Very gently he pushed open the library door and stood there. She did not see him. She was coming down the scale now, and then she paused; he kept still in the shadow of the door. Suddenly she sang

'*Early one morning just as the sun was rising*

I saw a fair maiden as fair as she could be' and he joined her and sang

'*Oh never leave me, oh don't deceive me – how could you treat a poor maiden so.*'

She played a crashing chord, and stood up. Her hands spread out on the keyboard; he came towards her.

He said 'Elizabeth,' and he lifted her hands and held them gently in his. He looked at her for a long time.

Then he said 'There is a bond.'

She drew in a long, deep breath 'between us both,' she said. 'Yes, between us both.' He pushed her gently back from the piano and stood with her in the centre of the room.

'Where is everyone?' he asked.

'Mary has gone out and Simon is on the river.'

'Then I shall do this,' he told her and he took her face in his hands and kissed her.

They stood holding each other, pressed together, as though they could never move apart. After what seemed a long time Elizabeth turned her head and looked out of the window towards the garden. She saw something that made her grow rigid with fear. Othello, Simon's dog who always accompanied him, padded past the window down the path. Simon must have just gone by, returned from the river.

'Look!' she said, 'It's Othello. Simon has come back. Oh God, he must have seen us.'

Greville just caught sight of Othello's black tail disappearing round the side of the house. A few moments later they heard a door slam somewhere in the direction of the kitchen.

'But it is so early!' Greville said, 'I told him I would join him later and perhaps fish myself.'

'Maybe there are no willing fish today. Would Othello come home on his own?'

'No, I am sure he wouldn't.'

'Oh, what shall we do?' she was in great anguish. 'We are mad!' she said, 'We never ought to have stood here, by the window.'

'I wasn't aware of where we were at that moment,' Greville replied. She laid her head on his chest.

'Neither was I,' she murmured. He put his arms around her again.

'Be calm, my darling,' he said, 'we shall simply have to wait and see how he is.'

Simon had seen them. He had caught two beautiful grilse and had been filled with triumph. He decided to return to the house and once and for all to seek out Elizabeth. Greville seemed to have disappeared for the time being and he would take his chance. They would eat one fish tonight; Jessie would be pleased to have it as supplies were running a bit low, and the other could go into the freezer or he might give it to a neighbour. He whistled to Othello who was searching along the bank for a possible rabbit, something strictly forbidden to the sporting dog, and started along the path towards the house. As he went by the library windows he glanced in at them as he always did, wondering what the time could be; he seldom wore a watch and usually he could see the bracket clock that stood on the mantelpiece. Instead he saw the two figures of Elizabeth and Greville standing motionless, like statues, in each other's arms. He had gone on rapidly and in through the back door. He laid the fish on the big marble slab in the kitchen and then rinsed his hands: mechanical actions, he still felt nothing, he was stunned. He went into the gun room and pulled out his fishing line so that it would dry. The familiar noise of the unwinding reel seemed to come from a long way off. After this he sat down in a chair and put his face in his hands and the pain came.

'I have been an idiot,' he said to himself, 'a total and utter fool to think that she could ever seriously care for me. I have literally been blinded by my passion for her!'

He stood up and left the gun room and went into the front hall. Here he stopped and listened; there was no sound. He went into the dining room and poured himself a large measure of whisky. He could not bear the thoughts that were crowding into his mind. If only she had never met Greville! If he had been alone with her she might have grown to love him. And he was so fond of his nephew, this made things worse. If only he had hated him, if he were a fiendish blackguard whom he could have saved Elizabeth from with justification; instead of this charming young man he had enjoyed getting to know these last few weeks. He poured out some more whisky, it wasn't helping at all. He went upstairs to his room and put on his faded old velvet jacket and a clean white shirt. I shall say nothing, he thought, I shall pretend that I never saw them.

Mary was out that evening, dining with some friends in the village, thus it was just the three of them who sat at the table in the dining room, about to eat the fresh salmon that Simon had caught and Jessie had cooked, accompanying it with a large jug of foaming Hollandaise sauce.

'A beautiful fish, Mr Simon,' she said, when she brought it in to them. Elizabeth wondered how on earth they were going to manage to eat anything and wished that Mary was there to help them. No-one spoke much. Elizabeth and Greville tried not to look too often at Simon or at each other.

After dinner, when they went into the library, Greville could not help catching Simon's eye, and the heartbreak that lay there: the wounded look that was at variance with his outwardly feigned normality cut Greville to the very core of his being. Simon said that he had several things to do in his studio. He smiled at them, bade them goodnight and left the room. Greville went and stood by the window.

'Look,' he said, 'a storm is coming.'

Elizabeth joined him. A bank of dark cloud was rolling over the evening sky, obscuring the setting sun. The rooks were cawing loudly, pleased, perhaps, that rain was coming. A cool breeze blew through the house.

Elizabeth said 'This is the end of the sunlight.' She turned and laid her head on Greville's chest. 'He knows,' she said.

'Like hell he does,' Greville replied. He pulled her down onto the sofa to be beside him. 'Elizabeth, has he said anything to you?' She moved a little away from him so that she could see his face.

She said, 'It is getting so dark.'

'Don't turn the lamp on,' he replied, 'I love the evening light, and this one suits my mood.' Then she answered his question.

'No, he has never said he loves me, but sadly I know that he does. I have been trying to avoid being alone with him because I felt he might tell me. Oh Greville, I never meant this to happen!' She cried the last bit out loud in anguish.

'Hush my darling, someone might hear and I have to talk to you. I am feeling terrible as well.'

She nodded, tears were starting to well up, her eyes swam with them. Then they spilled heavily down onto his hands. He was holding her, trying to comfort her.

'I did flirt,' she continued, 'but not seriously, just lightly as a silly girl does. You see I have been in awe of Simon ever since I first met him. He is beautiful and in a way remote, and a great deal older than I am. I revere him but I do not love him as a lover would. I like and love him as a friend.'

Greville nodded. He could see it all so plainly and he knew that Simon loved Elizabeth a great deal more than this.

'You don't feel that you would grow to love him in the other way?' He asked her.

She shook her head. 'Never,' she replied, 'I really never could. I love you Greville. Ever since I first saw the photograph that is here in this house, of you standing very straight with such a funny serious look on your face, I have loved you.'

'Oh!' He couldn't help laughing at this. 'That awful portrait photograph! My mother has one as well. I can't stand it. I was forced to have it taken when I left university, Vanessa insisted. How could you have fallen in love with that!'

'Well, I did,' she replied, 'although I might not have fully realised it at the time.'

The rain had started, they both turned to look at it spurting on the window panes.

'Oh what a tangled web we weave when we first fall in love,' he misquoted.

'Is it the first time for you?' she asked him.

He nodded, 'Oh yes. I have had a quantity of girlfriends and lovers but I have never felt like this.' She leaned her head on his shoulder.

'Greville, what are we going to do about Simon?' she murmured.

'Well, I was thinking perhaps I should talk to him. You leave here soon, and I go two days later. I could get him on his own.'

'But what will you say?' she sounded fearful.

'I shall tell him we love each other,' he answered slowly, 'and that we feel terrible about all this but it is the truth.'

'It is the truth,' she murmured. 'You know,' she continued, 'I feel like a murderer.'

He took her face in his hands and kissed her.

'Never, never say that,' he told her, 'and if you are a murderer I am a terrible thief.'

They sat for a long time in the darkening room. At length they heard the door open and Mary came in shaking out her wet mackintosh and struggling with her umbrella in the hall. Greville switched on the lights and went to greet her.

'Aunt Mary, you haven't walked back!'

'Only a very short way,' she replied, 'Adela Savage gave me a lift to the end of the avenue; we've been playing bridge!'

She went into the library to say goodnight and, finding Elizabeth there, she said,

'Oh, has Simon already gone up?'

'He is in his studio,' Greville replied, 'He had some things to do in there.'

'I see, well I think I shall follow; I am quite tired. Such a good thing for the garden, rain at last. Goodnight my dears,' and she left them.

Once in her bedroom she closed the door gently and sat for a moment on the edge of her bed. 'Oh dear,' she thought, 'things have been happening, and I'm not really surprised. Elizabeth has obviously been crying and Greville looks very disturbed. I do hope Simon will prove to be all right tomorrow morning.'

No-one at Merlinstone slept well that night and everyone came downstairs to breakfast a little later than usual. Simon appeared last and Greville and Elizabeth struggled to look normal. He helped himself to porridge and, smiling at them, sat down at the table.

'Well,' he said, 'this is sadly Elizabeth's last day. What would you like to do?' he asked her. She felt too choked for a moment to reply.

Greville said instead, 'How about we go for a ride? The rain is much lighter.'

She nodded. 'That would be lovely,' she murmured, 'But I'm happy to do anything, please don't feel you have to entertain me.'

Simon said, 'I'll just slip down to the river for a while, all this rain will have brought much needed water. I might join you later.'

Greville said 'Is there anything we can do for you, Aunt Mary?' Mary was tapping the top of her boiled egg; she laid down her spoon.

'I don't think so, my dear,' she replied mildly, and then opened *The Scotsman* which lay beside her plate, neatly folded. Greville suddenly felt as he had done during the war, a child again - aware that his aunt was in some way displeased, but not exactly with him alone.

Later that morning Elizabeth and Greville went for their ride. It was refreshing, the fine rain blowing in their faces as they rode their favourite way, towards the hills. After a while Elizabeth said

'He hasn't joined us.'

'Perhaps he's catching things,' Greville replied, and he glanced at his watch. 'It's after one, shall we go back? Aunt Mary will be expecting us; I should have said we'd take a sandwich with us and miss lunch.'

They turned their horses and cantered across the fields of rough grass. The rain had stopped for a while but the sky was still filled with billowing grey clouds. It had grown warmer and the damp air was full of the scent of wild flowers and honey. Greville felt almost optimistic.

'I thought he seemed a little better at breakfast, did you?' he asked Elizabeth.

She looked at him, 'I just didn't know what to think. He covers everything up so much,' she replied.

Back at Merlinstone they found Mary who suggested they should wait for Simon to return before they started lunch.

'It's a very light one so it will keep,' Mary said, 'some rather nice spinach and sorrel soup today from the garden and some salad and cheese. Simon told me he would be back before he left.'

They waited in the library. Greville sat on the sofa with Elizabeth and showed her some old photograph albums and Mary got out her knitting. The clock ticked, deep and slow, and at two o'clock it chimed. Mary looked up.

'How much longer do you think?' she asked. She was thinking of Jessie who was due an afternoon off. 'Shall we give him another fifteen minutes and then start?' Greville suggested. Finally they ate lunch without Simon. There was nothing unusual about his late return; Simon seldom wore a watch and was famous for failing to keep his appointments on time. Although, Mary thought, this was a little strange of him today knowing that Elizabeth was due to leave them tomorrow.

It was later during the afternoon that they became alarmed. Othello, Simon's dog, came bounding onto the lawn from the direction of the river. He was obviously distressed. He went to Greville and stood on his hind legs and pawed him. Greville waited for Simon to appear and when he did not he called Elizabeth. She came running from the house.

'I'm going down to the river; I'm worried about Simon, Othello's come home without him.'

'Wait one moment, I'm coming,' Elizabeth replied.

She snatched up her light raincoat and ran to join him and Othello bounded after her. Mary did not hear them go; she was in the vegetable garden which lay on the other side of the house. Greville and Elizabeth ran down the path to the river and started along the bank, pushing their way through the overgrown pathway. Herbage, heavy with rain, had fallen in front of them and they became drenched. Low branches, also heavy with rain, sent cascades of water onto their heads as they pushed them aside. The river gushed past them, gurgling like rich brown ale. Greville pressed on until he came to a clearing, and Elizabeth caught up with him. The river widened here, and the giant hemlock grew almost down to the water.

'This is a good pool, but he's not here,' Greville said.

Elizabeth said, 'Look, Othello's going on ahead. He knows where Simon is.' They followed the dog, who trotted in front of them.

'The next place is very deep,' Greville explained. 'If he is there he must have brought his body waders with him; I should have checked, they are always hanging on the hook in the gun room. When the river is in spate like it is today the whirlpool, as we always used to call it, becomes exactly that. I wasn't allowed to fish there as a small boy; it was considered dangerous.'

They came to the place he described, and still no Simon and still Othello looked back at them, whimpered and continued on. The water dashed now over a high plateau and down onto another stretch below, forming a magnificent waterfall. Beyond it the river curved to the right where a shallower pool emerged, lapping the far bank and a slice of silvery sand.

'Look!' shouted Greville, and there, floating on the surface, they saw a fishing rod.

'Where is he?' Greville whispered. He looked at Elizabeth; for a brief moment they stood in silence, then Greville said

'Oh God, look over there.'

He pointed to the opposite bank. Lying in the water, on the edge of the spit of sand, where the river swept to one side on the bend before it carried on through the wood, they saw the body of Simon - lying face down, his arms stretched out wide, half floating. Othello sat down and looked up at them. Briefly Greville stroked the dog's head.

'We must go over there,' he said, 'Before another spate of water comes and sweeps him away. Follow me; there is a bridge further down the river where we can cross.'

They raced on, Elizabeth feeling sick and weak and Greville burning with anxiety. They ran over the rickety bridge, followed by Othello, and then back along the bank towards Simon.

'We shall have to use all the strength we have,' said Greville, 'somehow we must drag him onto the grass.'

'But his face!' she said, 'We'll rip it on the stones.'

'We'll turn him over, then when we get him out we'll try and pump the water out; we'll try the kiss of life, we'll bloody try everything.'

They reached Simon's body and waded into the water; here it was not very deep. Greville said, 'You take the top part of his body, under his arms, and I'll get a grip on his waders and we'll haul.'

Inert bodies at the best of times are heavy, but bodies when bloated with water are far heavier. At last they managed to drag him onto the spit of sand.

'We'll do the revival job here as quickly as possible, then we'll get him to the bank,' Greville said.

First they tried pumping his back, Elizabeth holding up his head, and then they turned him over.

'I will try,' she said, 'I have been taught how to do this.'

She put her mouth to his cold wet lips, and thought how ironic it was that this was the only kiss she would ever give him.

Then she said, 'It does not work, Greville, he has drowned.'

Greville bent and closed his eyelids and they dragged him very slowly onto the grass. Then Greville turned to Elizabeth and said, 'Listen, you will have to be brave. You must run as fast as you can to the house and fetch everyone. Go to the farm, the stables, Aunt Mary; tell them to bring the Land Rover down here at once. The keys are on the mantelpiece in the

library; and tell them to bring a big tarpaulin to roll him in; they'll have one
at the farm. We must get him back to the house. I'm not having anyone
coming to bundle him into an ambulance yet. I shall have to ring all those
guys later. He is going to lie in his home. I shall have to stay here with him
and wait for you.'

She nodded, and flew away up the path. Her breath was coming in gasps,
her legs were bleeding and her hair was dark with sweat. Greville knelt
by Simon's body and Othello sat beside him and whimpered. Greville put
his arm around the dog and pressed him close and, bending his head, he
sobbed.

Elizabeth hardly knew what she was doing - she was only intent on
reaching the house. How could such a terrible thing have happened? How
could this darkness come after some of the happiest weeks of her life?

Down by the river Greville knelt beside his uncle's body; bending over he
saw that the strong fastening to his body waders had not been secured. Had
he forgotten to do this, he wondered? It was an easy oversight to make, and
a dangerous one. If you slipped and your waders filled with water you were
inevitably dragged down into the water and this was a hazardous place
when the river was in spate. One or two unlucky anglers had been drowned
over the years. Othello whimpered; Greville drew the dog to him again.

'You clever old boy,' he murmured, 'to come and find us.'

But how had this happened, he wondered? Simon knew every inch of
the river and understood all its moods.

Eventually they arrived; Mary and Jessie, Tom from the garden and all
the hands from the farm and the stables. They guided the Land Rover down
the track and hauled out a large tarpaulin and rolled Simon's body into it.
Then they heaved him into the back of the Land Rover. They returned,
some walking and others driving slowly, and in shocked silence, back to
the house. When they reached the garden they took Simon out and tried
to wring some water from his clothes and then, after Mary and Elizabeth
had draped the sofa in another dry tarpaulin, they laid his body on the long
sofa in the library. Othello would not be parted from Simon; he lay beside
him on the floor. Mary had become very pale and suddenly and silently
she fainted. Jessie and Greville carried her to the kitchen where Jessie took
charge.

'It is too much for her,' she said, as she sat Mary in a chair and pushed
her head towards the floor. 'Leave her with me; she'll be all right in a wee
while.'

Greville felt traumatised by this turn of events. Mary was their rock – she had been through so much of life with them and she had never reacted like this before.

'But then,' he thought, 'nothing like this has ever happened before.'

He went back to the library and thanked all the helpers, telling them to go to the kitchen and Jessie would give them tea, but when they did this and saw poor Mary they decided to go back to the garden and the farm. Later that night they all went down to the local to regale the neighbourhood with their tragic news. Elizabeth and Greville stood beside Simon for a long time as the evening came; they were unable to speak.

Then Greville said 'I shall have to ring the hospital, and, I suppose, the police. I shall leave relations until tomorrow. I simply cannot face my mother until the morning.'

In the end, after the local doctor had been out and the chief superintendent made what was really a courtesy call - he had known Simon well and had a great respect for him - Greville rang the undertakers who arranged to come for him the following day. Everyone was quietly kind and understanding. Elizabeth postponed her return to London for another day.

'I will stay to help you,' she said. He wished she would stop crying. Tears rolled down her face in a never-ending stream.

'Oh my darling,' he said, 'do try and stop. You will make yourself ill. Come to the kitchen and we'll see how Mary is and maybe a strong cup of tea with lots of sugar would be a good idea.'

They found Mary sitting very upright on a kitchen chair, Jessie had put a cushion behind her back; she was sipping from a glass of water.

'I am so sorry,' she said, 'I have rather let you down, you poor creatures.' Her voice was weak, hardly more than a whisper.

'Darling Aunt,' Greville replied, 'of course you haven't, we are all feeling the same.'

Later that evening, after they had packed Mary off to bed, Greville and Elizabeth found as many candles as they could and placed them in the library around Simon. He looked peaceful, Elizabeth thought, lying there on the tarpaulin, his face ivory pale. Little rivulets of water still ran down onto the floor, making small puddles, and turning the red carpet to black.

'We had better take care not to burn the house down,' Greville said as he brought in a branched silver candlestick from the dining room and lighted the tall candles.

'He looks beautiful,' Elizabeth whispered. They sat beside him in silence for a long time.

After a while Greville said, 'Death is so strange. He is here and yet he is not. There is an odd silence, different to the usual one if you are alone in a room. Do you know what I mean?'

She nodded. After a while she asked him, 'Do you think this happened because of us?' Brave Elizabeth, speaking the unspeakable. Greville looked back at her.

'How can we ever know? Several people have drowned by accident in that pool over a stretch of many years. He so easily could have slipped and I discovered he had not secured the fastening on his waders, a fatal error.'

'I wish we knew,' she said, 'Now it is a lifetime of wondering. I have a terrible feeling that I broke his heart.'

'If that is so I broke it with you,' Greville replied.

'What do you think Mary's opinion will be?'

'She will never tell us,' Greville replied. 'She is really heartbroken. She adored Simon; all through the war she worried about him and wrote to him when he was in prison. I remember so well she knitted an enormous khaki scarf and sent it to him through the Red Cross.'

The rest of the evening went by mostly in silence whilst they kept their vigil. They did not go to bed until the early hours of the morning and then they went to Elizabeth's room and lay in each other's arms – too exhausted and sad to make love.

The following day, on the evening before she left Merlinstone, Elizabeth went to find Greville. He was alone in the library, thinking his thoughts. The undertakers had been and taken Simon away and Mary had been persuaded to remain in bed. Elizabeth went in, closing the door behind her.

She said, 'Greville, I have something to say to you.' He looked up at her.

'Darling?' he said.

'I am going away, out of your life. I have quite decided this. We cannot stay together, after this tragedy – it would be wrong. I really do feel that I may have caused Simon's death. I could not live with you knowing this!'

'Elizabeth!' he cried out, 'Do you want to kill me as well?'

She shook her head; this time she did not cry. All her tears had gone and she was arid with grief.

'I cannot tell you how much this is killing me as well, but it would not be right, both of us together in happiness, and Simon dead.'

'He would not have wanted this,' Greville said, but deep in his heart he knew that she was right. They had to make a sacrifice. She stayed talking with him for a long time, until the moon came up and shone in through the windows, a tormented-looking moon half hidden by ragged storm clouds. The following day he took her to the train and she was gone, forever, out of his life. He went back to Merlinstone and wept bitterly.

CHAPTER XII

1981

Claire stood looking out of the large window in her flat over the panoramic view of London. She was waiting for her daughter Olivia to return from her visit to the London library where she had been doing some research for her book. What a luxury it was, she thought, to have time at last to stand for a moment and dream, after so many years of work. After having a job as well as being mother to Olivia and wife to Leonard, a time when she was always in a hurry leaving notes for everyone and cooking in advance, she had finally retired from being matron in a large London teaching hospital where her husband, a surgeon, also worked.

'But he will be retiring soon,' she thought, and her heart gave a little skip of delight. They had half made a plan to sell the flat and move to Scotland near to Merlinstone, Claire's old home. Olivia had been saying she quite wanted to move out and be more independent, sharing a flat, perhaps, with one of her friends.

She turned from the window and admired the large, light room, so different to all the other places she had lived in and so very different to her old family home in Scotland, Merlinstone, where her nephew Greville now lived. In contrast to her previous apartment this one was shining and modern. The long, white curtains had been expensive and the tables and chairs were tubular steel. A thick, white rug lay on the polished floor in front of the fireplace. The few paintings on the walls were mostly abstracts. There was one by her brother Simon, a landscape in the border country. On a table stood a photograph of herself and Leonard after their wedding and another of Olivia when she was a baby. There was also a photograph of her nephew Greville. Vanessa had sent it to her quite recently, as a kind of gesture of friendship. They had hardly spoken since she had run away from home to become a nurse at the beginning of the war. Now Claire picked this up and studied it. Greville – she had hardly seen him since he was a little boy. He is attractive, she thought, but he looks like Nessa far more than Henry, his handsome father who had been killed in the war. There was something faintly arrogant about him; strange, she mused, studying the photograph, she had not detected this when he was young.

Claire put the photograph back and sat down for a moment on the tubular chair. She remembered what had been worrying her that morning. Olivia was off to Scotland the next day to stay at Merlinstone with Greville, whom she had never met. She was writing the biography of her grandfather, the famous General Tarnoch, who was also Greville's grandfather and in whose house, Merlinstone, he now lived. Olivia needed to search through the many archives, which were stored in the house, relating to the General and his family. Claire was proud of her daughter. She had come down from university and had already written her first historical biography that had had great success. She wanted writing to be her career and had got off to a flying start. Claire hoped her second book was going to succeed as well. It was a daunting task. She thought perhaps she should warn Olivia about Greville. He had, she knew, rather a reputation with what she called 'the girls.' He had never married which had caused his mother, Vanessa, great sadness. He had left journalism and after a second career as a successful film director he had retired early to Merlinstone where he had been busy renovating and redesigning the garden and the house. He had made a great deal of money and was now happily spending it. The buzzer went in the hall. Claire jumped up and ran to press the button. It was Olivia. She would miss her daughter, she thought, with a sudden little ache in her heart.

*

Olivia:

My darling mother nearly drove me mad last night whilst I was packing. She kept coming into my room with new ideas.

'You must take warm clothes; Merlinstone can be freezing. I do hope you are taking your radio; there may not be one for you there and don't forget to take one decent dress, you never know.'

'Mum,' I said, 'I am going there to *work*.'

What was it she really wanted to say, I wondered? Later she came in with some paperbacks and I sort of found out.

'I thought you might like to take some of these; I don't think you've read them. You'll need some time to relax. They won't take up much room.'

'Really, Mum, I won't have much time for recreational reading!' I told her.

She put the books by my suitcase and sat down on my bed. I looked at her and sighed.

'I've been to Russia and back safely on my own, you know,' I said, 'this is only Scotland!'

'I know,' she laughed. 'You will ring quite often and tell us how you are getting on, won't you?'

'Of course I will.'

'The thing is,' she continued, 'I feel I ought to warn you, Olivia, Greville can be tricky.' What on earth did she mean?

'How?' I asked her.

'Well, you know, I don't want to be unkind, he does have a bit of a reputation.'

'Listen, Mum,' I said, 'I shall hardly see him. I shall be working hard all day and then I shall crash into bed at night. I'll lock my bedroom door if that would make you feel better!' She laughed.

'Good,' was all she said, and we kissed goodnight.

My parents were both up early the following morning to see me on my way. I hugged them and then hauled my luggage into the lift. My father had already taken all my writing materials, including my typewriter, down to the car for me.

'I'll ring you soon,' I called out as the lift doors closed and we sailed down to the ground floor. Outside I packed my things into the car and with a surge of excitement I drove away through the early spring morning.

The trouble with being an only child is everything hangs on you. You bear a great burden of loving and responsibility. I hate the way some people look at me narrowly and ask 'Are you the only one?' as though there was something weird about this simple fact. When I was little I used to make up stories and tell strangers dreadful lies about having loads of brothers and sisters and being part of a big family. I wondered, as I drove, if Greville had suffered from this as well. I knew that Henry, his father, had been killed during the war and Vanessa, his mother, had not married again or had more children. I wondered if this had affected him and if his romantic adventures were a kind of compensation. The sun was rising and so did my heart. I turned on my car radio and listened to the strains of Dusty Springfield – love, love, always love – all these singers went on endlessly about it. So far I myself had not yet succumbed. There had been the odd boyfriend but never, as yet, a real affair of the heart. I was 'virgo intacto' and 'heart intacto', pretty remarkable as well as unadventurous after three years at university. Perhaps, I thought, I should be proud of my purity. I laughed to myself as I wiggled the Mini through the rush hour traffic onto the road north. Anyway, I thought, thank Heavens my book will not be about love. It was to be a serious work, in which I would try to prove my grandfather, once lauded as a hero and now was being torn down and labelled a butcher who led his men heartlessly to their death, had not been like this at all. I hoped that I would still believe this after I had done all my research. I seemed to be living in an age when the demolition of heroes had become the norm. T. E. Lawrence was gay, vain and weak, Rupert Brooke a useless poet and a total narcissus, and countless others were being written about, reappraised and then condemned. Lewis Carroll had done odd things to children; this really upset me as I loved Alice the most of all my childhood books. Perhaps I should tackle this subject one day, and try to refute the accusations.

I do not remember quite where I was; I think it was probably as I approached the wonderful, undulating country of Northumberland that I started to seriously consider what lay before me. A tiny, cold twinge of apprehension started to creep into my heart. What if Greville proved to be somewhat hostile and irritated by my being there? Or what if he proved to be terribly lecherous and had to be fended off in the night? How would I deal with these situations? When I had first written to him telling him about my book and asking if I could come and stay and do some research he had not been very encouraging.

'I live a rather reclusive life these days,' he had written, 'I work on various projects of my own as well as running the estate. There would not be much entertainment for you here, but if you are happy to look after yourself and get on with your writing all should work out fine.'

'Humph!' I had thought, when I read this. I had got the message. He was happy for me to come to Merlinstone provided I kept my distance and didn't bother him. I wrote back saying that would suit me perfectly and that I would come to Merlinstone and would not need entertaining! After this correspondence my mother rang up Greville and said he had been all hospitable charm and everything was settled.

I stopped for some coffee, petrol and a brief scan of the map. It was at a bleak motorway café and I could already feel the sharp, colder air of the north. Then I drove on and crossed the border into Scotland and there, in the distance, were the hills. My stomach gave an excited lurch, this was my mother's country and therefore half mine. Before I reached Melrose I stopped again and examined Greville's instructions. He had interesting writing, I thought.

Turn left, turn right, I read, up a steep hill and through the small village of Merlinstone, about half a mile out of the village I would see some iron gates on the right, and an avenue of lime trees at the end of which was the house. It sounded simple enough.

The village was really only one street with a church standing at the end of it, beside a square house that could only be partially glimpsed behind a high stone wall, probably The Manse I thought. I came to the gates and a small lodge and bouncing and bumping over the rough surface I drove up the lime avenue. It seemed to stretch for a long way. The magnificent trees rustled and looked down on me, along with the independent, intelligent rooks that were busy making nests. It was many years since I had been to Merlinstone and I could barely remember it. I came to a smoother bit of drive and went on round the sweep of lawn to the front door of the house. I looked up at the stone walls. Not beautiful, I thought, but full of character, a great bastion of stone facing the world, and life, and the years. I switched off the engine and sat there for a moment imagining them as they must have been so many years ago – my mother and her sisters and brother, tumbling over the lawn, and General Tarnoch their father with Violet, his lovely young wife, on his arm. Whilst I mused the front door suddenly swung open, and standing there was, I supposed, my cousin Greville. I had not realised that he would be so tall. I got out of the car, smiling rather nervously.

'I'm Olivia,' I said, a fact that must have seemed to him quite obvious. He smiled back charmingly.

'Hello cousin,' he said, taking my hand. 'Welcome to Merlinstone. You've made good time, come in; we'll get your luggage later. I expect you could do with a cup of tea.'

His manner was easy and he seemed determined to put me at my ease. I was grateful for this as I was suffering from a bad attack of shyness. I followed him into the house.

'This,' he said, waving his hands towards the room around us, 'is where we used to have our grandfather's military relics. They were all in glass vitrines – things like uniforms and medals and letters. We called it The Museum. You can still go and see them; I had them moved to a house near Edinburgh that is devoted to wartime memorabilia.'

I followed him across the hall. The house had its own distinctive smell, I thought, of scented wood and damp stone.

Greville turned towards me, 'We'll go to the kitchen for tea,' he said.

Looking at him more carefully I thought he resembled his mother, my

Aunt Vanessa, rather than his father Henry whose face I only knew from photographs. He had been fair-haired and handsome in a boyish kind of way whereas Greville was slightly saturnine-looking. His hazel eyes were hooded and his hair that was thick and dark was only lightly touched with grey. He was wearing an old tweed jacket, an open-necked shirt and a pair of jeans. I felt slightly less afraid of him.

'Of course,' he said, as I followed him towards the kitchen, 'you can't have been here for years. Did you come here as a child?'

'Yes,' I replied, 'but I can hardly remember it.'

I noticed that the hall, as we went through it, had obviously been quite recently decorated. The walls were melon-coloured and large, antique jardinières stood beneath the windows filled with lilies and sweet-scented geraniums. It all looked discreetly expensive and I remembered my mother telling me that Greville had done a great deal to the place. We went into the kitchen which had obviously more or less remained as it always had been. In the centre, standing on uneven stone flags, was a large scrubbed top table. There was an imposing and ancient Aga cooker, above which washing was hanging to dry on a long rack. Standing by the Aga, a kettle in her hand, was an elderly woman with remarkable looks. Her white hair was drawn back in a bun and her twinkling eyes were the bluest I had ever seen. She had fine, regular features.

'Jessie,' Greville said, 'look who we have here, Claire's daughter, Olivia.' At this her face creased up with smiles as she held out her dry, strong hand in greeting.

'So you are Miss Claire's daughter,' she exclaimed. Her voice still held the soft lilt of a true highlander, from whence she had come, so many years ago, to work for the Tarnoch family. 'Well, it is a great pleasure to meet you my dear, that it is,' she said. 'I remember your mother when she was only a girl.'

Greville put his arm around the old woman's shoulders.

'Jessie is our left footer, Olivia!' he said, with a wink, 'She belongs to the other church.' Jessie pretended to smack his hand.

'Enough of that now, Mr Greville!' she protested, 'treating me like a foreigner!'

But you could see how really fond of him she was, and that she enjoyed being teased. 'Now off with you,' she said, 'you'll be wanting tea and I can talk to Miss Olivia later on. She must be exhausted. I'll get Edie to bring you some in the library.'

Edie was the girl who came in from the village to help Jessie in the kitchen.

'Is this THE library?' I asked, surprised.

'Oh no,' Greville replied, 'there is a much bigger one upstairs where I keep all the manuscripts and diaries belonging to Grandfather. I'll show you later when we do a tour of the house. This is the little library where I always congregate with family and guests, although I do use the drawing room for parties. Now come and sit down by the fire.'

There seemed to be a bewildering amount of rooms. I thought of my parents' apartment and how small it would seem in comparison. Greville sat down opposite me, and poured out the tea.

'I haven't seen Claire, your mother, for years,' he said, 'She broke away from the family when she had a tremendous row with my mother during the war.'

'I know,' I said, 'it is sad. She does see Theresa, though, quite often,' and then, feeling that this was perhaps rather tactless, I added, 'I am sure she and my father would love to see you some time. They may be leaving London and will be looking for a house near here if they do.'

He looked at me for a moment, unsmiling, and then he changed the subject and offered me a scone and raspberry jam.

'So you are writing a biography of our Grandfather,' he observed, 'that is brave.'

I felt uneasy but was used to family criticism so took his remark calmly.

'I enjoyed your last book,' he continued. I was surprised by this.

'You read the life of Mademoiselle D'Esté?' I said, my eyebrows raised.

'Oh yes – after all a successful biography by my cousin, whether I know her or not, aroused my curiosity.'

I felt a stupid blush creeping over my face so quickly drank some tea.

'You'll need to do a large amount of your own research for this one,' he continued, 'if you want to prove your point.'

'I know,' I replied, feeling slightly nettled. 'I want to portray the General as he really was, a sensitive man of his times, and a brilliant tactician. It is no good judging anyone from the past, by the jurisdiction and values of your own era.'

Greville nodded – he was serious now, and in sympathy with my opinions.

'That is quite true,' he replied, 'and the last book about him, apart from being too short and badly written, was set on destroying the final shred of any glory his memory had managed to maintain. It is sad but there was another author, Oscar Cornwallis he was called; he was writing a much more rounded and unbiased biography of the General, it was just before war broke out and he was killed in a raid and the book was never completed.'

'Perhaps,' I said, 'in a dreadful way that is my gain.'

'Yes,' Greville agreed, 'it could well be so. The others have enjoyed tearing the poor General to pieces. In the old days he was England's hero and Scotland's God!'

'Perhaps,' I said tentatively, 'you have some records of his early days. I would like to include a little of this in my work so that I can give a complete picture of him as a child and a young man.'

'You will find a large amount of records and general information in the old library,' Greville assured me. 'I thought you might like to write there and make it your den. We'll look at it after tea.'

When we had finished Greville helped me take my luggage up to my room. I was enchanted by it. The walls were covered in a Victorian wallpaper, faded now but still full of charm. It was patterned with great boughs of blossom on which were perched birds of paradise with sweeping tails. The bed had a brass bedstead and was high and covered with a white lace bedspread. There was a marble-topped washstand, the china jug and bowl patterned with large pink roses.

'Wemyss pottery,' Greville told me. On the walls hung watercolours by my grandmother Violet showing different aspects of the garden.

'It is wonderful!' I cried, almost clapping my hands. Greville looked pleased.

'This used to be my Aunt Theresa's room,' he said, 'I thought you would like it in here. It is quiet and when you are not working you can retreat here. I think,' he continued, 'that we had better do a tour of the whole house tomorrow. I have just remembered one or two things I have to do before dinner. I'll leave you to unpack. Dinner's at eight in the dining room.'

He left me abruptly. I was rather disconcerted by his remark about retreating to my room when I wasn't working. Was he expecting me to keep a discreet distance like a well-trained servant might have done in the Victorian era, I wondered? I was piqued that I would now have to wait before taking my typewriter up to the big library.

I went to the window and looked out at the garden, and beyond, the hills. Through the branches of the trees, not yet covered with leaves, I could see the glint of the river where my Uncle Simon had drowned. No-one had ever told me much about this. I knew that it had been an accident and a great family tragedy, and that Greville had afterwards gone abroad for several years. He had left journalism and had gone into films and had become rich. When he came home he had moved into Merlinstone, the house his Uncle

Simon had left him as he had no other heir, and had then spent a great deal of time and money on the whole estate, had re-landscaped the garden and renovated parts of the house. I could see from my window that there had been planning done on a grand scale. There were lawns and vistas and terraces, beds of lavender and wide stone steps. Impressive hedges were all carefully clipped and looked rich and dark like spinach. I was longing to explore. I unpacked my case and hung my few clothes in the magnificent walnut armoire that stood at the end of the room. My clothes hung limply on the fat, padded coat hangers, each with a little lavender bag tied to its stem – only my one dress had a more sophisticated air and looked vaguely worthy of its surroundings. I hung it in its plastic cover beside my faded jeans, and then I had a quick bath and put on a clean t-shirt and my least darned cardigan. The time was 7.45 – I went down the stairs admiring the paintings that hung on the melon-coloured walls; the collection my Uncle Simon had made that included many of his own paintings. I tiptoed across the hall, holding my breath, wondering why I was behaving like a shy child, and I pushed open the library door.

Greville was already there, standing in front of the fire. He was wearing a faded old blue velvet jacket, otherwise he did not appear to have changed. He was reading a paper which he put down when I came in.

'Drink?' he asked me.

'How lovely,' I replied.

I felt that this evening I really needed one. He poured some whisky into a glass, and, watching him, I thought how graceful his movements were, not realising, of course, that he had inherited this from his father. I wondered why this word was almost always applied to women and so seldom to men. Accepting my drink I wandered round the room examining the family photographs that stood on several of the tables. They all appeared to be of relations and animals, horses and dogs, and one or two were groups from house parties there must have been here long ago. Then, on the piano, in a large pale blue leather frame I came upon a photograph of my Uncle Simon. I gazed at it spellbound. He was wearing a white tie and a tail coat. Written on it in dark spiky writing I read 'Simon at Glengower Hunt Ball 1955.' I thought how handsome he must have been, this lost uncle of mine. He had an almost ethereal beauty that managed not to belie frailty. I suddenly felt intensely sad that I had never known him. At that moment Greville asked me abruptly

'Do you ride, Olivia?' I almost jumped and turned away from the piano.

'I wish I did,' I replied, 'but living in London I have somehow never learned to.'

He did not make any further comment or offer to give me lessons. I knew he kept several horses in his stables, my mother had told me this, and there was a groom as well who looked after them. Oh well, I thought, I'll just have to drive and walk, when I have spare time. I rather fancied riding a horse towards the distant hills. We went into the dining room. This was surprisingly bare and simple compared with the rest of the house. The walls were white and above the sideboard hung a large oil painting; it was a portrait of Simon. He was standing with his dog, the hills forming the background against a stormy sky. It was an arresting painting; he seemed to be looking at us deeply with his long, dark eyes and just a glimmer of a smile.

Greville saw my gaze and said briefly 'our uncle', and sat down, shaking out his table napkin with a sharp crack of starched linen. I sat down slowly, my eyes still on the painting.

'When was it done?' I asked.

'When he was twenty-one, quite some time before the photograph in the library that you were so hypnotised by.'

Ouch! I thought – that was a sharp remark. He changed the subject:

'Have a glass of claret,' he said. 'Jessie is giving us venison tonight,' and he leaned over with the decanter as I watched the dark red wine slip into my glass.

Edie came in and handed round the food, a venison pie with a flaky golden crust, mashed turnips laced with cream and finely chopped cabbage. I was hungry in spite of having eaten tea. This was followed by a lemon mousse and home-made shortbread biscuits. I took another sip of my wine; there was a delicious woody taste about it.

'You were a foreign correspondent for a time, were you not?' I asked boldly. The wine was helping me to feel less shy but I covered the glass with my hand when he offered me more.

'Yes, I was once,' he replied, 'then I went into films and I was lucky. It is make or break with that but I became a director and I made money. I decided eventually to pack it in and come back to Merlinstone – it needed me. My Aunt Mary who had looked after it, and me during the war, died and it was time to return and resurrect the place.'

I nodded. I knew the Tarnoch family had not been well off. After the General died it had been a struggle to keep the place going. Somehow they had hung on to it and it had still been there, waiting for Simon to come back from the war. Greville did not appear disposed to discuss his uncle any further, although he was happy to talk about his own childhood days with his Aunt Mary at Merlinstone.

When we had finished dinner I went to telephone my parents and told them I had arrived safely, then I returned to the library to find that Greville had disappeared. The tall guard had been put in front of the dying fire and one lamp had been left on. I switched it off and decided that I would have an early night. I felt suddenly tired – so much had happened in a single day and I was longing to curl up in that inviting room with its delicious-looking, lace-covered bed. I slept as I had seldom slept before, that first night at Merlinstone. It was like sinking into a sea of dark velvet. I think I may have dreamt but I could not remember my dreams. The next morning I was dragged back from my slumbers by a small noise in my bedroom. I sat up hurriedly, pulling the bedclothes up to my chin, pushing back my hair. I simply could not believe in what confronted me; I must have entered some kind of time warp during my sleep. Standing by the washstand, her back turned to me and her smooth red hair drawn back to the nape of her pale neck was a young girl. She was pouring hot water from a brass kettle into the china basin. I could see the steam from it rising around her. She wore a dark dress and a navy blue linen apron. She turned to me and smiled.

'Good morning Miss, I'm Simona, I come here during the daytime and help Jessie and Edie in the house.'

'Do you come here every day?' I asked, pinching myself.

'Well, more usually when Mr Greville has people staying. The bathrooms are a little way from the bedrooms on this side of the house.'

'What is the time, Simona?' I asked her. I had forgotten to unpack my travelling clock which still lay in my case.

'It is eight o'clock Miss, breakfast is at 8.30 but Mr Greville said you are not to hurry today as you may be tired after your journey.'

'That was thoughtful of him.'

'Yes Miss. Is there anything you will be needing?'

I shook my head.

'No thank you,' I replied and when she had gone, closing the door gently behind her, I leapt out of bed.

I dressed hurriedly, eager to start the day. As I brushed my hair I smiled at my thoughts. Mr Greville this and Mr Greville that, they obviously loved him, those who worked for him at Merlinstone, and he was undoubtedly spoiled. I ran down the stairs, humming to myself as I went; I was looking forward to discovering the big library. Greville was already in the dining room tapping a boiled egg with a newspaper spread out before him. He was dressed in riding clothes. I helped myself to a cup of coffee from the sideboard.

'Hi,' he said, looking up from his paper. 'Sleep well?'

'Wonderfully,' I replied. He noticed my solitary cup.

'Not much to start work on,' he remarked, 'don't you want an egg?'

Perhaps he was right - normally I skipped breakfast. I went back to the sideboard and helped myself to an egg and a piece of toast.

Greville got up and said 'I'm just going to change out of these clothes. Meet you in half an hour in the hall and we'll do a quick tour of the house.'

He was very brisk; I nodded, suppressing a strong desire to play truant and to run out into the garden and explore.

When Greville returned he said

'We'll go to the big library first,' and I followed him up the stairs to a broad landing where our bedrooms were.

We then went up another flight of stairs and a smaller landing. There were three doors – two normal size ones and the other very small and low.

'I think we'll do the Peele tower first,' he said and, producing a key, he unlocked the smaller door and bending low we went through and up another flight of very narrow, steep steps, at the top of which was yet another door. Greville opened it and a rush of cold northern air swept over us as we went out onto the narrow parapet. I caught my breath. We could see for miles from here. Greville stood beside me, pointing out all the landmarks and the history of the Peele towers. I was entranced.

'It is a magic land,' I said and he smiled, a smile of sudden and unexpected sweetness that made him look younger and less saturnine. I could not have known that this smile was for a memory of the past, for someone who had stood here years ago and had remained a dazzling image in his memory. I thought he smiled because he loved his home and all that lay around it and foolishly I expect that I thought a small part of his smile was meant for me.

'Anyway,' he said, 'we must get on.'

The smile had gone; he turned abruptly and I followed him down the steps back into the house.

'This is the large library,' Greville said, 'and the third door, the one opposite, is my den where no-one but me is allowed to go except by special invitation.'

I looked at him and saw that he was not joking. The large library was an impressive room. There was an imposing mahogany writing desk with many drawers and plenty of room for my typewriter. The walls were panelled and lined with books. Beneath them were cupboards where all the manuscripts were kept as well as family photograph albums and letters. One wall only had no shelves and here there hung a large oil painting, a portrait of our mutual grandfather. Greville looked up at it and said, rather dryly, 'I hope that will inspire you.'

He had been painted in his dress uniform, standing against a stormy sky and a suitably northern landscape. I looked with great interest. Although I had seen photographs of this portrait, until now I had never seen the original. He had been fine-looking, I thought, with his straight nose and impressive moustache. His long dark eyes were the eyes of Simon, his son, and held a gleam of amusement. Behind the rather stern exterior you felt he must have been kind.

'It was considered to be a good likeness at the time,' Greville observed. 'It's by James Gunn. He was quite a well-known portrait painter in those days.'

I liked the presence of the portrait. It would keep me company, I felt, in this large silent room at the top of the house. Heavy velvet curtains hung by the windows, strips of which had been bleached to a pale wine colour by the strong, northern light. No comforting electric kettle or jar of Nescafé to be seen, I would have to import them. Greville opened one of the cupboards beneath the bookshelves:

'You can search all through here,' he said, 'you'll find everything has been indexed and dated.'

He pulled open a drawer at the back of the writing desk and took out a book that was bound in dark green leather. Inside the yellowing pages were covered with elegant, flowing handwriting.

'Our grandmother's work,' he said, 'you'll find she listed everything. All the diaries and military stuff are in there, and all are numbered.'

I was feeling slightly daunted by the amount of data that surrounded me. He pointed to the far side of the room where a chest stood.

'In there are all the personal things like photographs and family letters.'

On a round table beside the writing desk were two telephones. I looked at Greville enquiringly.

'Yes,' he said, 'you dial nine on the red one and you get the kitchen. If you're lucky Edie or Jessie or even Simona will answer. You can ask them for a cup of coffee or anything you need. The other one is just an ordinary telephone for the outside world.'

'Goodness!' I exclaimed. 'Room service! I won't want to bother them. I can easily slip down and make one for myself.'

He shrugged. 'As you please,' he replied. He had become remote again.

We both left the room, me to find my typewriter and Greville to go out on one of his missions to the farm. At that moment Finn, Greville's labrador, came bounding up the stairs to find him.

'I'm here, old boy,' he said, and without further words he ran down the stairs and out of the house, his dog following at his heels.

I went back into the room and closed the door. The task that lay before me seemed enormous – to strip back the life and soul of my ancestor suddenly appeared a daunting task. Looking up at him I hoped that he was on my side. After this I fetched my typewriter and placed it on the desk in place of the large Moroccan leather bound blotter which I carefully moved to one side. I got out a whole pile of paper from a large shabby bag I always had with me whilst I wrote, and my bundles of pens, and found a place for these as well. Somehow these necessary items looked cheap and inferior resting on the rich green leather top of the desk. I felt like the little typist who was being employed to catalogue by the great family. Where was the author of repute, I wondered, who was here to start her momentous biography?

'I have come to put the record straight,' I told the portrait. 'I do hope that you will look favourably on me; I am not here to pry.'

Because this was precisely what I felt I was about to do. Reading diaries and letters and private papers did add up to prying – you were dealing with a person about whom you knew very little except the obvious things that everyone knew. I started looking for material that dated back to the year of the General's birth in 1861. I was so deep in my research that when the red telephone buzzed I nearly jumped out of my skin. I picked up the receiver and Jessie's soft voice sounded.

'Miss Olivia, I hate to disturb you,' she said, 'But you've had nothing to eat and it is three o'clock!' I looked at my watch.

'Oh Jessie,' I said, 'I missed lunch. I'm so sorry, I hadn't realised the time.'

'Now you must eat,' Jessie said firmly, 'hard work means you need food. I'm sending Simona up to you with a tray.'

With a click she had gone and a few moments later Simona knocked on the door and came in with a plate of delicious-looking sandwiches and a steaming cup of coffee. 'There now Miss,' she said, handing me the tray, 'you get around that; it will give you inspiration,' and with that she left the room and ran down the stairs. I worked on for the rest of the day.

When evening came I went out for a walk to discover the garden. It was a cool, lemon-coloured evening that smelt of spring rain. As I walked I reflected that Greville had obviously spared no expense where the gardens were concerned. The wildness my mother had always described, the sea of long grass where her brother used to hide had become stretches of closely-mown lawn. This was terraced down the hillside and edged with clipped yew hedges that were cut into impressive topiary. Wide borders stretched ahead beneath the hedges, filled now with spring bulbs that were just starting to bud among the herbaceous plants and shrubs that would burst forth later. Wide stone steps led gently down to other levels and gardens, some filled with roses, others with herbs and statuary. At the end of one terrace stood an astrolabe in the middle of a wide circle of paving that was patterned with pebbles and shells. The levels seemed to go on for ever with a new discovery on each one until I finally reached the last terrace, just above the wood, and here a fountain jetted up into the air sending out millions of sparkling drops of water that spewed down into a basin that was shaped like a giant shell. It was all so lovely, I thought, it was almost too good to be true. Somehow these wonderful gardens did not match the uncompromising, bulky face of the house itself. On my return I was relieved to find another garden much nearer to the house which I recognised from photographs my mother had shown me. This was somewhere unchanged that had always been part of Merlinstone. It lay to the back of the house and led up to the kitchen door - a real Scottish garden, being a mixture of vegetables, fruit and flowers. Beyond this stretched a row of greenhouses that I decided to visit on another day. The clock in the stable yard distantly struck seven. I had better go in and have a bath, I thought, and get ready for dinner.

Later, in the dining room, whilst we ate our roast chicken and sweetcorn fritters Greville asked me how my first day had gone among the archives.

'It went well,' I replied, 'there really is a vast amount to sift through and digest.'

'Well, take your time,' he told me. 'You can stay here for as long as you like and you can always come on a return visit if you need to.'

I was warmed by his suddenly friendly tone, if rather nervous.

'Would I be able to take some photocopies of some of the papers?' I asked him, 'to refer to when I am back in London. I will of course destroy them later.'

'I don't see why not. There is somewhere in the town where you can have that done. I'll find the address for you.'

I was surprised that he did not have one in the house; perhaps he kept it in his private den. Greville changed the subject. Turning to me with his suddenly charming smile he said,

'I have been meaning to tell you. They are going to unveil a statue in memory of our grandfather in Griselda Square in Edinburgh and they have invited me to do this, you know, pulling the cord and all that. When I talk of 'they' I mean the good burghers and citizens of the town who still revere his memory as do many in this part of Scotland. It has taken years for them to come to this decision and at last they have scraped up the funds; the town has masses of money really, they just sit on it and then there was endless argument as to where it was to go and who was to sculpt it. I used to fall asleep during the meetings – anyway a decision has been made at last and it is to take place on what would have been his birthday, the 19th of July. They are renaming the square Tarnoch in place of Griselda.'

'How impressive!' I exclaimed.

'Yes, thank God it has at last been decided; anyway I do hope that you will come to it, Olivia, I am inviting all the family.'

'I would love to!' I said.

'A lot of French are coming over,' he continued, 'he is still greatly esteemed in Northern France.'

We finished our dinner and I went upstairs for an early night. I intended to set my alarm and get up with the dawn the following morning; I had a great deal to get through.

At first the days went by marked out in a hard-working but peaceful routine. Sometimes Greville would go away for a few days, never explaining where he was going to – I did not like to ask. I did not feel lonely, I had so much to do and there was always someone friendly to have a chat with in the kitchen. When Greville was at home I took care not to press him with too many questions but I valued his opinions on the Great War and on our grandparents and their family. Sometimes, in the evening, I would go for a long walk and Finn, Greville's Labrador, came with me. We crossed fields and climbed hills and I ran, letting the northern air fill my lungs as we plunged over the rough ground, Finn bounding ahead of me. When I was feeling less energetic I went down to the river. Once or twice I saw Greville fishing there, from the bank in one of the clearings. I was careful to creep along and keep hidden so as not to disturb him. I wondered where my Uncle Simon had drowned. Greville never mentioned the subject so I did not bring it up. I concluded that it must have happened in the wide space of water they called 'The Whirlpool'. Jessie must have known about it but I did not like to question her. Although she was one of the warmest and kindest people I had ever met there was an hauteur about Jessie that forbade intrusion.

Occasionally my parents rang up. They were missing me, they said, when would I be coming home? I found it hard to explain that I had become obedient to a rhythm of work that I did not want to break away from. The weeks went by and we slid into the month of May. Spring arrives in the north at a more leisurely pace than it does in London. I dreaded someone might say 'Why Olivia! You have been here for a good many weeks!' I kept hidden in the big library, as much as possible, and then, one evening during dinner, the first blow fell. I realised it was said as a token of real friendship. Greville, who had been in an unusually cheerful mood all evening, put down his glass of wine and pushing his chair back from the table looked at me and said,

'I think, Olivia, that it is high time I did something for you. I have decided to have a dinner party.'

I looked up from my plate where I was devouring a delicious piece of creamy smoked haddock. I was horror-struck – but with a tremendous effort I tried not to show it.

'Why on earth should you do that?' I asked him. He looked surprised by my reply.

'Well, you deserve a little playtime, you have been working so hard and you haven't met a single person other than myself and the household since you arrived a good many weeks ago. I think you should meet some younger people.'

'I am perfectly happy,' I said, 'I really am, I don't need to meet anyone. Work is the main thing in my life at the moment. But of course, it is up to you.'

He laughed. 'I think you need a break, you are becoming too serious and I am worried about you, you need jerking out of yourself for a bit and I am sure that Claire, would agree.'

I felt rather angry at these remarks, after all I wasn't a child, I knew what I needed and it really was not his business. I shrugged.

'All right,' I said, 'give a dinner party, but please do not expect me to start a wild social life as a result.'

'I'll make a list,' Greville said, 'and ring around a few people tomorrow. There are one or two nice non-octogenarians living fairly nearby'; and humming to himself he went to the kitchen to tell Jessie about his plans.

I stayed on for a few moments, eating the last of my bakewell tart and cream. Of course, I ruminated, it had to happen sometime. I could not have gone on forever being a virtual recluse; and after all, if it was only a dinner party, I could return to my work the very next day, if my rhythm had not been too disturbed. It was this I was so frightened of happening, upsetting that precious rhythm, which was woven like a delicate spider's web around me whilst I worked. My parents understood this – they left me alone until I announced I was finished and ready to tear the web aside. 'Perhaps no-one will accept the invitation,' I thought, although I knew this was a vain hope.

My wish was not granted. All the guests accepted and Greville was quite jubilant. There was rejoicing in the kitchen as well; Jessie and Edie loved preparing for a party. I smiled with difficulty and tried to agree with them. I felt I was being an ungrateful wet blanket and might spoil all the fun by not entering the spirit of the thing. On the afternoon of the party I found it impossible to work. I had been sitting at my desk in the big library, gazing blankly at the portrait of the General, but seeing only the respectable garment I had to wear for the party and hoping that it would look all right. It was only three o'clock – the guests had been asked for eight. I decided to go downstairs and wash my hair. After doing this I felt slightly more prepared. I stood in my dressing gown looking out over the garden, my hairbrush in my hand. My hair was long and hung over my shoulders. Usually I gathered it together and twisted it into a ponytail but tonight I decided to loop it back on either side with two tortoiseshell combs that had belonged to my mother. As I brushed I thought my hair, which was usually a nondescript light brown, had gained a new richness. Perhaps it was the soft water. It crackled with static electricity as I brushed until it shone. I took my dress out of the cupboard. It was still in its plastic cover and I shook it free and slipped it over my head. I felt it slither over my body with the conspiratorial whisper of real silk, then I stood back and surveyed myself in the long mirror that was fixed inside the door of the armoire. My reflection surprised me; the cherry-coloured silk dress gave a sparkle to my eyes and was a radical change from my jeans and washed-out T shirts. I tightened the belt round my waist; it seemed I had lost weight since I came to Merlinstone in spite of all the wonderful food I had eaten. Next I hooked my only pair of good earrings into my ears, a present from my parents. They were rubies set in gold and had belonged to my grandmother. My shoes were my pièce de resistance – black suede with two small red bows. I did a twirl in front of the mirror and felt slightly more confident about the evening ahead.

I went down the stairs savouring the knowledge that I did not have to cook for the dinner party. My contribution would be to help Greville dispense the drinks. I stopped for a moment in the hall – the jardinières had been filled with fresh plants, and there was music playing. Greville had switched on the record player and adjusted the speakers and the whole

house was filled with the strains of Mozart. I went through the library into
the drawing room, which was seldom used. Tonight it looked welcoming
with a small fire in the grate and flowers arranged on the tables in wide-
necked vases. Greville was standing by a table covered in bottles and glasses.
He wore a wine-coloured velvet jacket I had not seen him in before. He had
no tie but had knotted a cravat around his neck and he wore a beautiful
cream shirt that looked like silk.

'Have a nice calming drink,' he said, and handed me a glass of champagne.
Then he drew back and inspected me.

'Nice,' he said, 'I like your dress.'

'My only one,' I replied, somewhat pointlessly. I am bad at receiving
compliments.

He took a scrap of paper out of his pocket.

'I never really told you who is coming tonight,' he said, 'very remiss
of me. We have two married couples, Lorna and Max Fergusson, small
landowners. You'll like him, she's a bit of a nightmare though. Then we've
got a young chap called Ivor Harcourt, just finishing Edinburgh University.
The family are friends of my mother's and he is bringing a girl with him
called Ruth. There is Guy Hamilton, a young land agent; he helps look after
the Glengower estate – not madly inspiring but nothing wrong with him
on the whole.'

I laughed at this. I was starting to feel a little better. Champagne had
worked wonders on me.

'One more couple,' Greville continued, 'the Craig-Millars; nice folk, I
play golf sometimes with him.' Greville waved some name cards at me.

'I'm going to put these round the dining room table,' he said. 'Won't be
a moment – help yourself to some champagne.'

I stood in front of the fire, my eyes glued to the windows. When Greville
returned he was carrying more champagne, an ice bucket and a large white
table napkin.

'They'll be here soon,' he said, 'Come on, let me fill your glass.' He came
towards me with a smoking bottle.

'Not yet,' I replied, 'I don't want to be drunk at the start of the evening.'

I watched him pour himself a glass, and it was at this moment that my
heart gave a great lurch and something terrible happened. I felt briefly
rather sick and moved away from the fire. I was experiencing a feeling I had
never had before, I was falling in love. We heard the scrunch of gravel as
the first car drew up at the front door. I could not do what I longed to do.
I wanted to run outside into the evening air shouting 'Damnation! Death

and damnation.' I saw Simona, neat in a dark dress and a white apron, cross the hall to let them in. Soon all the guests had arrived. There was laughter and talk and clinking of glasses. I hurried around, helping to hand them their drinks. I felt they were trying not to stare at me. Greville introduced me to everyone as his 'authoress cousin' and I immediately forgot every name. I could only think of one thing and pray 'Please, oh please God, do not let it be true.'

At last Simona came and told us that dinner was ready. I envied her deeply, standing there in her black dress and starched white apron not obliged to make conversation with anyone. As I went past her she gave me an encouraging little smile. In the dining room the long table, usually only casually laid, looked festive. Slim white candles burned in old silver candlesticks and Simon's portrait, half hidden in shadow, looked down on us all. Greville had seated me at the foot of the table whilst he sat at the head. I could see him between the candlesticks and was determined not to catch his eye. Simona went round carefully putting our soup down in front of us. It smelt enticing and rich. I picked up my spoon and turned to my left to engage Ivor Harcourt in a conversation about his university. After what I hoped was the correct length of time, we had just started on the roast lamb, I turned to Guy Hamilton who launched into farming and shooting and other things that I knew very little about. We moved on from champagne to claret. At least, I thought, I did know a little about wine. My father had taught me a fair amount and my mother, growing up at Merlinstone where the General had kept a good cellar, was quite knowledgeable. When I said how good the claret was my neighbour looked rather blank and said yes, obediently, but he himself always drank Rioja. This put a finish to that topic and we returned to the land again, this time fishing. Further down the table there was a great deal of laughter; Max Fergusson was telling a story and it was obviously going down well. His wife, Lorna, was watching him with indulgent pride.

The pudding arrived - we are nearly there I thought, helping myself to a slice of cinnamon and apple tart. I was back again with Ivor Harcourt tackling holidays in Majorca where I had never been. There was a lull as Greville, after making everyone accept another glass of Sancerre, tapped his glass with his spoon.

'God!' I thought, 'What is he going to say?'

A silence had fallen. Greville stood up and looked down the table at me.

'Tonight,' he announced, 'we are going to toast my cousin Olivia. She is staying here whilst she writes a biography of our mutual grandfather, the

General. It is going to be a blockbuster.'

I felt myself go scarlet and wanted to yell 'Stop!' Instead of which I fixed my eyes on my table mat. When I did look up it was straight down the table at Greville who was raising his glass and laughing at me. I knew, at that moment, that the arrow was cruelly wedged into my heart. Everyone stood up and, turning towards me, raised their glasses.

'To Olivia!' they all said.

They were pretty well away on the alcohol by then so I hoped they did not notice my scarlet face. I took a large gulp of wine and stood up also.

'To my cousin Greville,' I said boldly, 'and my thanks to him for putting up with me for so many weeks.' Laughter ensued and more drinking.

At last Greville announced we would go and have some coffee in the drawing room and we all obediently followed him. The fire had been made up and was burning brightly and most of the guests sank down into the chairs. Greville murmured to me,

'Olivia, could you please take the girls upstairs if they want to go there?' No-one did except Lorna Fergusson.

'I'd love to powder my nose,' she said brightly and followed me out of the room. She was a small woman, rather dumpy with short grey hair cut in a somewhat masculine style. She was wearing an old-fashioned style of dress, reminiscent of the fifties. It was made in a rusty-looking brocade and had a pleated effect across the bosom. She smoothed her skirt and said

'Max brought this material back from Cairo for me, after the war.'

I could see that she was proud of this. I had a sudden vision of a younger Max, having quite a good time in Cairo whilst waiting for the Germans to advance, rising one day with a bit of a hangover and going down to the bazaar and buying the brocade for Lorna, perhaps because of a twinge of conscience after the night before. I was jerked out of my reverie by Lorna looking round and remarking,

'So this is your bedroom – very nice.' I turned on the dressing table light.

'The bathroom is just down the passage on the right,' I told her.

She took no notice of this and plumped herself down on my bed.

'Such a lovely house,' she went on, 'you will miss it when you go back home.'

I did not reply but went over to my dressing table and picked up my comb. Then Lorna asked,

'How is Greville behaving?' I looked at her blankly. 'Oh, you know what I mean. Has he made a pass at you yet?'

'I don't know what you are saying,' I replied; 'he is my first cousin and I am simply staying here to write my book.' Lorna paid no attention to this.

'He is terrible, you know,' she continued, 'although he may have calmed down a bit these last few years. When he first came back to live here he ran after every woman in the county! He nearly broke up Caroline Norland's marriage, to say nothing of many others. No-one was safe!' She lowered her voice a little and glanced towards the door.

'They say the ministers threatened him; they told him he would have to resign from being an elder of the kirk if he carried on like that; his reputation was becoming so scandalous and it would have been a tragedy. The Tarnochs were the pillar of the church in the old days.'

I went on combing my hair as she carried on talking to my reflection in the mirror.

'But then,' she continued, not in the least put out by my blank expression. 'Some say it was all because of that French girl, Elizabeth somebody – the girl his Uncle Simon was supposed to be in love with. People say Greville was in love with her as well and she broke both their hearts!'

Oh, the temptation to ask her more about this! But I still did not say a word. An icy hand had touched me. Lorna's eyes were glinting. I could see she enjoyed an audience, even a silent one, to expound to.

'Of course there was an awful lot more we never found out about. Simon drowning, that was terrible, we never really understood why that happened. It was all very odd.'

'I know nothing about any of it, except my Uncle Simon drowned whilst he was fishing,' I said coldly. 'I think we had better go downstairs and join them. Do you want the loo or not?' Lorna got off my bed at last.

'I'd better take my chance,' she said, with a simper, and thankfully I watched her leave the room.

Left in my bedroom I buried my face in my hands. I was racked with shock and pain and, I must admit, with curiosity. Jealousy was by far my strongest emotion and it devoured me. Not the casual affairs Lorna had so enjoyed talking of, they were bygones, the thing that had upset me was the name Elizabeth. Some days before I had been wandering round the house and had come upon a room that I had hitherto not discovered. It was on the other side of the house, and on going in I was certain that it must have belonged to Simon. There was a small, framed photograph of him on the dressing table and one of his paintings hung on the wall. I wandered round idly, pulling open one of the small drawers beneath the dressing table mirror. In it, right at the back, I found some pieces of paper that had been torn, it seemed, from a notebook. It looked like a poem someone had written. The writing was blotched and impossible to read except for one line: 'Elizabeth is the sun, and all the glory in my veins is gold.' I read it again and then again. I folded it and put it back in the drawer. I was certain it was written in Simon's hand. 'Elizabeth is the sun.' The words went through my head for the rest of the day.

When Lorna returned I gave her a fake smile and led her back to the drawing room. The other guests were drinking their coffee and there was the pleasant feeling of soporific surfeit that comes after a good dinner. We had been upstairs for longer than I intended and I thought Greville gave me a rather questioning look when he handed me some coffee, which I ignored. I went and sat beside a couple I had not yet had the chance to talk to. Lorna was asked if she would like a drink and answered 'sticky green please,' and rolled her eyes at Greville who smiled calmly back. He could deal with her, I thought, I was not going near her again.

Eventually, well after midnight the guests started to leave. A tide of exhaustion swept over me. I helped Greville collect the coffee cups and put them back on the tray.

'Thank you,' I said, 'for an entertaining evening.' Greville stood still for a moment and looked at me.

'I hope you really did enjoy some of it,' he said, 'it's good to have a gathering occasionally. I trust taking Lorna upstairs wasn't too much of a nightmare?'

'Oh no,' I lied, 'that was fine. I'll say goodnight now. Must get back to work tomorrow', and with that I went up the stairs to bed.

Once in my room I pulled back the curtain so that I could see the night sky. Owls were hooting and a sickle moon suddenly came out from behind the clouds. I was trying to remember something. What had been her second name? My mother had mentioned her to me in the past – and then it came to me, she was called Elizabeth de Saint André.

I fell asleep from sheer exhaustion and woke too early, when it was still dark. I lay there and wondered if, by some miracle, I had been cured of my stupid madness but no, the arrow was still there, wedged in my heart. Cupid must have split his sides, he must have rolled over with laughter watching me lie there, more in love than ever. When at last the hands of my clock reached seven am I got up and crept down to the kitchen. I made myself some strong black coffee, took two aspirins and decided to get dressed and then go up to the big library and start work. I also decided that I would try to avoid seeing Greville as much as was decently possible without appearing to be rude. Jessie sent me a sandwich up from the kitchen for my lunch.

'Don't go overdoing it now,' she warned me, 'you must be tired after the party last night.'

But overdoing it was exactly what I planned to do. I meant to work so hard that I would not notice my heart or anything else relating to it. After forty-eight hours of managing to avoid Greville I decided I would have to emerge in case it looked rude to have been elusive for so long.

It was Thursday – I remembered he had said that he would be away for a night. I decided that I would join him for lunch. I heard the stable yard clock strike and I left, carrying a pile of books I intended returning to the little library. As I went down the stairs I heard a door close on the landing above and footsteps descending behind me. I had reached the eleventh step; I counted them later so that I would always remember which one it was. It was one of those odd, three-cornered shaped steps that often occur on a staircase when it forms a corner. I backed against the wall, holding on to my pile of books so that Greville could get by.

He stopped and said 'Well, here you are at last! I thought you must have run away.'

'I have been working on a rather tricky bit of research,' I replied, willing myself not to blush and to sound casual. Slowly he took my face in his hands, bent his head and put his mouth on mine. The kiss lasted a long time and I returned it. Then he drew away.

'I'm off for a night,' he said, 'going over to the west, so no lunch for me today. See you tomorrow evening.'

He continued on down the stairs, and out through the front door, whistling to Finn who came bounding to join him. I heard the door slam and the car engine start outside. My legs started to give way and, letting the books slither down the stairs, I sank on to the eleventh step.

For a few moments I allowed myself the intense luxury of believing that he loved me. For a few moments I was filled with a wild joy. Then I went down to the library and replaced the books; I wanted to believe the impossible. The horrible words of Lorna Fergusson kept returning to me, 'Has he made a pass at you yet?' I could not get them out of my mind. I ate very little lunch. Afterwards I went into the garden and ran as fast as I could down the steps and over the terraces and beyond. Eventually I collapsed onto one of the elegant iron seats. How stupid I had been! I never should have returned his kiss. I should have pulled away sharply and run down the stairs or, better still, I should have hit him.

It took courage to face Greville the following evening. I was determined not to appear cowardly or act as though his kiss had affected me in any way. When I had finished working I changed into a clean pair of jeans and a fairly respectable white jersey. To give me a bit more confidence I put on my only other pair of good earrings my Aunt Theresa had given me for a confirmation present. I had been so thrilled by them and loved her forever after for not giving me a small gold cross on a chain or a prayer book. They were jade hoops with little diamond clasps.

It was nearly eight o'clock when I heard the car. I was still upstairs in my bedroom. I came down very slowly. Greville was in the front hall looking at his mail. He said, 'Hi Olivia! I'll just grab a drink and we'll go into dinner – mustn't keep Jessie waiting.'

During the meal our conversation was a little stilted. I was determined to be as normal as possible. He did not enquire after my work but simply said he had been looking at some land he was thinking of buying as an investment. I replied politely and when we had finished he said he was going to his study to deal with his correspondence. I said 'fine,' and went into the library. I was furious with him. He had barely seemed friendly. He had just managed to behave with the necessary politeness you might expect from a stranger.

From that day I avoided Greville as much as I could. It was easy during working hours and I was thankful that he was out for most meals. I took to having sandwiches in the big library or eating with Jessie in the kitchen. The arrow was still there, wedged into my heart. I had hoped that it would fall out, along with my shame and disgust, but I was disappointed. Something puzzled me about Greville. I kept thinking it over when I was not concentrating on my book. I knew, deep down, in spite of Lorna Fergusson's pronouncements, that he was not an evil man. Why, then, I wondered, did he bother to kiss me? He must have so many others to choose from.

It was a few days later that Greville tapped on the door and came into the big library where I was working.

'Sorry to disturb you,' he said, 'Just wanted to tell you I am going away for a few days.' I looked up from my typewriter.

'Fine,' I said.

'Also,' he continued, 'I thought I had better remind you the statue unveiling is only two weeks away. My mother is staying with the Glengowers for it and then coming on here for a short visit. Your parents have let me know they will be abroad and will have to miss it.'

'Yes,' I replied calmly. 'They are very sorry about this. They booked a holiday in Egypt ages ago. Anyway,' I continued, 'I shall be leaving you quite soon after the unveiling, if that is all right with you.'

'Perfectly all right,' he replied courteously, 'you know I said to stay for as long as you needed to. You can always come back if you need more research,' and with that he closed the door and left me.

I drew in a long, deep sigh of regret and relief. Going away again, I thought – perhaps some siren awaited him somewhere; I would never know. I wondered if he knew how I felt about him and my cheeks grew hot with shame. I told myself not to be so stupid; after all, just one kiss, what was that? It could have meant nothing to either of us.

To work that day was impossible. What would I do with myself instead, I wondered? Drive to the pub and get very drunk? Go for a long walk, then have a hot, scented bath and read one of the thrillers my mother had insisted I bring with me? Drive into the town and buy ridiculous things with money I had saved and intended not to spend – a new outfit for the unveiling, an outrageous hat that would put Greville to shame? I was forced to laugh at this last idea and I felt slightly better.

I left the big library and closed the door, uncertain still on my next move, and then I saw that Greville had left the key in the door of his study. He had gone off in a hurry and had obviously forgotten to put it away as he always did, in a rather bluebeard-like manner. I felt a rush of excitement and I went straight to the door of his room, turned the key and stepped inside. Holding my breath I stopped on the threshold and looked around me. I felt wonderfully wicked and I knew that this was what I needed to feel. His very private room, I thought, and I am here at last. Several paintings hung on the walls, all by Simon. I walked round and examined them. There were photographs dotted around, one of Henry Sinclair, Greville's father, with his mother Vanessa; it was a wedding photograph. How young they looked, I thought. Even then Vanessa had an air of rather tough sophistication and Henry looked serious, and undeniably handsome. Perhaps it had shocked him, the knowledge of what he had undertaken.

I tiptoed round the room, fascinated by the different objects – a Spanish shawl and an old cricket bat, portfolios, presumably full of work by Simon, a folded Oriental screen and a standard lamp, the shade rather moth-eaten and tilted to one side and then I saw an old ciné projector and a large, rolled-up screen. On the floor beside these were some boxes. I lifted the lid of one and found inside numerous spools of film. Trembling with excitement I pulled out all the equipment and unrolled the screen. I dragged the projector across the floor and found a suitable socket for the plug. I knew how to work the mechanism; my father owned one of the same vintage and I had often helped him set it up. I went through the spools – they were all carefully dated. I came to one marked E, S and G 1956. I pulled the heavy velvet curtains over the windows to block out the light and then I turned on the projector and slotted in the film. There was a whirring noise and a mass of jagged shapes and flashes like cubist confetti danced over the screen. 'Come on,' I murmured, 'please, please work for me,' and then it began. First came jerky images of Merlinstone. It was obviously summer; there was a lot of long grass and bobbing wild flowers. Jerk, flash, jerk the film went, and then, very faintly I made out two figures walking through the grass. One figure broke away and ran towards the camera. It was a young girl – I knew at once that I was watching Elizabeth de Saint André. Even in these old, black and white images you could see her radiance. She was wearing a summer dress; it had short sleeves and candy stripes. Her fair hair sprang back like flames, and then in a flash she had gone and we were on to something else. A young man, whom I realised was Simon, came towards the camera and then Elizabeth joined him and linked her arm through his. They stood there for a moment, smiling. Greville must have been filming, I thought. Next, in the last spool Elizabeth and Greville appeared in the screen together. To start with they were fooling around, doing some sort of dance. Then they stopped and stood for a moment looking at each other, the picture moved closer, I saw Greville's face as he put his arm around Elizabeth's shoulders. They are posing for Simon who must have been taking this part of the film. They smile at the camera. She is so lovely; I am empty even of jealousy. I realised that she had a quality other beautiful women did not have. And Greville, I could hardly bear to watch him. Click, they had gone, the spool had finished. That day in summer at Merlinstone was snuffed out. I packed the spools back into their box and took out others. I watched my mother and my aunts; I saw Aunt Mary and Greville when he was a little boy. Who had taken these, I wondered? They were fascinating, but all the time one thing stood out in stark relief before me. Greville would never love me or, for that matter, anyone else, for Greville was in love for ever with Elizabeth.

Had Simon loved her as well, I wondered? Lorna Fergusson had said as much – and could this possibly be the reason why he had drowned in the river? Was he driven to do this in his despair – or was it an accident? I knew that several anglers had drowned in that pool; and was this also the reason why no-one spoke about it? Poor Simon – my heart bled for him as I contemplated his unrequited love. 'For Elizabeth is the sun, and all the glory in my veins is gold,' I remembered again the line in the poem I had found in the dressing table drawer. 'But the sun burns,' I thought, 'it can consume you.'

Very carefully, so that I did not leave a trace of disorder, I packed up the spools and the projector and screen and replaced them exactly as I had found them. When I was satisfied I pulled back the heavy, velvet curtains. I felt like a criminal who had just completed a successful crime. But what sorrow it had brought me! Although I had known in my deepest heart that Greville would never love me I suppose I had still treasured a faint spark of hope. I could see so clearly now that this was useless – those flickering images, those few jerky moments on that screen had shown me how much they had loved one another, on that far-off summer day.

I returned to the big library after locking the door of Greville's room and, leaving the key in the door as I had found it, I sat down at my desk and thought for a long time. The film had explained so much about him – his inability to commit himself to any woman, his dalliances that never ended in partnership, even for convenience or companionship's sake. I wondered if he ever imagined if any of them would. It had become a kind of habit, I thought, to have an affair and then move on. Had he considered having one with me, I wondered? If so he had changed his mind very quickly. Soon I would be packing up my things and returning to London. I told myself that my little sorrow was nothing when compared with those of the First World War. Lately I had had bad dreams and sometimes nightmares. I saw bodies piled up in trenches, all around me lay the dead and the dying. One night I dreamt of the General. He was on his horse and he was yelling his lungs out. I saw his wide open mouth, all red, with flecks of saliva. There was a thundering noise and I heard him order his men to go out and die. I woke and found that I myself had been yelling in my sleep. I lay for a moment, rigid with fear, engulfed by the terrible atmosphere of the dream; thankful that I slept on the other side of the house where no-one could have heard me scream. The whole saga of the war was getting to me and I had started to feel exhausted during the day. I vowed that the next book I wrote would be more about peace and happiness, and less about conflict.

Greville was away for ten days, during which time I did a large amount of work. Being on my own and knowing that I would soon be returning home gave added impetus to my writing. On the day of his return I resolved to be friendly and welcoming. He arrived at five o'clock and we had a cup of tea together in the kitchen. He greeted me quite normally; it was later that evening I noticed a change in him. We had a drink in the library before dinner and he handed me my glass without a smile. He did not speak to me at all during dinner. I made an attempt at conversation but when he did not reply I decided that I would no longer try to engage him. I wondered what on earth could be the matter with him. I knew that I had replaced everything in his room exactly as I had found it. I had taken great care to do this. He could not possibly have known I had been in there; and no-one else in the house knew either. Jessie, Edie and Ishbel had all been out that afternoon; and yet somehow I felt oddly certain that he had discovered my intrusion. After our silent dinner he said a curt 'Goodnight,' and went upstairs. The evening was fine and I went out into the garden. I felt bewildered and, I hated to admit this to myself, I felt afraid.

The following day I avoided breakfast and sought refuge in the kitchen for lunch, with Jessie and Edie who were as ever cheerful and kind.

Jessie said 'We'll miss you when you go, Miss Olivia, that we will!' and I felt perilously near to tears. I would far rather Greville had ranted and raved at me, shouted 'You meddling bitch,' hit me, even, anything would have been better than his icy stares and his silence. And even now I wanted to reach out and put my arms around him to drive away his anger.

Friday came, the day before I was due to go to Edinburgh for the unveiling of my grandfather's statue. I was upstairs in the big library, sorting out some of my papers with the view of packing them for my journey south, when Greville appeared in the doorway.

'Just to tell you the unveiling tomorrow is for four pm. We are asked to be there a good hour beforehand. I imagine you will want to take your own car.' I looked up and smiled at him.

'Yes,' I said, 'I shall do that.' He nodded and left the room without any further remark.

'Bastard,' I growled, behind clenched teeth.

That evening, standing in my bedroom looking out as I so often did at the darkening sky, I thought how sad it was that I was leaving Merlinstone under such dark clouds of estrangement. It seemed an age ago that I stood here on the day I arrived, full of expectant excitement, longing to begin my work and Greville being so charming and helpful. I wondered whether I should go to him now and ask him to tell me what was wrong. If he accused me of going into his room and meddling I would admit, openly and honestly, all I had done. On the other hand, if his manner had nothing to do with this at all, it would be a foolish and unnecessary confession.

'And anyway,' I thought, 'it is really up to him to explain.'

I awoke the next day with a deep sense of foreboding. The early summer had suddenly fled and a cold, grey sky replaced the blue and white one.

A light rain was falling. I got up early and went and had breakfast in the kitchen with Jessie. Greville had asked her as well as Edie and Ishbel to the ceremony but they had all decided to stay at Merlinstone instead and await our return. Edie and Ishbel had really planned to go to the cinema together, I found out later when they confessed this to me with much giggling, and Jessie said she was too busy; she could hear all about it when we returned.

After breakfast I carried my typewriter down to my bedroom so that it would be ready to go into my car the following day. Greville was nowhere to be seen. I had an early bowl of soup for lunch and then I went and changed. I put on my slightly more respectable black jeans and my navy blue coat which was quite smart in a retro sort of way; it had once belonged to my Aunt Theresa. I let my hair go loose, and put on the beret I sometimes wore to church. I wondered why I felt like a schoolgirl again and not the sophisticated writer I hoped to seem. Greville had already left, Jessie informed me. She explained to me where Griselda, soon to become Tarnoch, Square lay, and I drew a rough map on the back of an envelope and bade her goodbye. I was feeling distinctly apprehensive.

I drove into Edinburgh and found the square with surprising ease. A large crowd had already gathered. I decided that I would hide myself on the outskirts and brave going up towards the statue later when it had been unveiled. It stood there on a plinth, swathed in a St Andrew's flag. I could see Greville and Vanessa in the distance, chatting to a group of dignitaries all wearing smart, dark clothes; most of the women were wearing hats. There were men in uniform, some obviously were from France; they looked elderly, with white moustaches. I glimpsed my Aunt Theresa and her husband and I pressed myself into the outer edge of the gathering hoping to avoid everyone for the time being and I was lucky – no-one noticed me. I watched as a very elderly lady smothered in furs was being given a chair to sit on. I guessed she must be Gloria Glengower. A silence fell and the crowd waited whilst Greville said a few words into a faulty microphone. Then a detachment of soldiers marched in, dressed in the uniform of General Tarnoch's old regiment. They were followed by several men wearing black gaiters, the clergy I thought. The soldiers were part of a military band and they struck up and played whilst a few more people arrived, rather hurriedly, obviously aware they were late. There was a pause and I craned forward to watch Greville go up to the statue where a man handed him a plaited rope which he pulled and the flag collapsed to the foot of the plinth to reveal the bronze statue of our grandfather, tall and magnificent, gazing out over the square. Clapping ensued, Greville spoke again, complimenting the sculptor and saying a few more words about his grandfather (our grandfather, I thought, as I listened to him).

The band was about to strike up for the last time when I saw her. She was standing on the far side of the square on the edge of the crowd. Like me, she looked as though she was trying not to be seen, but in her case she had been unlucky, most people had left that side of the square and were making their way towards the statue. I watched the very slender figure, wearing a dark cloak with a hood which she had pulled forward to partially conceal her face. In spite of this I knew, without any doubt, this was Elizabeth de Saint André. I saw her turn sharply, her hood fell back revealing her fair hair. She looked in flight. Then I saw Greville detach himself from the crowd. He ran across the square and I saw Vanessa gesticulate in amazement as he went. No-one else seemed to have noticed. They were all making their way towards the Civic Hall where refreshments awaited them.

I knew at once what I must do. I ran from the square to my car. My legs felt weak with fear. I jumped in and drove away as fast as I dared. I had not been able to wait and greet my relations and I only hoped they had failed to notice me. I had to get back to Merlinstone as soon as I could and then I would load the car and leave that night. I knew that if Greville managed to catch up with Elizabeth he would take her back to the house. He was a man with a desperate, lifelong mission that nothing could deny.

I decided I would drive through the night, back to London and home. When at last I reached the house I ran in to the kitchen to find Jessie. I burst into the room where she was sitting with Edie and Ishbel who were regaling her with tales of the film they had seen. They were all drinking strong tea.

'Miss Olivia!' Jessie exclaimed, 'You look winnowed!'

I said sorry, but I must pack up at once as I had to get home.

Jessie said 'Sit down now, and have a hot cup of tea.'

'I can't,' I replied, 'I can't,' and suddenly I was clasped in her arms sobbing my heart out, my face pressed against her starched linen apron. Forever I shall remember my tears, darkening the white linen, and the feel of her strong arms around me.

'There you are,' she said, 'cry it all out, whatever it is, and then you'll drink some tea and we'll all help you get your things packed up.'

After a few moments I raised my swollen, tear-filled face and accepted a cup from Edie.

'I shall be all right now,' I said, 'and thank you all so much, I'll go upstairs and pack right away.' Jessie gave me a long look and said no more to detain me.

Packing took me longer than I intended. I kept remembering things I had left around the house. Jessie found my gumboots in the gun room and my file on the Tarnoch family life before 1914 was missing. I found it eventually under a large album of photographs. At last I had loaded the car and splashed cold water on my face; I pulled back my hair and twisted it into its usual ponytail. Then I went to the kitchen to say my goodbyes. Jessie pressed a small thermos into my hands and a package of sandwiches.

'We will miss you,' she said sadly, and the other two agreed. She gave me a quick little kiss.

'Now mind you stop often enough and don't you dare get sleepy; those roads are dangerous enough even when you're awake!'

I got into the car quickly before I could start to cry again, and blowing a kiss I drove away, all three of them standing in the doorway waving to me as I went. The sky was darkening. How dreadful it would be, I thought as I drove down the lime avenue, if I were to meet headlights coming towards me on the drive! One woman comes, another goes. But no lights whitened the tree trunks except my own. I swung out onto the road with a sigh of relief. I went through the village and then I headed south. Far away in the west a streak of lemon light still lay across the sky. I could see the dark, lumpy shapes of the hills, and I felt a sharp pang of sorrow at leaving the north. But the security of my own home awaited me, and the long task of finishing my book.

I was determined to reach London by morning. There were moments during the journey when I longed to pull off the road and sleep. I got out and did exercises and slapped my face. Then I drank the coffee and ate some of the sandwiches. On and on I drove, it seemed an endless journey. I wondered what Greville would think when he reached home and found that I had gone. I reckoned he would be relieved, especially if Elizabeth was with him, and I was quite certain that she would be. I drove over the Carter Bar and into England, and the beautiful county of Cumbria enfolded me, whitened by moonlight. I drove fast, like a fugitive, fleeing from the grief of love. It was dawn when I reached London. I felt I had arrived in a foreign land. I pulled up outside the flat and was so stiff I could hardly climb out of the car, but I had made it. With a sigh of relief I hauled out my case, dragged it into the hallway and pressed on the button for the lift. Inside the flat it was very silent. My parents were still away in Egypt and there was nothing in the fridge but I hardly cared. I drank some water and flung myself down onto my bed and slept until noon the following day. My Scottish saga was over and now the real hard work on my book would have to start.

CHAPTER XIII

Back in Edinburgh Greville had flown across the square, following the rapidly retreating figure of Elizabeth. She hailed a taxi and he saw her jump in and slam the door. He hailed another and shouted to the driver

'Follow that blue cab in front as though your life depends on it, I'll make it worth your while.'

The driver, fortunately, was amused by this request. They plunged into a labyrinth of smaller streets, until the blue taxi pulled up outside a small hotel.

'Wait here,' Greville commanded, 'I want the passenger to get out and go into the hotel without seeing us.'

'Are you 007, sir?' the driver asked; Greville ignored this remark. He could not see Elizabeth from where he sat, and he did not want to wind down the window in case she noticed him, but his driver gave him a running commentary.

'The lady's got out of the cab, she's looking in her handbag, like all of them she's taking her time about this, now she's paying and she's going into the hotel. I'll have to move soon, this street is getting busy and we're not supposed to stop here.'

Greville got out of the cab.

'That's alright, I'll walk up to the entrance.' He pressed a wad of notes into the man's hand.

'Bless you, sir,' he said, and with a large wink he drove away. He would have a good story to tell them when he got to the pub tonight.

Greville sauntered into the hotel. He went up to the desk and put his hand on a small button and rang the bell. A door opened and a young man arrived, peering at him through a large pair of horn-rimmed spectacles.

'Can I help you, sir?'

'Yes – I hope you can. I think you have a friend of mine staying here, a Mademoiselle Elizabeth de Saint André, or she may have checked in using her married name – Madame Turrenc.'

The young man flicked through the register.

'Yes,' he said, 'a Madame Turrenc is staying here. I will ring her room. Who shall I say wishes to see her, sir?'

'Greville Sinclair,' he replied. Unbearable moments followed. 'Oh answer, Elizabeth,' he prayed, 'Please, please answer.'

The young man spoke quietly into the receiver.

'A Mr Sinclair here to see you, Madame. Shall I send him up?'

Another terrible moment – the young man turned to Greville.

'Madame Turrenc says yes please will you come upstairs. Her room number is fourteen.

The lift is over there on the right. She is on the first floor.'

Thank God! What would he have done if she had said no? The lift rose and he said to himself be calm, be calm. The gates drew back and he pushed open the door. He went along the thickly carpeted passage and at the end he stopped. Here it was, no. fourteen. The key was in the lock, he turned it and entered the room. She was sitting on the bed. She had removed her cloak and she was wearing a dress in a particular, hyacinth blue he always associated her with. She was thinner than before and at the moment she looked very pale. Her hair sprang back from her face as it always had, like flames. She was staring at him with her amazing eyes very wide; he remembered how much they had reminded him of the eyes in a classical statue – perhaps it was something about their rims. She slipped off the bed and came towards him holding out her arms. He held her to him.

'Why, oh why did you run away you mad, silly girl? Do you realise I might never have caught up with you.'

'I was afraid,' she answered, 'I had not planned to do that but I was suddenly terribly afraid.'

He kissed her and they sat down together on the bed.

'Is it really you?' she asked him softly, and taking his face in her hands she looked at him - and then she smiled.

'Yes, it really is.'

They sat together for a long time in silence, like two people who have been shipwrecked and have somehow survived a violent storm. After a while she came out of her dream and said,

'But Greville, all those people, the visitors from France, your mother, your Aunt Theresa, what must they be thinking now you have left them?'

'I don't care,' he replied, 'I don't care about anything in the world except to be here with you.'

And indeed, on the other side of Edinburgh in the Civic Hall, Vanessa was trying to hide her bewildered rage. People were starting to realise that Greville was missing. Some were expecting him to reappear at any moment and were looking expectantly towards the door. Vanessa went round chatting and being as calm and friendly as possible.

'I so want to speak with your son a moment, will he be here soon?'

'Yes, I am sure he will be,' she replied to an elderly French general who had asked the question, 'He just had to leave us for a moment to make a telephone call.'

Vanessa had not noticed Elizabeth in the crowd, but someone else had. Gloria Glengower, who had enthroned herself on a chair and was about to accept a large piece of chocolate cake which was being offered to her by Theresa, may have been old but she was far from short-sighted. Now, as she bit into the cake, she smiled. She had seen Greville leave, like a streak of dark lightning, and unlike most of the guests she had noticed the cloaked figure of Elizabeth as she emerged from the crowd.

'The de Saint André girl, I swear it was her,' she thought. 'A woman now, no longer girl but I still recognized her gait.'

She finished the cake and accepted an iced biscuit with a radiant smile.

'I hear you are going on to stay with Greville, Theresa,' she said, wondering if indeed this would still be the case.

Back in the hotel Greville took Elizabeth's hand and pulled her up from the bed.

'I am taking you away now,' he said, 'you are coming back to Merlinstone.'

She put her hands on his shoulders.

'Greville,' she said, 'I cannot go anywhere with you until I have told you something – something so serious that when I have told it you may never want to see me again.'

'Tell me now,' he demanded, 'if you have any pity for me, Elizabeth, tell me at once.'

'That would be impossible,' she replied, 'it would take too long. Perhaps I had better tell you when we have arrived at the house, and then I can always leave the next day.'

'What!' he cried. 'Are you crazy? You are never ever going to leave me again! I know what we will do; we'll go to a restaurant I am fond of in the town. It is late enough now for us to drive. I really could not bear the suspense after all these years; I must know what it is you have to say.' He grabbed her case and she threw her cloak over her shoulders and he dragged her out of the room.

'This will look like an abduction,' he said, and they started to laugh, as they used to all those years ago.

After the bill had been settled they took a taxi to a restaurant where Greville had often dined before. The head waiter greeted them with deference and guided them to a table at the far side of the room, discreetly placed on its own in a small alcove.

'A table for lovers,' Elizabeth thought, and she smiled. Greville looked at her.

'You are too pale, my darling. You need a drink,' and he ordered a bottle of wine and when the waiter returned he ordered their food and then hoped that they would be left on their own for a while. The restaurant was filling up and the staff would be busy. Then he turned to Elizabeth and raised his glass.

'Don't be afraid,' he told her, 'Tell me everything. Nothing, however awful it may be, will ever change my feelings for you.' She drew in a long, deep breath.

'I shall get to it as directly as I can,' she said, 'Many gaps can be filled in later. It is not possible to tell you the story of my life in the short time we shall have here!'

He nodded.

'Go on,' he said.

'Well,' she continued, 'After that awful time at Merlinstone when we parted I went on studying my singing. Madame decided to leave London and I went with her to Rome. When I finally launched on my career I had moderate and then greater success.'

'You had enormous success,' he interrupted her, 'I used to read about you and God how it hurt! Elizabeth de Saint André in Paris, in New York, in Rome, at Covent Garden. Once I nearly came to one of your performances but I could not bear the thought of the agony of it – and then I read in a newspaper somewhere, when I was making one of my films, I think it was in Morocco, that you had decided to retire. You were so young and successful. A little later I read that you and your husband had separated – and then silence.'

'I know,' she said, and had a sip of her wine. 'I married my Svengali and it did not work out. I never loved him and I should not have married him, poor man, but he persuaded me and in many ways I relied on him. Around this time my father got in touch with me and begged me to come home as my mother was very ill.' She paused. Greville said,

'But why did you stop singing when you were at the height of your career?'

'Wait,' she said, 'You will see why – I will try to explain. It was partly, I suppose, my broken marriage but mainly it was because of something my mother told me before she died. It was strange but I think it was on this journey across Europe, back to my home that I realised I had never stopped loving you; and that all other relationships had been, and would be, hopeless. I arrived home feeling tired and sad but it was wonderful to be back at the chateau after so long. My father met me; he was in a terrible state about my mother. They had tried everything, he said, but now they had given up and she was just lying there, waiting for her death. I spent as much time as possible sitting with her. She was very brave. She wanted to talk to me about the past and the secret work she and my grandfather had been in with the resistance during the war. One day, when I went into her room she said 'I have not taken any painkilling drugs today. I want to be clear-minded because I have something important to tell you, Elizabeth.'

I nodded and sat down beside her bed and listened. She was obviously in great pain and then she told me, and I do not think anything in my whole life except Simon's death and leaving you, had been as awful as her story proved to be. She related how she had had a passionate love affair just before the war, in England, with your father Henry Sinclair. She had fallen desperately in love with him. She had to leave him and return to the chateau and her father, never knowing for certain if she would see him again. When she arrived back home she discovered that she was pregnant, with your father's child, and I, Greville, am that child. I was born at the chateau in one of the coldest winters they have ever known, the midwife only just managed to get to her in time. My mother was lucky – she was young and strong and it was an easy birth. My grandfather had accepted her pregnancy with kindness and understanding. He never asked her who my father was fearing, my mother thought, that she might have been raped on her journey back to France. My mother did not write to England and tell Henry what had happened. She did not want his pity, she said. She christened me Elizabeth Mary after your aunt, of whom she was very fond. The following summer the miracle happened. Your father, who was then in the SOE, came to France on a mission and dropped from a plane near to our town Mont Rouge. He made his way to the chateau. He had been ordered by London to link with my mother and grandfather who had further instructions for him as to where he was to go. He was to set up a cell. My mother waited for him shaking with fear and excitement. They made love, in the kitchen I think it was, until the small hours of the morning. My grandfather was away so my mother was in charge of the messages for your father. She said nothing about my presence until just before she took him to her room to snatch a few hours' sleep when she told him she had something to show him and they went into the room where I was fast asleep. He must have been stunned, poor man, when he saw me lying there and my mother explained to him who I was. And then, before they went to bed they had a terrible argument. She told him that when he returned home he must seek a divorce from Vanessa, your mother. Henry was greatly distressed. He told my mother he adored her but that he could not leave his family – it was unthinkable. My mother replied there was no other way. I can just see her saying this, she could be like steel. She loved him and she must have him totally. Henry left early that morning. He was due to return to the chateau for a night before he returned to England. Your poor father, he must have been exhausted. My mother told him she hoped that when she next saw him he would have changed his mind.

On the final day, the day that Henry was due to return to the chateau, my mother received a message telling her to warn him not to go to the venue where the plane was to collect him, his departure had been delayed for another night. Henry returned to the chateau and my mother questioned him again and he still said no, he would love her forever and always help and support her, but he could not leave his wife. He left that evening; she did not give him the message that would have delayed him and saved his life. He stole out from the chateau in the darkness but he was never to see England again. He was arrested by the Gestapo before he reached the stretch of ground where he expected the plane to land. They took him away and shot him in a high place behind some giant grey rocks. As they marched him there he must have glimpsed the chateau again, lying below them. I cannot bear to think how he must have felt.' Elizabeth paused, and Greville ran his hand gently over her hair.

'My darling,' he said to her. She looked up at him.

She said, 'Do you know that when she told me this my mother did not show a flicker of remorse. After this tragedy she married a young man who had always been her admirer, he came from Normandy and I grew up loving him, thinking he was my true father. He was gentle and kind and devoted to my mother. He is there, now, in the chateau. They had another child, Antoine, my half-brother, and he will inherit our home. According to Napoleonic law it will go to both of us but I shall relinquish my share of it to him as I shall not wish to live there when my stepfather dies. When I talked to my mother about Henry she simply said, 'He belonged to me.

I could not allow anyone else to claim him.' She was like that, there was this ruthlessness in her none of us could understand, and she was utterly unrepentant to the last. I cannot tell you, Greville, what my feelings were like! I loved Pierre, it was a dreadful shock to discover he was not my real father. But to discover, also, that my mother was capable of such an unforgivable deed was the greatest shock to me. I could no longer sing and I abandoned my career. This discovery and my separation from my husband just overwhelmed me.'

Greville put his hand over hers.

'It makes no difference you know,' he said, 'I still love you exactly as I did before.'

'Is that really true?' she asked him, and he nodded. 'I feel the same,' she told him.

'But it will be incest!'

'I don't care,' he replied, 'no-one need know.'

To his great relief she smiled.

'Did your stepfather ever know the truth?' he asked. She shook her head.

'No, my mother simply told him the Gestapo had caught her lover and killed him. She did not tell him that it was her fault this happened. He will die never knowing the truth.'

'And so will everyone else,' Greville replied, 'including my mother. But what a story – it explains so much that for years I have found hard to understand.'

They saw, to their surprise, their food had been put down in front of them which they had forgotten to eat – delicious-looking fillets of sole and hollandaise sauce. A waiter was standing beside their table looking at them enquiringly. Greville picked up his fork.

'So what made you come to the unveiling today, how did you know about it?' he asked her.

'I had to see you again,' she told him. 'After my mother died and I was alone in the chateau with Pierre I became ill with a sort of nervous exhaustion and depression. I tried to hide it but it was almost impossible to do this and my stepfather grew worried about me. One day I was asked to go and visit some cousins of my mother's who live near Arromanches in the north of France. I used to spend wonderful summer holidays with them when I was a child. Pierre thought it would be good for me to go and he packed me off, rather against my will. Whilst I was there I read in a local paper about the forthcoming unveiling of General Tarnoch's statue in Edinburgh. Several dignitaries from Arromanches were going to attend it.

When I read this I knew that I had to be there. I had to see you again and tell you my story.'

'And you nearly didn't see me, you silly girl,' Greville said tenderly.

For the first time she really laughed and he saw, for a moment, a flash of the old Elizabeth he had known all those years ago.

The waiter returned to their table with two plates of strawberries and thick cream. When he had gone, Greville picked up Elizabeth's hand and kissed her wrist.

'Why did you run away?' he asked her.

She said, 'When I saw you all standing there I suddenly lost my courage. Your mother and all your relations, and seeing you again looking so like you have always looked, I was overwhelmed, I just could not face you all. I planned to ring you up later, from the hotel.'

'Look at me,' he said to her. 'You must believe me, Elizabeth. What you have told me makes no difference to my feelings about you at all.' She nodded.

'I know,' she said. She felt suddenly flooded with happiness and exhaustion.

'I am taking you home now,' he told her, 'back to Merlinstone.'

They left the restaurant and went out into the cool, dry night to find the car.

'I shall have to telephone,' Greville said. 'I should have called from the restaurant. I want to tell Jessie to get another room ready.'

Jessie heard the telephone ringing and throwing down her knitting she ran from the kitchen to answer it, praying that it was not going to be bad news. A voice said

'Jessie!'

'Mr Greville!'

'Listen, I am on my way home and I am bringing someone with me, could you possibly get the Lily Room ready for them.'

'But I was giving that room to your mother!' Jessie replied. 'You said she was coming here tomorrow – with your Aunt Theresa.' There was a short pause.

Then Greville said, 'They will not be coming after all, Jessie, I am putting them off.'

'Very well, Mr Greville,' Jessie sounded shocked.

What on earth could have happened, she wondered, to cause him to do this? The Lily Room was the prettiest one in the house. The walls were covered in a William Morris paper that had hung there even before Violet

Tarnoch's arrival as a bride.

'This someone he is bringing must be important,' she thought. 'I wonder who it will be!'

She went to the room to see that everything was in place. Edie had laid a fire in the grate of the old fireplace, and she decided to light it. A fire in a bedroom was a decidedly welcoming thing and the early summer night was cool. Not very long after she had done this she heard wheels and she went to open the front door. Greville was getting out of the car, then he stooped and gathered someone up in his arms. It was a woman, very slight in build, wearing a black cloak. She appeared to be fast asleep. As he carried her into the hall Jessie looked at her and gasped.

'Mother of God! It is Miss Elizabeth!'

'She is exhausted,' Greville whispered, 'I am going to lie her on her bed,' and he carried her up the stairs.

Jessie followed him in silent amazement. They laid her on the bed and she stirred a little but she did not wake.

'I think we'll leave her,' Greville said. 'I'll come back later with her case.'

He closed the door gently and went back down the stairs, Jessie following him.

'Miss Olivia left this evening,' she said. Greville looked at her as if he had forgotten Olivia's existence.

'Oh, did she?' was all he said. He went into the library and stood in front of the fireplace in his usual stance. He felt triumphant and elated. Fate had, for once, dealt him a winning hand. He had got her back at last and this was the only thing that mattered in the whole world.

*

My parents returned from Egypt, looking suntanned, and full of stories about the places they had been to and things they had seen. My mother hugged me, and then she said,

'But you are so pale, Olivia, and far too thin! Did they starve you at Merlinstone?'

I assured her that I had eaten enormously and that Jessie was a wonderful cook. Since coming home I had arranged my work in the little room my parents had allotted me and I had been working hard on my book. Sometimes memories of the big library came back to me, the portrait of the General, the panelled walls, and I would do my utmost to sweep them aside. I told my mother that Greville and I had got on fine together, and I described his newly planned gardens and the things he had done in the house. My mother sighed and looked wistful.

'Home,' she said, 'melon-coloured walls must look wonderful. We were very sad, Olivia, to miss the unveiling. Do tell me about it.'

This was rather dangerous ground as I did not dare mention my Aunts Vanessa and Theresa as I had not spoken to them or even, to my knowledge, been seen by them. I skirted around the subject and instead I launched into a description of the sculpture and the visiting dignitaries from France whom I had not met either but she was unlikely to discover this. I had written a polite and somewhat formal letter of thanks for my stay at Merlinstone to Greville, and a much warmer one to Jessie. I gave away my red silk dress that I had worn for the memorable dinner party at Merlinstone. I could ill afford to part with it but I could not bear to be reminded of that evening. I had been drilling myself never to picture again the moment when Greville had looked down the table at me, between the candlesticks, and raised his glass. The arrow was still painfully wedged in my heart but I was growing more practised at ignoring it. Just occasionally, a memory would return, like, for example, the kiss on the eleventh step.

I tried not to think of or imagine Greville and Elizabeth together at Merlinstone. In spite of this images came to me of them, standing on the hillside in the rough grass. I could see the sky and the sunlight and even hear the buzz of the wild bees. If it became too much I would leave the flat and run down the street to the pub where I drank myself stupid.

It was autumn when I finally finished my book. For such a complex task it had really taken a relatively short time to complete. I had put in more hours than I ever would have thought possible, which deadened the pain. On the day when I wrote the final words I went into the kitchen and found my mother making jam from blackberries she had bought in the Portobello market.

'I've done it!' I cried, 'Just one more draft and all is finished and I can send it off to my publisher.'

I twirled round the kitchen and licked the jam spoon and my mother laughed.

'It is lovely to see you like this,' she said. 'I know these last months have been hard for you.'

'It has been a miserable, long wet week,' I suggested.

'I didn't say that,' she replied. She has a wonderful, wide curvy mouth when she smiles. She stood there with the jam spoon in her hand, looking so happy. I gave her a hug.

'Let's have tea,' I said, 'and crumpets with masses of butter and jam, and let's call Dad. This is a celebration.'

The following morning I woke early and lay for a few moments on my bed, my arms stretched above my head. Something had happened; the arrow had loosened. I felt light-hearted, even happy. Soon it will fall out, I thought, and be gone forever. I knew that my luck was turning. When I finally packed up my manuscript and sent it to my publisher some of my old apprehension returned, but it did not cloud my feeling of rediscovered freedom. A few weeks passed and I heard nothing. Then, one day, the telephone rang.

'Olivia?' a voice said, when I answered it. 'It's Edwin Ransome here, sorry not to have been in touch sooner, various things got in the way. I am delighted with your manuscript. Can you come and see me next week and we'll discuss publication?'

I replied that of course I could, and planned to go and see him the following Thursday. Full of happy anticipation I set off for Oxford. I could tell from his voice that Edwin Ransome was pleased, even excited. As I drove down the motorway I ruminated on how lucky I would be if my second biography proved to be any kind of success; it was hard to follow up the triumph of the first one.

Later, when the book had been published, I was amazed by the reviews.

'Sensational young writer does it again,' one journalist wrote.

Another more weighty and literary one wrote, 'Olivia Elliot has almost persuaded me to take a different view of the great General Tarnoch. Her work is finely argued and well researched; she is certain of her subject and has an original slant.'

I was asked to book signing sessions by fashionable sellers and various clubs and societies invited me to come and talk about my biography. My parents were delighted for me and I even had a congratulatory letter from my Aunt Vanessa. I kept passing shop windows and seeing my volume on display in its glamorous red jacket. I allowed myself a short spell of euphoria; I sent a signed copy to Greville and received a polite but rather formal reply, telling me no news of himself.

It was a little while after all the excitement about the book had died down I decided that I would go abroad for a kind of exploring holiday. I had always wanted to go to Iran, or Persia as my mother called it, so after much preparation I loaded a backpack and went. My father was about to retire from medicine and my mother wanted us to move to Scotland so that she could be near her old home. I left them in a state of excited house-searching. My travels in Iran could fill another book; I was enchanted by

the country. I had promised myself one night of luxury in the Shah Abbas
Hotel in Isfahan, after my weeks of camping, or staying in makeshift rest
houses – there were no hostels as such to be found. The idea of one night
of civilized comfort was a beacon that I could keep in my mind as I trekked
onwards. I had allowed myself a lot of time and not having to hurry was a
luxury in itself. It was in this far country that I met someone called Meredith
Cochrane. We did not meet in the Elburz mountains or beside the Caspian
Sea, we came across each other in the bar of the Shah Abbas Hotel.

  I arrived in Isfahan in a state of happy exhaustion, aware of the fact
that I did not look a suitable guest for such luxurious surroundings. The
hotel stands near to the beautiful Blue Mosque, and is lined with the same
turquoise-coloured tile work. It breathes luxury. I went to my room at once
and pulled my only clean shirt and jeans out of my bag. After washing
my hair and trying desperately to smarten myself up, I slung several bead
necklaces round my neck and pulled on a pair of sparkly sandals, and then
I went downstairs to the bar. This was smaller, darker and more friendly.
A serious-looking barman glanced at me in a fairly welcoming manner; he
was shaking something in a silver cocktail shaker. The bar was empty, it
was rather early I supposed – Iranians must keep late hours rather like they
do in Spain. There was only one other person, a tall, slim, youngish man
sitting on a bar stool and awaiting his cocktail. He, rather like me, looked
as though he had tried to smarten up what was a thoroughly tattered
wardrobe. Boldly I went and sat on a stool and smiled at him. I suddenly
felt quite desperate for a drink; he smiled back over his glass. He had an
amused expression, and his eyes danced as he looked at me. They were
an intense, warm blue, if this is possible, in his deeply tanned face. We fell
into conversation, and soon after this we fell in love. I found out his name
and that he had been travelling in search of plants for his nursery back in
Scotland, which was, it transpired, near to Merlinstone. He was not staying
at the hotel but had come here to meet a friend who had failed to turn
up, an Iranian botanist - an interesting man, he told me, but Iranians did
tend to be unreliable when it came to making plans. The evening stretched
on. Meredith gave me dinner and then we danced, and I could see myself
cancelling my journey home and staying on, in a cheaper hotel, whilst I
went with him on a plant hunt expedition. And this is exactly what I did.

    When we returned home I went to live with Meredith, in a small grey
cottage where he has his nursery of rare plants. My parents bought a
manse near to us. They accepted my situation, and the fact that I was now
pregnant, calmly, and when our son Carol was born they rejoiced. We were

completely happy. The only strange thing was that none of us mentioned Greville. My mother did say once that she must ring him up as she so wanted to see Merlinstone again, and when I told Meredith about him he said he thought he had met him once. There had been a gardens open day to help raise money for charity and he had gone to Merlinstone out of curiosity. He had always heard about the terraced lawns and the rejuvenation that Greville had brought about the whole place. He said there had been a woman, taking money at the gate; she was extraordinarily beautiful, there was a kind of radiance about her; he did not know her name. I knew at once this must have been Elizabeth. I often thought of getting in touch with Greville but I somehow did nothing about this. I knew that I would see him again but when, I did not know. I was tied up with so many things – my new home, my parents' house and our baby, and most of all I was so happy, loving Meredith and enjoying being loved in return; I did not need anything more. I knew that I would start to write again, but I felt a break from this was one of the things I needed most.

The interruption to this state of affairs came one autumn day about a year or so after I had moved into our new home. I was sitting in the kitchen reading the local paper; Carol was in his high chair contentedly sucking a rusk. I was about to put the paper away and attend to him when something caught my eye. Inside the front page I read that there had been a fatal accident near to Merlinstone. It had happened on a roundabout where the main road ends and you turn off left for the village. A lorry had collided with a car, the driver of which was a lady named Elizabeth de Saint André. She had died instantly. The journalist added that the inside of the car and the road were scattered with white flowers that she had been taking with her. Somehow this added a touch of beauty to the description of her death – it seemed fitting for Elizabeth to have been flower-strewn at her tragic end.

I folded the paper feeling deeply disturbed by this news. Poor Greville, how was he going to be able to bear this, I wondered, losing the only person he really loved and whom he had found again after so many years. My heart started to bleed for him. Carol had finished his rusk, and was staring at me, his blue eyes very wide; I picked him up out of his chair and hugged him to me.

'You must be careful when you learn to drive,' I murmured to him, my mouth against his soft baby hair.

Later that day I rang and told my mother about the accident in what I hoped was a matter of fact manner.

'Olivia,' she said. 'I know all about Elizabeth. You can't live up here without knowing that he found his beautiful lost love and brought her home! This really is terrible news.'

I wondered what else she knew; I had never told her about my love for him.

'I shall write to him,' she said, and I agreed.

I sat down that evening and wrote a letter. It was quite short, and, I hoped, warm. It was a difficult one to write. It seemed so strange that I knew so much about her and yet I had never met Elizabeth. My mother wrote a letter to her nephew and received a polite reply. In his letter he said that he did hope that she and my father would go over one day to Merlinstone and visit him and her old home.

I, on the other hand, received no reply to mine. I swallowed back my resentment over this and did not mention it to Meredith. It is strange, I thought, that although I no longer loved Greville as I once had - my heart was totally given to my own man – the scar still remained and I supposed that it always would. And then a surprising thing happened. A few months after Elizabeth had died the telephone rang. Meredith was out dealing with some plant orders and Carol had gone with him. He loved to play on the floor in his office where he rolled around some toy flower pots and tiny plastic flowers my mother had given him. I picked up the receiver and heard Greville's unmistakable voice at the other end.

'Olivia?' he said.

'Yes,' I replied, 'it is.'

'Oh good, have you got a moment?'

'Of course.'

'I want to thank you for your kind letter; I know that I never did. And I would so like to see you again and this guy I hear you are with.'

'Well that is one way of putting it,' I replied, and I couldn't help laughing. Years of shy resentment went rolling away. 'It would be lovely to see you.'

'Well, come over then and have some lunch and bring your man. What is his name?' I told him. 'That's right, someone did tell me, Theresa I think, and I had forgotten, and of course bring your mother and father.' There was a pause. I hesitated, then I said

'That would be lovely. Can I bring our little son Carol as well? I have no-one I can leave him with.'

'Wonderful!' Greville sounded surprisingly pleased by this idea. 'Please bring him as well; I'll try and dig out some old toys I think we still have in the big library.'

'You have,' I replied, rather daringly, 'you have our grandfather's teddy bear with one ear in the big chest.' Greville gave another laugh. I started to feel excited and happy about the plan.

In the end I drove to Merlinstone with only Carol as my companion. My parents were away and said that they would love to go another time, but they had to be in London to collect some furniture that was still in store. Meredith was also away on business, and was disappointed but could not change his plans. I went feeling suddenly shy and apprehensive. It was a beautiful day, reminding me of my first arrival at Merlinstone, except now it was autumn and the last time had been spring.

I drove up the familiar lime avenue, my heart beating rather fast, Carol beaming at me; he loved the car, I hoped this sunny mood would continue. We parked outside the front door and I lifted the baby onto my lap. The front door opened - I am ashamed to admit that at this moment my stomach dipped a little and I lifted Carol out of the car. He has not changed much, I thought, as I watched Greville come towards us. Perhaps he was paler than usual; there were dark patches under his eyes but his hair was streaked with no more silver than before. He bent and kissed my cheek and then put his finger under Carol's chin and tilted up his face. I think this was love at first sight for both of them. Whilst I held my breath praying the baby wouldn't cry Carol beamed, and Greville beamed back at him.

'Come along in,' he said, 'and we'll have some lunch. We're having it in the kitchen, better for your little man, I thought, and easier for Jessie – she isn't getting any younger.' I followed him into the house.

'Jessie!' I exclaimed. 'How wonderful! Is she really still here?'

And in a few moments Jessie's strong arms were around us, me and Carol together, and we were all laughing and crying at once. Jessie still looked one of the most handsome of women, and in spite of appearing slightly lame she had not changed at all. Lunch was laid on the kitchen table that was covered with a starched white tablecloth. An ancient high chair had been placed beside the table, the kind you expect to find in an antique shop.

'The General's chair from his childhood day,' Jessie said. 'I found it in the attic. See it has a row of beads here for the bairns to play with whilst they wait for their food,' and she swung Carol up into the chair without further ado. I was amazed by his good behaviour. He was still beaming and surveying the room and all of us with pleasure. Jessie was his instant slave, I could tell that, she could not take her eyes off him.

After lunch, having Carol curled up on the sofa in the library for a nap, contentedly sucking his thumb and cuddling his great-grandfather's one-

eared teddy bear Greville had faithfully dug out of the chest, we went into
the garden for a talk and a stroll. Greville spoke of Elizabeth with surprising
ease. I expected him to be in a state of great despair but this, I could clearly
see, was not the case. Although he was obviously missing her deeply there
was a strange calm about him, a kind of certainty someone might have if
their lover had merely gone away on a long journey and was due one day
to return. And later, much later on, I discovered this was indeed the case.
Greville knew without a doubt, that he would see her again, although he
never mentioned this. His time with her had changed him: I felt he had
known so great a happiness it would sustain him forever. He told me that
he was pleased about my book being a success.

'You are a credit to us, cousin,' he said, with almost his old mocking
manner, and sadly, as of yore, I blushed.

Before we left for home Greville said

'Please come back soon, I have so enjoyed seeing you both, and I would
love to meet Meredith and see your parents again,' and I promised that we
all would.

When we reached home I saw with a leap of joy that Meredith had
already returned. He was standing, as he often does, his hands in his
pockets, surveying his plants in the nursery garden. He came running to us
when he heard the car and swept Carol up into his arms.

'Well,' he said, 'how was your visit; did it go well?' I told him that it had
and that Greville wanted to meet him.

After my lunch with Greville at Merlinstone we started to visit him
frequently. Meredith got on with him surprisingly well and the two formed
a warm friendship. Greville loved to have Carol there as well. Sometimes he
sat him on his knee and drew pictures for him. When I saw them together I
realised how sad it must be for Greville not to have had a family of his own.

It was about a year later when Greville told me that he was ill and that
there was nothing the doctors could do for him. I had noticed that of late
he had become gaunt and there was sometimes a strange and distant look
in his eyes which I associated with his missing Elizabeth. We were sitting
together in the library watching the autumn wind blow the leaves over the
lawn.

'They give me up to a year,' he said. He spoke quite calmly in a fearless
kind of way as though he had expected this to happen. I felt a great surge of
grief, and words were hard to find. Eventually I said, 'Please tell us Greville,
Meredith and I, if there is anything at all we can do for you.'

'Just come and see me,' was his reply.

This is how it became a routine for us to visit him. I would often go over on my own when Meredith was busy, sometimes leaving Carol with my mother if I did not take him with me. All through that long winter Greville sat in the library by the fire with a rug wrapped over his knees and talked to me. He wanted to tell me everything. It was his way of remembering the past and of reliving happiness. He never mentioned having had any suspicion that I had entered his den on that fateful day when I used the ciné camera; and I never mentioned it either.

A nurse came to look after Greville. She stayed at Merlinstone as it was too much for Jessie to manage everything on her own. I watched him grow so thin that he seemed transparent. They gave him blood transfusions in the hospital but eventually he refused to have any more. He was slowly fading away.

It was on the day of a heavy snowfall that he told me the truth of his relationship to Elizabeth. We were sitting by the fire as usual, in the library, and Jessie brought us in some tea. Greville looked out of the window and said, 'You must go home, don't leave it too late, the roads will be bad and Meredith will be worried.' I promised I would do this. He had been talking to me for a long time and he appeared exhausted. I poured him out some tea and held the cup for him whilst he sipped it. I was trying to digest all he had told me that day - the terrible truth about his father's death, about his love for Elizabeth, he could never stop telling me about this, over and over again, and how strangely sweet her singing was, and wild. Sometimes, and I am forced to admit this, I did feel the smallest prick of envy. After this he told me about Geneviève, Elizabeth's mother, and the last grain of envy mysteriously left me. All I could feel was pity for his father, Henry, walking into his death and for Vanessa, left alone and destined never to marry again.

'It is a full circle,' he said, looking up at me from his chair, 'everything has come full circle.' I bent and kissed his cheek.

'I must go home, my dear cousin,' I said, 'I'll tell Jessie that I have to leave now.' He nodded and took my hand.

'My dear Olivia,' he said and closed his eyes, and I left the library.

As I drove back through the snow that night my head swirled with all the things Greville had talked about, and the snow spiralled against the labouring windscreen wipers. I was very relieved when I saw the lights of our house. Meredith was in the kitchen giving Carol his supper, anxiously awaiting me.

'I was so worried,' he said, hugging me. I clung to him for a moment. 'You are so cold darling, let me get you a hot drink.'

'I think I'll have some whisky,' I replied and he fetched a bottle from the dining room. I knew that I would never see Greville again. I told Meredith the extraordinary tales that Greville had told me about Henry and Geneviève.

Greville died that night, and Jessie rang me up the following morning. Alina, the nurse, had found him lying in his bed, looking as though he was peacefully asleep. Jessie told me calmly, although I could tell she had been crying. The last in the line of male Tarnochs to go and no-one left to carry on at Merlinstone. The winter that Greville died was the longest that I can ever remember. The snow seemed as if it would never go. Sometimes there was a little thaw and the sun came out and Carol and I found aconites and snowdrops struggling to lift their heads and then down it all came again.

I was alone late one afternoon with Carol, Meredith was away and I had just ventured over to see my parents. I was feeling creative again and was thinking over a theme for a new book. Somehow it refused to gel so I decided to leave it alone for the time being and was on my way back to the kitchen where Carol was waiting for me, sitting in his high chair, when the telephone rang in the sitting room. I put a biscuit into his small fist and retraced my steps. I had hoped to hear Meredith's voice at the other end but instead a strange man asked

'Is that Mrs Cochrane?' It was a dry, cool voice with just the tinge of a Scots accent.

'Who wants her please?' I asked cagily.

'My name is Hector Fleming,' the reply came. 'I am the late Mr Greville Sinclair's solicitor. I am calling you from Fleming and Calvert, my Edinburgh office, not far from Academy Street. I probably should have written to you but I felt it might be easier if we were to speak first and if possible arrange a meeting. When would suit you, Mrs Cochrane, to come in here and see me?'

I was surprised.

'What will this be about?' I asked.

'It is about Mr Sinclair's will and it involves you. I would like to meet with you soon if possible, we have been somewhat delayed already by some documents being mislaid but luckily they have turned up and we have got everything together.'

'Would next Thursday be all right?' I asked him. 'At about four pm? My little boy will have had his nap by then, I am afraid I shall have to bring him with me.'

Hector said this would suit him well and we rang off with brief but cordial goodbyes.

When the following Thursday came, I scooped up Carol, who was luckily in a good mood after his rest, and strapped him into the child seat. Then I folded the push chair and crammed it into the boot. The world was still snow-covered, everything black and white and above a steel grey sky that was already darkening towards evening. As I drove towards Edinburgh I wondered what on earth Greville could have left me. Perhaps a little jewellery, I thought, some that had belonged to Violet, our mutual grandmother. I had not expected to be bequeathed anything by Greville and I was touched that he had thought of me.

I parked the car in a half-empty square and transferred Carol to his push chair, then we set off at a brisk pace. I soon found the old building – Hector Fleming had given me clear instructions – there was a smart brass plate on the door that said Fleming and Calvert Partners. I rang the highly polished doorbell, a buzzer sounded and I pushed open the door, hauling the pram behind me. The hallway was dark and a flight of green-carpeted stairs led steeply upwards. I hoisted Carol into my arms. He was looking around with wide, amazed eyes, and together we staggered up the stairs, realising too late there was a lift we could have taken, hidden in the darkness of the hall. I put Carol down on the last step and took his hand. A tall lady in a trim coat and skirt of a dark green material was standing in the open doorway ahead; she was smiling and looking owlishly at us from behind a large pair of horn-rimmed spectacles.

'Mrs Cochrane?' she asked politely.

I gasped 'Yes' and Carol gave her an alarmed look.

'Do come through - Mr Fleming is waiting for you.'

We followed her through a small office and then into a larger room. Everywhere was panelled in dark, polished wood. There was one picture on the wall, a portrait in oils of a venerable looking man in a suit with a somewhat expanded waistcoat across which a gold chain and watch garlanded his stomach. He had white hair, round silver-edged spectacles and a small moustache. He looked down on us benignly. Hector Fleming, for I realised it must be he, sat below the portrait and now rose from his seat to shake hands with us. The writing table before him was piled with files and papers. He was an exact, although slightly younger, version of the portrait that hung above him.

'Thank you Miss Simmons,' he said to the owlish lady, after he had greeted us. Then he looked at us and continued, 'Very nice to meet you Mrs Cochrane, and this young man?'

'This is Carol,' I told him. He bowed stiffly to Carol who looked solemnly back. Then he said 'Man' rather undecidedly. I sat down quickly and drew him onto my knee.

'Will you be comfortable there Mrs Cochrane, with the bairn?' Hector Fleming asked politely. I assured him we were fine and he took his place before us, drawing forward as he did so a large bundle of files.

'Miss Simmons will bring us refreshments soon,' he told me. I started to feel like the Queen. All this procedure, I thought, for what would probably turn out to be a small Victorian brooch, it was amusingly old-fashioned.

Hector Fleming cleared his throat and looked directly at me. His eyes were a cool, clear grey. I could see he might seem intimidating if he chose but today he was obviously determined to play a genial role. Carol appeared to be fascinated by him.

'Did you know Mr Sinclair well, Mrs Cochrane?' he asked me. I was a little surprised by this question.

'Well yes, I suppose I did,' I replied. 'I stayed with him at Merlinstone for quite a long time whilst I was writing my biography of our grandfather, and of course we are, or were, first cousins.' Hector Fleming nodded.

'Did he ever discuss his will with you?' he asked. I was almost shocked by this question.

'No,' I replied quickly, 'he never mentioned it.' Hector Fleming smiled.

'Well in that case I must warn you that what I have to say is bound to come to you as a very big surprise. Mr Sinclair has left everything to you and your husband, Mrs Cochrane, and then all is to pass on to this wee man here, your son. You have inherited the house and all its contents. There is a proviso to say that you are to hand a painting or two on to your two aunts and your mother if you wish to do so. You will get all the land, the houses and the outbuildings.' He seemed to go on and on, enumerating the items I was to receive. Finally he said 'and added to this you inherit his entire fortune. I hope you will not think it impertinent of me to add that I think you will need this; it is quite a place to maintain. And of course there are death duties and tax but compared with some unlucky people they will not be overwhelming. Mr Sinclair has been very astute with his affairs.'

I wanted to say 'Crikey.' I wanted to laugh and then to cry. Instead I lifted Carol off my knee and put him gently on the floor. He trotted away and was soon happily playing with an empty waste paper basket, rolling it across the floor. Hector Fleming rang a small bell and Miss Simmons came in with a large tea tray laden with a silver teapot and china cups, as well as a plate of scones and a fine-looking Dundee cake.

'Mr Fleming,' I said, my voice came out in a hoarse whisper. 'There is one thing you must know. I am not Mrs Cochrane yet – Meredith and I are not married, we will be one day,' I added, hoping he would not be shocked.

'I think I did know this,' he replied, 'but I did not like to presume.'

We sat together drinking the tea in a companionable manner. I felt like a patient in a friendly A and E department being given a helping hand by a senior doctor. After a while Hector rang for the tea to be cleared away and when Mrs Simmons had done this and left us, closing the door very quietly behind her, he turned to me again.

'Please forgive me,' he said, 'if this question appears too precipitous; you will obviously need to return home and discuss everything with your, well, with Mr Cochrane. But do you think that you will feel able to take all this on? To live at Merlinstone as I know Mr Sinclair so hoped you would?'

I looked back at Hector Fleming and suddenly I smiled. I felt clear-headed and inspired, and thrilled, oh so thrilled.

'Oh yes,' I replied firmly, 'obviously I shall have to discuss all this with Meredith but I want to live there with every bone in my body.'

Hector Fleming really smiled this time, and the smile reached his eyes that crinkled at the corners in a much more kindly manner.

'I am so glad, so very glad,' he said. 'It would have meant so much to Mr Sinclair to have known this.'

'I am sure he guessed that I would,' I replied. And inwardly I thought 'he does know, wherever he is.'

'There will be a great many documents to sign,' Hector continued, 'and we shall have to be in touch with the bank, but for now I expect you will want to go home and talk with your family.'

I gathered up Carol and Hector came with us to the lift. I said goodbye to Miss Simmons as we went through her office.

'Goodbye Mr Fleming,' I said, taking his hand, 'I shall await your summons. This has been an extraordinary day.'

The lift doors opened behind me and then closed and we went down to the ground floor. I packed Carol into his pram and we went out into the cold dry evening. Stars shone above us in the blue night sky and car lights flashed by.

Once I was driving I felt a little steadier. This had indeed been a really extraordinary day. Only this morning I had woken with the usual knowledge that I was Olivia, mother, lover, writer, not financially very well off but happy, searching for a theme for my next book. Now, in a matter of hours, I was changed. I was rich Olivia, owner of a wonderful house, an enormous garden and land of great beauty, of fields stuffed with flowers and field mice, tall lime trees that sent up spiralling columns of rooks – all these were mine, and so much more – paintings, libraries full of books, silver candlesticks with ivory-coloured candles that would glow softly in the darkness, bedrooms with deep brass-headed beds and flowered wallpapers that generations before me had looked at and been comforted by.

What would Meredith think of it, I wondered? I was a little worried about this; would he embrace the idea of such a great change? He so loved our little house and his family life, he was happy searching for his plants and growing his nursery. But he was also adventurous and, in his own small way, successful. Now he would be able to expand. We were nearing home, and with a leap of surprise and joy I saw Meredith's car parked outside. He had returned early. I would be able to tell him, and how badly I needed now to do this! How I longed to feel him holding me. Taking Carol's hand I ran into the house; a door closed and Meredith came towards us.

'Thank heavens you are back!' he said; 'I got home early and I was worried, it is late and the night is so cold, I wondered where you both were.' I went to him and he clasped us both.

'Listen,' I said, 'You must come and sit down and hear me. Perhaps we both need to fetch a drink first. I have the most extraordinary news to tell you.'

*

We talked far into the night. After I had put Carol to bed we sat and talked again. Meredith was stunned by my story. I worried about what he would really think deep down in his heart. It took us many nights and days to arrange our plans and to fully realise how greatly our lives would change. To start with Meredith was loath to leave our house and his small but productive nursery, but by degrees he began to see how advantageous it would all be and how he could expand his business.

My mother and father were delighted for us and supported all our plans. Both my aunts were surprisingly unworried by our news. Theresa and her two children had no interest in inheriting Merlinstone. Bernard, her younger son, had already gone to live in Australia and Alexander, the elder one, would eventually inherit his father's farm and estates in Argentina and was at present working in London. Vanessa, the one person I expected to have difficulties with, was quite the reverse! Ever since my successful book about her father she had become far more friendly towards me. She was delighted with the book, and since Greville had had no children she was pleased that Carol would one day inherit her old home. She even went as far as offering a small olive branch to my mother who accepted it with mild reservations. At least it was a beginning, she said.

We have been living at Merlinstone for nearly two years now, and I have finished the book that I decided to write at the very beginning when I came down from the tower, intent on telling this story of the Tarnoch family and the Matrix, the house that now so happily contained us. It has been a busy, sometimes exhausting, time of change and re-establishment of the nursery and all Meredith's plans, and my entire life. Carol is the least fazed by everything. He took his transplanting quietly and with what seemed like great pleasure. Sometimes he asks where Greville is, Grev he always calls him, and I explain as best I can that although we can no longer see him he is here with us for always, until the end of time, and indeed I know I am not lying. The other day I went to the green hillside where Greville and Elizabeth so often took a picnic, and where they are now both buried, as they requested, side by side. Their graves are marked by beautifully carved headstones. It was a warm, sunny day and the bees were working loudly on the hillside and I looked away over the rolling country thinking, as I always do, how beautiful it is and then suddenly, and so swiftly they were gone again in a second, I saw them; Greville and Elizabeth walking in the shaft of sunlight – and laughing together. She was looking up at him and holding his arm and then they were gone, as quickly as a rainbow can fade they went in to nothingness.

I returned home later in a quiet and thoughtful mood. Carol was out; he had gone over to my parents for the day. If he had been with me would he have seen them also, I wondered? I went up to the top of the tower to think. It was wonderful, I reflected, that they had looked so happy. Since then I have told no-one about this, not even Meredith. And what of Simon, I wonder, is he happy also? There is such joy in this house that I think he must be. I salute his paintings every time I pass them on the stairs on my way to bed.

The End